CURSE
OF THE
AMBER

KATHRYN TROY

CURSE OF THE AMBER

CITY OWL PRESS
www.cityowlpress.com

Cover Design by Mibl Art. All stock photos licensed appropriately.

Edited by Tee Tate.

For information on subsidiary rights, please contact the publisher at info@cityowlpress.com.

Print Edition ISBN: 978-1-949090-36-9

Digital Edition ISBN: 978-1-949090-35-2

Printed in the United States of America

BOOKS BY KATHRYN TROY

Curse of the Amber

A Vision in Crimson

Dreams of Ice and Shadow

1

ASENATH

The sun seems to have forgotten Wales. I didn't think there was any place on Earth that could make me long to be in Egypt again, but I couldn't escape the memories that flooded me. I shivered in the absence of the Valley's merciless heat, where for summers on end its oppressive dryness sucked the life out of my lips and baked my skin into hardened, sand-beaten clay. That dryness had followed Ramesses, Amenhotep, Aken-aten, and his son beyond the world's suffering down to their resting place, and kept the divine kings ready in the dark, empty stillness.

But the day's oppression had always faded with the sun. The perfection of those nights on the Eastern Bank, at our host Hani's home —that was what I missed. Invigorated by the fresh, life-giving breeze off the Nile's surface and snuggled between my parents under thin woven blankets was a warmth I knew I would never feel again. The cold and damp of Britain, once the stronghold of the Druids, was relentless. The gnawing feeling at the pit of my stomach grew, and the thought I'd pushed away more than once made itself more insistent.

This was a mistake. I shouldn't be here.

My fingertips numbed to the statuette in my hand, a solid representation of the wet chill in the air. Its faceless form was as alien to me as the bog in which I crouched. The shape of the stone fetish was at least interesting, a long, slender column with a severe "V" etched into it. It held more promise than the dozens of thin rings fashioned out of iron, bronze, and even gold, heaped together in a tangle, the clay pottery, now in shards, and scraps of linen that appeared to be tossed desperately into the bog as a last-ditch effort to avoid Roman destruction. But I couldn't enjoy it for what it was. It was inscrutable, too disconnected from anything familiar. Its primitive, obscure expression reminded me of my own cold thoughts, and as I squeezed the chilled stone in my hand, I doubted if I would discover anything that had once been warm—made of flesh and blood. We were as deep down as the famous bog bodies had been, more so in certain places, and still we had nothing, or rather no one, to show for it.

I lifted my head, trying to shake off my melancholy and averting my eyes from the stone carving that would not reveal its secrets to me. I was too low down to inhale even a whiff of air that wasn't saturated with the grassy pungency of the bog wall. From my vantage point, huddled low in a deep, man-hewn pit, the sodden depression of the bog appeared even more overgrown on all sides. Birch trees poked out of humble clusters of willows, red-speckled buckthorn, and mountain ash. Except for these trees skirting its outermost edges, the sunken area was wide and open. The cauldron bog retained its secluded atmosphere, despite being carved into a series of waterlogged cavities.

My somber mood deepened when I saw my advisor approach. Up until then I'd been successful at avoiding him. I deliberately didn't linger, and always found a reason to visit another pit when the one we were in suddenly emptied of other researchers. I'd resisted the wrenching feeling in my gut too long, but as our excavation wound down, it was impossible to ignore, with nowhere for my thoughts to hide—there was nothing left of what used to be my life.

"How's it going?" Alex asked, and knelt beside me.

"Fine," I answered, not bothering to look up from the peat I was brushing off of a link of iron rings sunken into the over-saturated soil.

After a long, awkward silence, he said, "It's okay, you know."

"What is?"

"If you don't…if *we* don't find one."

I swallowed hard. The only place for my rising fury to go was back down.

"I just don't want you to think that this whole thing was a waste—"

"A *waste*?" I shot back. "I've got enough to keep me occupied for the next decade, thank you." It was true, but that didn't make the prospect of studying human sacrifice *sans* a human sound any better. Nothing would tell us as much about the Druids as human remains that had, willingly or otherwise, undergone their practices. It may have been more than anyone else expected, but the bar had been set impossibly high. A human discovery might have been the only way to exceed my father's own discoveries in the Valley of the Kings and earn the same level of respect in my own right.

"All right, all right," Alex said, contrite. "I didn't come over here to upset you."

"Then why are you here?" There was more bite in my voice than I meant, but he had that amused eyebrow raised again, the one that made my anger meaningless and painted me as a silly, wide-eyed novice with dreams of finding the next Tut.

"I thought you might need a refill." He offered me a cup of coffee.

A gruff "thank you" was all I could manage. My brain had reached maximum capacity for caffeine, but it went down easy. Milk and two sugars, just the way I liked it. Damn.

He reached out for me but caught himself before his fingers could find their way into my hair, frowning before he lowered his voice.

"Will you come tonight, Asenath? It'd be a shame for you not to see the room. You picked it, after all."

Memories of Alex's firm, feverish grip on my hips, his moans in my ear, passed unbidden across my mind. Some days it was so easy to look at him and just see the charming, somewhat quiet young man always at my father's side, more often than not covered in two-thousand-year-old dust.

"Will you tell *her*?" I asked.

His silence hit me like a stab in the gut. It was self-inflicted—those rosy pictures and all his stale promises were just a veil, a childhood infatuation. I saw him then as he was—his chocolate-brown hair had dulled, the sharp line of his chin softened; so, had the brilliance of his eyes, their dark fathoms fading. Small lines crept at the corners of his eyes and mouth. I bit my tongue as a distraction. The imprints of his touch on my skin would fade, if I let them.

I sipped my coffee again. It had a bitter taste the second time around. When I let the silence settle between us, he rose to his feet, stifling a groan on the way up. He disappeared again to the other side of the dig, and I went back to work.

I ended the day uploading my latest round of pictures as usual. Dr. Pryce, the head of the Aarhaus team, walked into the makeshift tent and took up the seat beside me.

"Good evening, Miss Hayes."

"Hi, Dr. Pryce. I'm almost done here."

He nodded. "Time for your daily report. Carew was preoccupied, so he asked me to come in his stead."

"Preoccupied with what?" I asked, then mentally kicked myself the moment the words escaped my mouth. It was too familiar, but my patience with Alex was thin. Dr. Pryce didn't seem to notice, and only smiled, a sly thing with a hint of amusement. "Right," I answered, shaking my head. "Well, according to today's soil readings, we're anywhere from fifteen to twenty-five hundred years down, and some of the wells were definitely dug by human hands."

"Wells," Pryce repeated, bobbing his head thoughtfully, "but no mounds."

"That's right." I felt my face flush hot under the electric lamps swinging overhead. The Druids hadn't built permanent structures, making them an elusive lot. But I'd hypothesized that impermanent markers, made of dirt and mud, had been either destroyed or overlooked completely. The clunky peat-cutting that locals relied on for fuel had raised almost every bog body ever found by sheer accident. Any significant difference to the topography would have been ripped apart before anyone had realized its importance. I had at least hoped to map out some pattern to the ritualized deaths bog bodies had endured and give more substance to Julius Caesar's accounts of human sacrifice among the Druids. But without markers in the ground as a reference, or actual victims to study, deciphering the meaning of these haphazard bits and bobs wouldn't amount to a whole lot that we hadn't known before.

I think Pryce read the disappointment on my face, and tactfully changed the subject. "It's taking us longer than we thought to hit our marks," he said. "It's unlikely that we'll be able to complete the site, this time around at least."

I blew air out of my lips in a loud puff, deflated. He'd caught me. I had tried not to be concerned by it, but we *were* behind schedule. Cerriglyn Bog couldn't support the weight of bulldozers. The ground was too unstable. We'd been left to do the grunt work with smaller machines, sometimes only by hand. It made just reaching our intended depth a daunting task. I pursed my lips and wondered if I would ever feel the African sun on my face again, or see Hani's familiar, wizened face. He was probably still there, giving respite to obnoxious tourists, those he decried for destroying his homeland with their discarded water bottles and used-up film canisters. A hollow feeling deepened in my chest at the thought, threatening to swallow me up. I did my best to shake it off.

"Let's narrow the field, then," I finally answered.

Dr. Pryce smirked and pulled a copy of our working map from his back pocket. "I thought you might say that."

"Am I that predicable?" I asked.

"Predictable? No. But *capable*? Yes, you are that, Miss Hayes. So, what do you think?"

I examined the map centered around Cerriglyn Bog. Bordering its northeastern edge was the forest, with fainter lines indicating its prehistoric boundaries intersecting the topmost sectors of the bog. Along that corner crawled a small creek. Minus the geographic features, the map was blank. Staring at it was like gaping into an abyss, and that overwhelming feeling crept back up again, settling in my armpits and down the center of my back. I hoped Pryce couldn't smell my fear.

I closed my eyes, wishing for the meticulously plotted charts of the Valley of the Kings, its pristine, orderly rows and markers instead of this yawning nothingness. But it too, once, had been only a mass of nondescript, transient dunes. I looked at the map again, the one in my mind's eye laid over it like a transparency. The bog beneath came to life, reacting like watercolor paper dipped in ink. Invisible markers blossomed in neat, ordered lines, woven together by unseen pathways into a modest village, one as close to the wetlands as safety would allow.

"Let's pull it in here," I said, pointing to the northeastern sector where the environmental markers overlapped—where the bog met the forest and where it touched the bank of the creek. "Take half your team out of the south and move them to the center." Those in-between spaces would have been the most sought after, the ones deemed sacred. If we didn't find anything bigger than chicken bones there, I doubted we would find them anywhere.

"Will do," he said, restoring the map to his pocket. "You know, Miss Hayes, I never really thanked you for thinking of us. This is the most exciting thing that's happened to our department in decades."

"Of course," I answered quickly. "You're right here. I thought it would be wrong not to. Although I'll admit that my intentions were not entirely altruistic—your Celts might be able to tell me something that the pyramids can't." That was the main reason I'd gone along with Alex's suggestion in the first place—I was seduced by the idea of bringing Druidism out of the shadows and drawing a line straight back to the practices that made pharaohs divine kings and praised wetlands as sacred.

Pryce smiled. "You *are* your father's daughter, Miss Hayes."

I turned my face from him and bit my lip. The sting of tears that should have run dry long ago tried to push its way forward again. I tried to console myself with the thought that, had I not already been thinking about them, it wouldn't have hit me as hard. But even I wasn't convinced.

Pryce cleared his throat. "I apologize, Miss Hayes. I—"

"It's fine," I assured him, blinking to clear my eyes. "Thank you for the compliment."

"I'd ask you to stay longer, if I didn't think Alex would have a fit. Lord knows he wouldn't get any work done without you." He rose from his chair and left me with a knowing grin.

*P*ryce's parting words left me wondering just how much Alex *was* supposed to be doing as my supervisor. I shifted restlessly in a moldy dorm bed, abandoned in the nadir of the academic year. Today was not the first time that Alex was seen to shirk his duty. Sneaking breaks and doing his utmost to *not* tire himself out as much as the next man was second nature to him. It stung to have my work, my conclusions, be subject to his opinion. But it was too late to switch advisors and explaining the more pressing reason for wanting the distance was out of the question.

In the starkness of the brisk night, my boots called to me. Their plush lining was irresistible at the ridiculously late hour. I'd never get any sleep if I didn't clear my head and at least try to keep warm. I pulled the barely upholstered desk chair next to the window. After pushing down on the window to confirm that, yes, in fact, the wind was coming *through* the closed frame, I set the chair in front of the window, so that the frame sat at the leftmost corner of my vision, leaving the rest of my view looking out onto the bog which lay in the distance. Thick grasses and clusters of myrtle clutched each other in the darkness, shivering violently in the wind. Moonlight bounced off their tangled, indefinable edges, and the more I peered into the Welsh countryside, the more it divested itself of its false bluntness. The bog and its surrounding brush revealed whispers of greens, blues, purples, and yellows in its multi-layered blackness. Calm crept softly over my frazzled brain as I roughed out the scene before me in charcoals, paying attention to the angles and proportions before treating its colors and textures. I willingly lost myself in the quick strikes of my hand against the paper. Thoughts of anything but how to render the window frame fell from my mind. I considered whether to keep the aged, peeling texture of the white frame intact, or to restore it to a gleaming pristineness set at odds with the watery chaos beyond. As I worked, the untarnished frame looked too unnatural, so I weathered it once more. I worked until my eyes became blissfully heavy and drifted down into sleep.

I was still working on the image of the bog in my dreams. My charcoal strokes had become bloated with water, bleeding my greens, my blues, my whites, and my blacks together until the bog was nothing but a dark mass, a bottomless chasm. Obsidian waves shifted and swayed—something was rising to the surface. I couldn't run, couldn't scream or blink the image away as the rising wave took shape and glided across the surface of the bog. A shrunken, wrinkled face emerged from the watery depths. Its twisted mouth wrenched open to reveal a blank expanse. Vacant eyes glowed an unearthly blue, staring straight into my soul.

I woke gasping for air and wiped a sheen of cold sweat from my forehead. Raindrops pattered onto the floor beneath the window, its brittle borders unable to keep either wind or water out. The edge of my picture, laid on the nightstand, was visible out of the corner of my eye. The rain glistening on the windowpane reflected on the paper in the moonlight, making the colors look blurry and wet—alive, almost. I was afraid to turn my head, afraid in the way that you can be only after waking suddenly, still too tied to your dreams to know they aren't real. Those glowing, luminescent eyes still stared at me, *through* me, at the edge of my mind. I held my breath and looked. The only things on the paper were what I had put there—high grasses peering into the window frame, that crumbling barrier against the creeping dark without. It was splintered and cracked, losing its power to keep the fen at bay.

2

QUINTUS - 62 A.C.E.

The rain showed no signs of abating, and the dull showers against the hull settled permanently in my mind. The small hours in which the storm clouds took a breath flitted past as a dream, too brief to be trusted. The belly of our warship creaked and groaned, and no amount of warm, dry clothes would have felt sufficient to snuff out the chill that had taken hold in our very bones as we wound our way around Britannia. The risk of injury or death when I'd been dispatched to Gaul five summers ago had been greater and more certain, but at least the weather had been pleasant.

Our morale might have fared better if our ship had pointed us toward anywhere other than the forests of Mona, the last sanctuary of the Druids. General Paulinus had wiped the Druidic cancer from Mona last spring, we had been told, yet the unease of the three hundred beating hearts aboard grew as we traveled farther and farther into Britannia's unseen depths. Sleep was a wary business, plagued by dreams laden with oak trees and screeching women wielding firebrands beside white-clad priests in the very groves they held sacred.

Our ship pushed its narrow bow into a billowing white cloud that hung so low that it did not cease at the water's edge. We stood in formation on the upper deck, shields and swords gripped tenaciously, in defiance of the slick clime that obscured all and invited men's minds to see shadows in dark robes. Soreness and fatigue faded, pushed away like a forgotten memory. Knees bent, ears pricked for a sudden command to attack, we stood in a tight column prepared for venomous shrieks or sharp orders, half-expecting both. My gaze sought in vain to pierce the veil of the grim fog. For a fleeting moment, I considered the possibility that Britannia did not exist at all, that it was a trick of the mist. Nothing lay before us but vapor, thickening in its grayness as it adopted the guise of something solid. Every breath of terse silence sharpened us into focus. There would be no hesitation now, if Druids materialized on the coast. We were strung as tight as Ulysses's bow, itching for the word that would loosen us.

As if in mockery of the uneasiness that had hung over the ship since we entered British waters, the sun made its long-overdue appearance at this moment, puncturing the dense clouds. The charged air dispersed, revealing, for the first time, the complete emptiness of the beachhead. Sweat collected on my skin as we disembarked swiftly and silently, not yet convinced of our solitude.

Thunder boomed across rapidly blackening skies.

"Oh, son of a whore!" our commander howled.

Nervous laughter crackled through us like wildfire at the curse, and we thanked Neptune for a safe landing. Storm clouds brewed several miles northwest of us, lying in wait as we commenced our march to the Strait of Menai, and then crossing on to Mona. We were, without question, going to be sleeping on mud when night fell.

The fatigue in my limbs that had once been pronounced became comfortable and familiar, and I existed only in varying states of wetness —mild dampness, sweat-induced stickiness, or drenched. The land was uneven, and my boots took a serious beating, digging into the mud to conquer slick hills and swollen streams. Clinging close to the shore kept us in thick fog most of the way. The sloshing sound of our boots was the only thing keeping us from crashing into one another. Camping upon the banks of the strait, we lit more fires than was our custom to suck the wetness from our marrow and give our minds the much-needed rest.

On our final crossing to Mona, the dread we had felt on our first landing rushed back upon us in all its fury. The darker, more translucent clouds that now flanked us clung to the charred underbrush, as did the last smoldering fumes of fire. Celtic curses spat out in the throes of death seemed to echo faintly in the air, trapped like so much water. But questions of whether Paulinus had truly dealt the Druids of Mona a fatal blow no longer preyed on superstitious minds as the air cleared. Laying those doubts to rest was a great weight lifted from us, and we proceeded with confident ease through the ruins of the grand forest that had been home to the unruly cult. There was nothing to fear in the burnt, hollowed oak trunks lying fallen in twisted heaps of blackened brush. Mangy, half-starved rabbits dared not venture too close to us, a bastion of order and discipline forged in iron.

Another day's worth of marching brought us at last to our stopping point, a wide, flat area where the construction of fortifications was already underway. A hill composed entirely of felled oaks supplied carpenters with the endless means for heavy planks and beams. Walls had been erected, with large stone markers firmly plotting the layout of Legate Lucius's permanent abode, the necessary trenches already dug.

The men I had traveled with were ordered to make camp at the eastern side of the established tents housing the others, engaged now in the filthy work of building a more permanent position. I was dismissed from the column, allowed to make my way to the Legate's tent for my new orders. The front flaps opened to a large space, decorated sparsely with a long wooden table flanked by tall candlesticks, chairs, and an inkpot. Lucius sat hunched over the unfinished map before him, his fingers covering his mouth in a posture of deep thought. He did not look much older than he had been when he had first taken me along in Gaul, when I'd been an eager soldier. The man's dark eyes had softened around the edges, but they brightened when I cleared my throat to greet him. He had never stood on formalities with me in private and didn't now, rising from his seat.

"Quintus," he said, clapping me on both shoulders as he neared. "How was the journey? Without incident, I hope?"

"Nothing but rain the whole way," I answered with a smile.

He chuckled. "I'm sorry to tell you, there's no getting used to it but come, warm up, get some food in your belly, and change out of those clothes. Your boots look like shit."

"They feel like shit," I said, taking off my helmet for the first time that morning and shaking my hair out. I followed Lucius to the supply room, where I was thankfully furnished with a new set of garments. Once I was suitably dressed, I rejoined Lucius in his charting room, now replete with a hearty repast of bread, nuts, and dried fruit. I was most grateful for the wine as it warmed its way down my throat to my very toes and soaked into my chest for a much-relished thaw.

"Thank you again, Legate," I began, "for inviting me to share your tent. I learned a great deal on our last campaign from your fine model of proper governance. It's more than I would receive from another more prone to petty bureaucracies, or corruption."

"Yes, I am a dying breed. You honor me, Quintus. But, in truth," he said, waving a dismissive hand at me, "you were with me in Gaul because of my allegiance to your father. You stand here today on your own merits."

I bowed deeply.

"How *is* your father?" he asked. He leaned forward in his chair, half in interest, half to clutch a tempting morsel of fruit from the platter farthest from him.

"He is well," I answered.

"And his leg?"

I tilted my head to the side, contemplating his question, reluctant to betray Father's stubborn pride. But it wasn't anything Lucius did not already know. "Getting worse, though he continues to hide it."

Lucius snorted. "He was lucky to come out with it still attached. I knew then that it would never give him a moment's peace."

"I keep telling him to sell the tavern and retire, or at least hire younger men to do the grunt work." I spread my open palms before me. "But you know him."

Lucius chuckled, partaking of another handful of almonds. "He'd sooner *eat* his leg than admit he needs the help."

I nodded. "My mother is there, at least."

"And how is she?"

"Fine," I answered. I stiffened my back at the query. Thinking of her brought my forgotten melancholy back to the fore. I knew how much she suffered when I'd marched to the edge of the world for months on end with no guarantee that I would return. She'd not been young when she had me, and long had she endured the sympathetic looks of other mothers before my arrival, their broods tangled all about them. She doted on me, and I on her. But as I had matured, her loneliness had grown acute again, and she yearned for a child of mine to bounce on her knee, to occupy her days in my absence. I longed to give her what she craved.

"And you, Quintus?" Lucius asked. "Have you thought more of marriage since last we spoke?"

I pressed my lips together into a thin, forced smile.

"Your parents are growing impatient for grubby little hands," he replied with a conspiratorial glint in his eye. "You having a woman to warm your bed wouldn't be so bad, either."

"You think I don't want that too?" I replied. I'd long ago lost interest in the casual encounters with women afforded to soldiers, their faces nothing more to me than a series of faded impressions that ran together. As silly as it seemed at my age, I longed for the intimacy of a kiss. I envied the affection and companionship my parents shared, but my heart had not yet found its echo. Even if it had, I would not have made the best impression—suitors so far from home and fighting to stay afloat rarely did.

"Well," Lucius said, interrupting my thoughts as his hunger was finally sated, "there's nothing to be done for it right now. Not here, anyway. Despite the disgusting conditions, we're making good progress on the garrison. For now, this is sufficient for business with the locals."

I shifted in my chair. "I was under the impression there weren't any."

Lucius rose from his seat and beckoned me to follow. We exited the tent and walked round the far side of it, ascending a modest hill overlooking the island's interior, covered for the most part in dense forest. In the valley between the forest and the hill's incline was a line of roughly two dozen large, round structures, topped with conical thatched roofs. Between them, clusters of fair-haired men, women, and children shuffled about, fulfilling their daily duties, but at the pace of a dwindling, disoriented populace.

"Are they Druids?" I asked, absently watching a small girl struggle to carry more fruit in her apron than it would bear.

"There's been no sign of any sacrifices, human or otherwise," Lucius replied, shrugging.

"Have they been uncooperative?"

Lucius weighed the question. "I went down there to ask them who I might speak to, someone to represent them, and they just stared at me like dumb mules before returning to their business." He waved his hand in a sweeping motion over the placid scene below. "Either their lives are *so* simple they don't have a leader, or—"

"Or their leader is dead," I finished.

He nodded. "I want you to figure out which."

I shifted my weight from one foot to the other, folding my hands behind my back. "And if it's the latter?" I asked.

Lucius sighed. "If these people didn't appreciate our strength before, they do now. They need to be shown the value of Roman protection, of our fairness. But I can't collect tribute from people who are either dead or too scared to work."

I grunted in agreement.

"That brings me to the other matter I want you to address." He spoke more quietly now. "Not every man is accounted for," he said. "The last thing we need is soldiers harassing the locals or forcing themselves on the females. That's what set Boudicca's rebellion off in the first place. Quintus, I want Mona settled and producing copper within two years."

Two years. He hadn't specifically said he'd need *me* for two years, but his utterance made my heart sink. I was not averse to a marriage in the provinces, if that's where my heart should find its echo, but I could not abide making my home so far from my parents. I had realized my mistake too late—my experiences best suited me for a life abroad, and I was duty-bound to it for the sake of supporting my parents as they aged. Lucius's words confirmed the worst. I frowned. Returning home past my prime would damage my prospects even further. But failure in Britannia would bring disaster.

When I did not respond, lost again in my own thoughts, Lucius beguiled me.

"You're quick with languages, Quintus, and your father's tavern has given you the best education on navigating different customs." He smiled at me then, his voice full of confidence in the task he heaped upon me. "Be my eyes and ears with them, and for now, my mouth. Let them know we want them to thrive. And find where my missing men have got off to. Can you do all that?"

Victory in Britain was ours to secure, its spoils ours to share. If I wanted to keep the tavern going and provide for a family of my own, this was the only path before me.

"I won't disappoint," I answered, resigned to my fate.

His smile widened, and he offered me a second glass of wine. "I never doubted that," he said. "Sooner than later, we'll need to start them constructing the Imperial Temple, too," Lucius added. "Give them a proper channel for worship."

I swirled the remnants of my wine at the bottom of my glass. "There is, of course, a third possibility," I mused.

He looked up at me, puzzled. I met his eyes as I completed my thought.

"That their leader is good at hiding."

---

3

*T*he following day was the first decent one since leaving Rome. The sun penetrated through the thin clouds of the morning, casting its warming glow upon my face. I rose and looked out over the promontory that abutted my tent. The hills and streams in the distance glittered, the greens and blues made prismatic as light flitted from countless dewdrops. The landscape sparkled like a collection of fine gems and was almost beautiful.

I did not trust the mild morning and donned my dark woolen cloak before venturing out. To identify the local leader, if one existed, and determine the degree of latent hostility, I first required a linguistic tutor. I entered the village, cautious but hopeful that a little kindness would gain me entry into their circle.

The people of Mona scurried about under the watchful gaze of the soldiers stationed in pairs along the path from the first of the thatched roundhouses to the last. Men were drastically outnumbered, and so the few there were struggled with the arduous task of repairing a house damaged by fire. When a bundle of straw meant to patch the roof slipped from an older man's grasp and threatened to crush him, I intervened. The man stared at me, wide-eyed, as I shouldered the burden, passing it to the younger man above. He was equally stunned, but I outstretched my arms farther, offering it to him. He finally took the load from me as he blinked back to his own senses. With the straw safely in his grip, the man disappeared to the far side of the roof without a word.

I tried again at the next house, hoping that my help would loosen their tongues. But they were as implacable as Lucius had found them; Britons of all ages either bolted from my sight or accepted my aid in stubborn silence. I swallowed my annoyance and turned to examining their dwellings. Each structure was perfectly indistinguishable from the next. They were all approximately the same size and construction; no roof towered above the rest, no door or lintel marked the dwelling of a person of elevated rank. Neither did I spy traces of hasty removals or alterations in the absence of such signs.

As I lowered my silent inquiries to the garments of those around me, the sound of quicker, louder movements to the left caught my attention. I followed my ears and came upon a dirt path beside a rivulet flowing with great speed, as if to escape the fracas forming at its edge. Cowering on the bank was a small huddle of females, ranging in age from very young to startlingly old. They retreated backwards into the water as a pair of soldiers advanced, seizing their baskets, and threatening to toss them into the rushing waves. The women were wide-eyed, as though they were caught between fear of the soldiers and losing a morning's worth of foraging. Grasping hands outstretched one minute to regain their findings and shrank back the next. The man who stood closest to me pulled the contents of the basket apart. A green plant extended over his hand like a squid as he lifted it, each branch covered in pert, bristly needles. The women trembled like petrified rabbits.

"*This* is forbidden," the soldier barked, shaking the plant over the water and causing the dirt to lose its grip on the roots and be carried away in the brook. "You'll obey, or you'll be as dead as the rest of them!"

"Halt!" I shouted. The soldier and his silent partner spun around.

"Quintus, tent-mate to Legate Lucius," I said sternly. The pair promptly saluted me. It was unnecessary, but I was in no mood to correct them. "State your names."

"Cassius," the first responded.

The second followed with, "Cato."

I nodded, taking in the names in tandem with their faces as they stood at attention. As I approached, Cassius held out the basket to me. It contained several other plants and mosses.

"We came to the stream to fill our skins," he explained, "and found these wenches not at their work." He darted a sinister look over his shoulder.

"You found something in common, then?" I replied, keeping my tone cool. Cassius stammered, not quite sure how to respond. Finally finding his voice, Cato elaborated for his partner.

"These women were collecting plants at the water's edge, sir. Witches' plants."

"Witches' plants?" I repeated. My ears pricked up at the word, but I maintained my composure. Better to hear the whole story and judge for myself.

"Yes, sir," Cato continued. "These plants aren't edible, sir, not fruited, sir, and they were all plucking with their *left* hands."

At this, I raised an eyebrow. The concern in their eyes, their fear, was pronounced. It was understandable in this place, where the cries of the barbarously pious could be heard mingling with the night wind's howling. But I knew from many raucous nights in my parents' tavern that the best way to stop a fight without starting it again was to reprimand both. The women had fallen silent, aware that my intervention was not certain to aid them.

I gestured for the soldiers to leave their confiscated goods on the ground. "To your posts," I said.

Neither man resisted. As they passed me, I put a friendly hand on Cassius's shoulder and spoke low into his ear. "If you notice anything else, come directly to me."

He pressed his clenched fist against his chest in acknowledgment as he departed. I turned my attention back to the jumble of women as they dispersed. I narrowed my eyes at the crone who bent forward to retrieve the basket that Cassius had lain at my feet. She took hold of the woven handle, but I pinned it to the ground under my boot.

The woman crouching at my feet looked up at me, and I immediately realized my mistake. This was not the crone, but a young woman of striking beauty. Her eyes startled me as they peered up at me, imploring me with a widening expression. I instinctively withdrew my foot. She rose, her precious findings at hand, never taking her remarkable eyes from me as the rest fled.

"Thank you," she said in perfect Latin, confounding me further.

My mouth ran dry. I swallowed, not sure what to say, the logical workings of my mind temporarily arrested. She smiled at me, her pale, sallow cheeks suddenly flushed with color. I felt a rising heat reflected in my own countenance. The lady broke the silence.

"May I complete my search, or...or should I return to the village?" she asked. She began to back slowly away from me when I did not immediately reply.

I cleared my throat and straightened my back before answering. "What is the purpose of these?" I inquired, tearing my eyes away from her stare to gesture at the basket's contents.

"To heal. There is no harm in it," she replied.

I blinked, taking a small step back from her to catch my breath. The river and sloping hills behind her had begun spinning without warning. They resumed their regular place just as quickly, undermining the legs which kept the rest of my body upright. The woman locked eyes with me again, closing the small gap between us and looking coquettishly at me through veiled eyelids. My heart thundered in my chest as she spoke.

"You may come, if you wish."

I was eager to accommodate her; her knowledge of Latin was an invaluable asset. But my words came slowly, floating from my mind to my lips on a river of honey. So much was my speech impaired that the poor girl repeated her query before my mouth formed an affirmative answer.

Her lips peeled back in a wide smile, showing the teeth in the back of her mouth. Every one of her features was extraordinary, and as I walked downstream beside her, I could not bring my gaze away from her face.

Her eyes, which flitted back and forth between mine and the brook, were a cold gray, set widely apart with a sea of pallid flesh and a sharp, pinched nose in between. Her pale, thin lips were drawn tight as she led the way in silence. She had hair like fire that refused to be constrained by her woolen cap. The cap was tied beneath her chin, which sloped abruptly away from her face, making her whole head appear disproportionately small. Taken together, she was possessed of a rare, strange beauty.

I frowned as she knelt down and dipped the long, thin fingers of her left hand deftly into the rushing stream to retrieve an aquatic plant with round, bright green leaves. I didn't appreciate being so ill-used and quickly discarded, her only desire to go about her business unscathed.

"I mustn't look over my shoulder. But I haven't forgotten you."

Forgotten? I pressed my fingers against my brow, straining to remember all I had meant to say. We were closer now to the forest than the village, and my awareness of my original intent toward this woman and her companions buzzed obtusely in my ear.

"Why do you come here, so far from the rest?" I asked, unsure.

"For the samulos," she replied, lifting the plant in her outstretched hand before placing it delicately atop her growing pile.

"And the other?" I stalled.

"The selago is good for the eyes and driving away evil spirits. The older woman who was with me, Sarah, has a thin veil of white covering her eyes. The smoke of this plant should help remove it." For a moment, the cloud in my head lifted ever so slightly, and I pressed my opening.

"Who taught you that?"

Her face puckered into a scowl, and I bit my lip in regret.

"Am I a Druid, do you mean?" she retorted, placing her basket on the ground at her feet and planting her hands on the hips of her thick woolen dress. "Yes. What does Rome know of Druids? Is the worship of rivers and groves older than your ancestors' ancestors so odious?"

"It is when lives are stolen in the name of it."

"We praise life, my lord. We don't take it," she rebuffed. Her hands relinquished their defiant stance and turned to an anxious wringing. I resisted the urge to reach out to them, to uncurl those worried digits in my palms.

"Those that were cut down," she whispered, "invoked the gods' anger with their corruptions." She inched closer to me, making my heartbeat thrum in my ears.

"You claim your practices are nonviolent?"

"We offer sacrifices to the spirits," she admitted, "but no more than an ox, and that only in times of great need. That is permissible under Roman law, is it not?"

I nodded.

Her eyes widened, drinking in the light of the noonday sun. Staring into their lusterless hue was like sprinting through fog and diving headlong into a chasm.

"It is Calan Mai, and the spirits are upon us. Would you have me shun them?"

My tongue stuck to the inside of my mouth and barred me from answering.

"Would you deny them their due?" she pressed.

Something nagged. Before I regained my senses, the lady took a deep breath, and turned back toward the village. A chill wind rushed by as she passed. I lingered, disoriented, but she faced me again, and extended her hand.

She led me into one of the thatched huts. In the center was a hearth, dug in two concentric circles, which contained the flames as it warmed the space and illumined the darkened corners in which people hunched over their work. A woman in the easternmost corner steadily ground barley, while a child at her feet funneled the resulting powder into a clay vessel. Another duo knelt along the southern wall, squeezing whey out of what looked to be fresh cheese.

Before me was an impressive array of pots of all sizes, fired in plain clay. Larger still was a collection of amber, fashioned into a multitude of earrings, pendants, and brooches wrought in iron and gold. Some of the larger pieces held petrified insects, their wings frozen in the golden ochre of the woods. Others held spiders; their legs splayed out in eternal rest. The largest encased a fledgling bird, its barely hatched carcass curled about itself.

"Beautiful, are they not?"

I spun around to find the peerless beauty grinning in satisfaction at having found my interest piqued.

"Why so many?" I queried.

"The amber is as sacred as blood," she explained, "and can bring good fortune." Reflecting upon her own words, she picked up a small, clear specimen and pinned the brooch by a thin iron ring on her left shoulder. The result was immensely flattering.

"And these?" I asked, turning to the collection of jars.

The familiar aromas of thyme and sage filled my nose as she unplugged them for me. There were other, earthier scents I didn't recognize.

"Those soldiers," I asked, "were they the first to trouble you?"

"Begging your pardon?"

"Have you been harassed before?" I asked, half-afraid of the answer.

She inclined her head toward me. "Should I have been?"

"No, no, of course not," I replied. "It's just that there are a few men whose whereabouts are unknown, and I thought—"

"I see. It's most likely they've stumbled too far and gotten themselves lost. It's a common thing. I had another girl about my age helping me." She stopped, taking a step closer, her eyes as wide as an owl's. "Maybe they're together," she said with a grin. I felt my face redden and looked away quickly to hide my embarrassment.

"Tomorrow marks the dawn of spring," she said, leading me out. "We would have a bonfire, a feast, and an offering. You are welcome to attend, if it eases your worry. You need have no fear of us."

"Live lawfully, worship within reason, and give to the Divine Claudius *his* due, and you'll have nothing to fear from Rome," I replied in a firm voice, convinced of the fairness of my statement.

"Let this be our first act together, then," she declared. "Do you see where those two peaks meet, in the north?" She pointed to the mountains that lay beyond the forest. "Follow the peaks into the wood after sundown, and they will guide you. It is to the spirits who dwell beneath that we make our offering."

"Who shall I say invited me?"

"Hedra," she answered.

I came away satisfied, having made headway in my task, and in so doing having pleased a great beauty.

○

*L*ying atop my bed and staring at the ceiling, I found I couldn't remember Hedra's face. Features that had struck me as remarkable and distinctive now faded and slipped away, out of my reach. The lady's voice was equally hard to recall in her absence, and I found it difficult to make sense of the scraps of conversation that lingered in my head.

I had meant to ask Hedra of her birthplace; I was sure of it. Knowledge of our language and laws this far north was a rare thing indeed, and I wondered whether her Roman education had derived from elsewhere.

I was not entirely convinced by Hedra's claim that the villagers felt no grief at the violence that had been visited upon their priesthood. Their scared faces alone were proof they had been deeply affected. Whether or not they still harbored a futile resentment was unclear. Even more unclear was why I had agreed to witness a spiritual celebration that very well might incur Rome's returned wrath upon Mona.

I was sullen and distracted, and I made haste in quitting my tent at the appointed hour. I followed as straight a course as the forest would permit on my solitary march toward the mountains, coming upon row after row of stalwart oaks and yews interspersed with hostile birches, with no indication that I was nearing the opening of the wood. A thin branch swung back and bit my cheek when I attempted to brush past it. The wound was superficial but stung all the more in spite of it.

The sun was long gone now as I penetrated deeper into Britannia's wilds. Vapor rose up from the ground itself, creeping among the brush and bracken. The day's warmth vanished, leaving behind only cold shadows as the boughs overhead interlaced to blot out the moon. Dense as it was with rich undergrowth, the forest appeared abandoned by birds, critters, and beasts. Nor did the wind pass through its leaves, but the burgeoning fog—yea, the trees themselves—moved of their own accord, winking in and out of existence as the mist drifted and overwhelmed the grove.

My boot caught on something solid, and I stumbled. Bending down, I was met by the crude impression of a face carved into a long, weather-beaten stone. Represented only by two small circular impressions and a thin line for a mouth, its simplicity and grim expression unsettled me. I stood again slowly, acutely aware of my surroundings. I was deeper into the unknown than I had meant to go. The aspect of the wood had shifted. What had been a desolate space was now choked and menacing. The trees behind me stood taller and closer together, closer to *me*, like the strings of a purse drawn tight.

I surveyed my locale with wary eyes. The forest was so thick it was impossible to push forward. I contemplated retreat but turned abruptly when I heard a faint song. It was interrupted almost as soon as it had begun by the crisp snapping of movement just beyond. Cruel laughter was carried on the mist. I was on *their* ground now.

I drew my gladius noiselessly and squeezed between two unyielding tree trunks. I stepped through to a wide, flat expanse of grasslands grown knee-high. The ground sloped downward, and less than a quarter-mile out of the depression, the soil seemed spongy, in some places submerged altogether. Moonlight shimmered off the watery surface, its depths nearly translucent in the cool night. The surface of the lake sat undisturbed, excepting of a pair of tranquil geese. Without warning, their serenity descended into violence, their wings beating furiously against the night sky. Their shrieks stretched to the innermost recesses of my soul and shook me to my core. An image of blackened harpies flooded my memory at the sense of something moving behind me. I spun rapidly, swinging my weapon high in the air. Its sturdy blade cut through the fog and stopped short—my arm halted when I beheld Hedra, as stiff and unmoving as a stone pillar.

The cries of the geese were no more. They were gone; whither I did not see. Hedra first eyed the edge of the blade which touched her throat, then me, with haughty impatience. I blushed and quickly sheathed the weapon. She took a step closer, fixing me with her eyes. The coil in my stomach refused to unfurl, but her gaze swallowed me up, and I followed her obediently down into the bog.

4

___

ASENATH

*W*hen I noticed I'd written the same description for the last four statuettes and had repeated their catalogue numbers, I stopped. I rubbed my eyes to stay awake without subjecting myself to what I thought would have been my fifth coffee of the day. I packed away the last batch of properly catalogued items on the university truck and uploaded the latest round of photographs before stretching my limbs with a walk.

I left Alex doing God knows what and lumbered stiffly around the site. I was careful not to slide down an eight- or nine-foot drop which was more peat than solid dirt. The soil was deceptive, sometimes offering stable ground, but always with the threat of sinking into its bottomless patchwork lakes. The twin peaked mountains in the sky above me were perfectly aligned with the horizon, and I raised my camera to capture them. The perspective was a little too symmetrical to be interesting, but the mountains themselves looked majestic, with their crests peeping out from a thick white blanket of fog that threatened to roll off the mountain and over us before nightfall. Others had quickened their pace at the change in the air as well, anxious to be gone when that tingle on your skin told you fog was coming, the heavy kind that stopped you from seeing your hand in front of your face. Not being able to see whether your next step would land on peat or water was a frightening thought. The twilight breeze nipped at us, hastening our fingers as they sorted and packed tools, took the last soil samples for the day, and spread waterproof tarps over wide patches of the bog. We staked them down to prevent flooding, should the grim clouds be more than bluffing.

I came to the edge of the site and spied a solitary head crouched at its work in the northernmost sector of the excavation. According to Pryce's topography, the very edge of the forest had still reached here two thousand years ago, sloping steadily down toward the bog. Working from the outer boundary of the site inward, a young man about my age was farther out than most. He was so absorbed by his task that he hadn't noticed the rest packing it in.

"Hey," I called from the top of the slope, causing him to look up at me. "Time to call it a day. That's good work." I surveyed the near-pristine lines that he had etched out of the peat with a care and precision that put the stubborn, shapeless green muck to shame.

"Yeah, I just want to get this meter squared out," he answered, returning his face to the uneven wall of peat in front of him. He had marked out the edges with impossibly clean right angles and was aiming to smooth away the bulge in the center. "I won't sleep a wink tonight otherwise."

I smiled, appreciating that addiction to order that made a great excavator. I snapped on a spare set of latex gloves from my pocket and jumped in. My right foot sank down to the ankle, and the guy had to grip my wrist to right my balance as I pulled myself out. I whistled.

"Careful, doctor," he said, pointing at the dark, shallow impression where my boot had been. We watched as the peat slumped to fill in the depression, like a quicksand pit resetting its trap.

"This area is very unstable. That's why I marked it out first," he explained.

"I'm not a doctor yet," I said, feeling the strange need to correct him.

"You will be eventually. If you don't sink, that is."

"Right." I chuckled, trying to find a solid foothold where there was only sludge. "Christ, this is really sinking here. Why didn't you shout for help?" I asked.

"No need for shouting. You came, didn't you?"

I nodded, laughing. "Right again." He had an easy smile that was contagious. It lifted a huge weight from me as the day drew to a quiet close. I took the right corner, as it was the one closest to me, and he stationed himself at the left. We slowly closed the gap between us, pulling at the peat with small tools, sometimes by hand. I caught him stealing a glance in my direction more than once, and something fluttered in my chest, something that hadn't in a long, long while. He could flirt with me in public if he wanted to, and no one would look at him funny or ask uncomfortable questions—the kind that Alex avoided, and that made me feel insignificant, like I'd imagined the last two years.

"You can call me Azi," I said, working up a good sweat that felt heavenly after so many hours hunched over a mud-covered table.

"Then I guess it's only fair that you call me Jakob," he answered in a glib voice before fading back into the quiet concentration which I had disturbed.

The wall hewn into the peat before us was a little more than nine feet high. Stretching my legs to stand on my toes only made me sink farther. When I finally loosed the chunk above my head that I'd been working on, it came down quickly, and I had to dodge to avoid a face full of peat. I cleared the heavier piece of rubble at my feet. The electric blue of my gloves contrasted starkly with the turf that was progressively blackening as night began its stealthy approach. A wooden shard was encased in the peat which clung to it, lending the mud its weight and substance. I rubbed the peat away, and my thumb caught a curved indentation on the underside of the wood. I turned up the electric lamp to the right of me and held the rotted, stained wood in front of it. What my fingertips had felt was only faintly visible, but the pad of my index finger confirmed that it was there—the thin, scored impressions in the wood, the physical substance of which had long ago been dissolved by the acid in the peat.

I turned my eyes quickly upwards to where the chunk of peat had fallen from. "Hold up," I said, raising the lantern over my head to get a better view.

"What is that?" Jakob queried, following my gaze to the striations in the dirt that had been just out of reach.

"Willow branches," I said, my attention roving slowly over the continuous line of riddled dimples and thin, deep incisions in the peat above our heads, seeking a conclusive edge. The angle of the needles' impressions overlapped in a horizontal pattern. My heart beat double-time; the hair on the back of my neck stood on end. This was different from the other signs of human activity—more significant. "These branches were laid flat," I mused, excited, "put here deliberately. Hold this." I passed Jakob the lantern and pulled at the camera strap under my windbreaker. Jakob held the light a foot higher than I could, casting the striations in such an acute contrast that what had been faint in my hands was now unmistakable.

"Just like that," I said, rotating the focus of my lens to sharpen the view. When I inched closer to the wall to bring it into focus, something solid poked at my hip. I took the shot, several times to be sure, then looked down. Another clump of peat fell away as I stepped back. My heart stopped. What had poked me, and what was now exposed to the open air, was a finger.

Jakob's line of sight caught up to mine, and was immediately accompanied by an "oh, shit!"

My mouth gaped, camera hanging limply from my hands. I'd uncovered so much with my parents, had seen so many preserved kings and queens, but never had we actually discovered a mummy for ourselves. This was my first.

"Azi!"

I heard Alex calling me impatiently. His voice sounded a million miles away. I didn't take my eyes off that tanned, leathery finger, all the fine lines and creases of the knuckle made distinctive in the glow of the lamp as the sun dipped away to my left.

"Alex!" I called back, my whole-body rigid with excitement. I was ten years old again, and ready to explode.

"Come on, Azi, we're done for the day!" he shouted.

"I don't think so!"

His boots sloshed quicker and closer together, hearing the triumphant tone in my voice.

"What?" he cried, stopping at the edge of the pit, out of breath.

I tore my gaze from the digit to Alex, and simply pointed. His eyes widened, and he shouted to Pryce, who was not far behind, before coming into the trench with us. Jakob pushed the lantern into Alex's hands the minute he descended, and without further discussion, we chipped slowly, slowly, slowly away from the peat in front of us. Lanterns from the rest of the site were snatched from their posts and brought here, surrounding us in a bright yellow haze as Jakob and I fought the fog as hard as we could without being careless with what lay in front of us. A small crowd had gathered—students who had caught a second wind on the eve of discovery, and even some new faces, colleagues whom Dr. Pryce had called when the unearthing of the first bog body on Anglesey was imminent.

The crooked finger that had heralded the body was connected to a hand, then an arm, then a shoulder. Seconds and minutes passed like hours as I traced the curve of the deflated, once powerful shoulder up the neck, careful not to dislodge the rusted hair that fell lazily there until I caught sight of the jawline, still intact. My brush was caked up to the hilt with peat as I brushed at the chin, seeking and finding lips, the bridge of a nose, and finally, two eyes.

Cheers pierced the golden-speckled night. I couldn't catch my breath. I just continued to gaze in silent awe at the head that hung solemnly before me. The eyes were firmly closed as I dusted off the brows and forehead, causing some hairs to come loose from the peat and fall across the face. The eyelids were closed, smooth and calm, but his lips, the fine lines still distinctive, were puckered. At turns, he appeared in sleep and in agony, like he couldn't decide which. Taking in the whole of his face, as well as the individual angles and features, the man was striking, so vivid in his un-sleep that I just stared for a long time, taking in his portrait with painstaking detail.

"Just like Tollund Man," Jakob finally said. "Like he's sleeping and is gonna wake up any moment. He's perfect."

He nudged me back to my senses, gesturing to the camera hanging loosely about my neck. My fingers felt the coolness of the night as they fiddled with the settings, allowing for the abysmal lighting conditions. I didn't dare use a flash on such delicate skin, settling instead for perching Alex's hand in just the right position to cast a revealing light on the face.

"Can't you hold still?" I cried. Alex's hand shook and it frustrated me to no end. He scowled, but I got my shot.

"Your turn," Alex said to Jakob, handing him the lantern dismissively and looming over the body. He offered his hand to me to help me back to where he was. "Come on," he said, pulling me back and taking the camera off my neck. He made to hand it to Jakob, but I caught the grip.

"No," I insisted. "This one is *his*."

Jakob was as embarrassed as Alex was seething. I stood firm.

"It's *ours*," Jakob finally interjected. He pulled at the bottom of my windbreaker and wrapped a muddy sleeve around my shoulder, the deliberate squishing sound he produced causing me to laugh.

Alex took the camera from me with a grunt, but I didn't care. I smiled broadly and didn't let his sour attitude spoil the moment. Jakob was light on his feet, carefree as he switched places with Alex, who did his best *not* to touch me as he stood beside me. I was still smiling, only this time it wasn't genuine. He stepped away from me as soon as he could.

"Can we get out of the mud now, please?" he whined, extending his arms above his head to be hoisted out of the pit by two other grad students who had brought the wide, flat planks that would keep the body safe as it was extracted from the bog.

I lingered, not taking my eyes from the body as planks were shoved under his feet, behind his back, and on either side of him.

"Sorry," I whispered, as the man's face, hidden from the world for millennia, was once more packed in dirt and the final plank of his coffin nailed shut. I brushed my numbed fingers against the wooden box as it was lifted by stalwart hands out of the bog. Dr. Pryce hoisted me out of the trench for the night, shaking both my hands heartily and kissing my cheeks in congratulations.

"Can you believe it?" he said, his hands trembling in mine, his eyes lit up like a schoolboy's.

"Not hardly." I couldn't tell which of us was shaking the other.

His smile stretched all the way back to his ears. "Well, you've done it now. No going back," he said. "I really wish I could keep you. You could teach this old dog a thing or two." His smile settled into a thin, even line as he said, "Your parents would be proud of you."

"They sure would," Alex said, coming up behind me and pressing his fingers into my shoulder. "I am too."

I took in Alex's face for the first time in days. The smile there seemed genuine, but for some indefinable reason, I wasn't entirely convinced that it was. There was something about the way his bottom lip pushed against the other that made me uneasy. It reminded me of a pouting child who had discarded an unwanted toy and only regretted it at the sight of another's enjoyment. After all his sweet talk about trading the desert for the bog and carving out a name for myself not linked to my parents, he appeared simultaneously surprised and disappointed—I couldn't decipher why, and it bothered me.

I drifted away from the site, following the floating lanterns and the obscured men who carried them like formless wraiths wandering toward their vehicles. A whistle turned my attention behind me. Jakob, carrying the lantern we had used in the pit, swung it above his head and to the right at a blue pickup.

"Can I buy you a drink, doctor?"

"I told you, I'm not—"

"You will be after today," he interrupted. "So how about it?" He lifted the lantern again, illuminating both our faces. His eyes glittered like emeralds.

"You can buy me two."

5

"There's another one!"

I leaped out of my chair at Jakob's declaration and raced with him back to the northwest corner of the site where all our efforts were now concentrated. Not even a quarter-mile from where our first body had been found, Alex and two others were unearthing another corpse.

I ran so wildly my foot slipped at the edge of the pit and I slid down to the bottom. Jakob yanked me to my feet and tried, unsuccessfully, to wipe the muck from my back.

"I'm fine, I'm fine," I insisted, wading over to where Alex was digging. "What did you find?"

"A leg, so far," Alex answered, wiping his forehead on the corner of his elbow and smearing mud on his face.

I smirked. "I thought you didn't like getting dirty."

Alex's face turned beet red. "It's my dig. What else should I be doing?"

"*Your* dig?" I repeated, incredulous. "Since when?"

The hue of his cheeks deepened to a dark purple, but the man standing to Alex's right sliced through the dense air.

"I've got an arm," he declared.

I cocked my head, studying the depression beside the shriveled, leathery leg that Alex was exposing up to the hip. The tanned edges of the abdomen sunk back into the peat, then disappeared.

"I don't think the left one's attached," I said. "You would have come across it by now."

Alex grudgingly looked up from his work and nodded his head in the affirmative. "Go over there and look for it," he snapped, pointing off to his left. His helpers looked up at him, then at each other, before turning their eyes back to their work without saying a word.

I opened my mouth to bite his head off, but Jakob pulled me away to hunt for the detached limb. "Come on, forget him," he whispered.

"That arrogant bastard," I cursed under my breath.

"I know, I know. Don't worry about it. What do you want tonight? Indian?"

I grimaced. "I do love Indian, but again?"

"All right—burgers?" he suggested.

"Yeah. On me this time."

"Deal. So, what will we call this one? Anglesey Man B?" Jakob asked, pulling away a chunk of peat with a hand-held trowel and tossing it to the ground behind him.

"Anglesey Man—is that what we're calling ours?" I asked.

"What else would we call him?"

"Anglesey Man," I repeated. "I like the sound of that."

"Uh—how do you like the sound of Anglesey Man C?"

I turned to him, confused.

"Call me stupid, but that's *another* right arm."

A third limb hung suspended in the peat right in front of us. It was only paces away from the others.

"Didn't find your leg," I shouted over my shoulder. "Will another arm do?"

I lost all track of time as we carved the corpse out of the bog. He was submerged upright, like the others. The head was in slightly better shape than Anglesey Man B, but a chunk of his shoulder was caved in, and both of the legs were missing.

"Look, look!" I cried as I brought the level of excavated mud nearer to his head.

"Those don't look like willow branches," Jakob commented.

"No," I said, scanning the impressions encircling the head like a halo. "They're thick and braided, like wicker."

"A *wicker* man? Seriously?" Jakob quipped.

I grinned. "You got it. I want to make a mold of this. What do we have?"

"There's a plaster set back at the lab, I think. I'll make a run." He kissed me on the cheek and scrambled out of the pit.

"Thanks!" I shouted and pulled my camera out of my bag to take a dozen more shots. I felt a lumbering presence gather over my shoulder and turned around to find Alex glaring at me.

"What the hell was that?" he grunted.

"The impressions here are different from the other one. These are more woven than botanical."

"Not *that*."

"What?" I asked.

His eyes narrowed to murderous slits. Laughter bubbled up in my throat so fast I almost choked—he'd seen Jakob kiss me.

"What?" I dared him. "What's the problem, *professor*?"

He remained silent—I knew he would. He would never say anything out loud, in public. Why he'd brought it up at all was a mystery.

He swiveled on his heel and rejoined his team without giving me an answer. There was no talking to him after that. On our last day, when I showed him the cargo list for what we were taking back with us, he exploded.

"Are you insane? This was *our* dig!"

"And we only found as much as we did because of Pryce's help," I countered.

"Is it Pryce, then? Did he pressure you into this, because if he did, I'll—"

"*No*," I insisted.

His eyes widened. "Then how in God's name could you let them keep *two* of the bodies? Two!"

"Because I want Anglesey Man!"

"Who cares which ones we get?"

I shook my head, furious that the first honest conversation we were having about this excavation was over turf. His protests rang in my ears as someone desperate to stay relevant, to take control of a project he'd given minimal thought to. It was obvious now that he'd never expected this dig to matter at all. Why encourage me then? Why waste my time? I couldn't wrap my head around it. But he'd left me to my own devices so long that I hated him stepping on my toes.

"Anglesey Man is the most complete—he'll tell us more than the others will." When he didn't respond, I played my trump card. "It's *my* name people will see first on anything published," I reminded him, balling my hands into fists at my sides to keep the rest of me from shaking. "*I* made the proposal. *I* made this dig happen, and *I'm* taking the body I want back with me." Anglesey Man was the one I wanted. His was the face that came to me in my sleep, that possessed my days and would fill the pages of my dissertation. He had had an effect on me, more than the others. Whether it was because he was the first, or because of the conditions, I couldn't tell. But the prospect of leaving him in another team's hands was too much of a sacrifice.

I took several deep breaths, curling my toes inside my shoes, finding any way I could to squirm in my place without letting Alex see. He stayed silent for several seconds, each tick of the clock stretching to its extremity. His face reddened with every passing moment. The animus in his eyes told me he hadn't forgotten our publication agreement, and that his annoyance stemmed from the fact that *I* hadn't either. I relaxed the pressure of my fingernails against my palms and blinked, trying to cool my own ire before either of us said something we shouldn't. Alex caught the gesture, and thankfully followed suit.

"Fair enough," he answered, the fire fading from his cheeks as the hard-set line of his lips upturned in one corner.

"Thank you," I said, relieved. He came closer, standing a head taller than me and looking down into my eyes. I was afraid he would kiss me and went stiff as a statue.

Satisfied, he laughed under his breath. "Good for you." With that, he left. I rubbed my eyes, passing my hand quickly through my hair. I groaned at the prospect of having to do that again, greasing the small wheels in my head that might just conjure a way for us to never have to work together again. At a loss, I groaned louder.

○

"*I*t might be a while until you hear from me, but I promise to share everything," Dr. Pryce said, taking my bags out of his trunk and laying them on the sidewalk outside Cardiff airport.

"I'll do the same," I said, extending my hand.

He laughed, bypassing my hand and opening both his arms in a jovial embrace.

"Safe journey, Miss Hayes. I hope we can work together again soon."

"I'd like that." I took my leave of him as he moved to bid Alex goodbye.

Jakob didn't know what to do with himself, and simply smiled at me. He finally decided to take his hands out of his pockets as he drew closer to me and reached for my hand.

"Thanks for everything," I said, squeezing his fingers and wishing I'd chosen to stay silent instead. It would have been more elegant. His gaze darted to the ground as he gave a subtle nod. He tugged on me, bringing us closer together, and left a tender kiss on my cheek.

"It's been my pleasure," he murmured against my neck.

I licked my lips, my heart quickening. "Mine too." The corners of his mouth twitched in a smile against my skin. "Goodbye, Jakob."

"Bye, Azi."

Our mouths touched so lightly that I wasn't sure if I'd felt his lips or only dreamed them. He held my fingers until the last moment. He snaked his hand back into his pocket as I looked over my shoulder and the glass door slid closed behind me.

"Let's move it. I want to grab a drink before we board." Alex's voice broke my trance, and I looked at him blankly, disoriented. I stifled a hard, shuddering breath. I wanted to scream at Alex or run back through the doors. I cared more about Jakob in that moment than I did about the man standing beside me—the one I'd loved my whole life. I didn't know whether to laugh or cry. Settling on neither, I hauled ass to the gate.

"*H*ere," Alex said, throwing the slim, neatly shrink-wrapped airplane blanket off his seat and onto my lap. "After weeks in that Godforsaken dorm, you need this more than I do."

I'd been perfectly comfortable in Jakob's apartment for those last two, but I kept that to myself as I layered his blanket on top of my own, settling into my chair and pulling up my satchel on the spare seat to the left of me, taking out first my sketchpad, then my charcoals.

Alex surprised me by arresting my hand in his own, touching me more softly than I had let him in a long time.

"Pryce was right, Azi," he started, examining my fingers as he folded them into his own. "Your parents would be very proud of you." I swallowed hard, not wanting to think about Alex *or* my parents at that moment.

I don't remember falling asleep, and I certainly do *not* remember resting my head on Alex's shoulder. Yet that's the position I found myself in when the captain announced our descent into Providence. I felt a cozy compression on my hair release as Alex lifted his cheek off my head, waking the same moment as me, and stretching his arms upward. He didn't seem to care at all, going about his regular business of retrieving his carry-on from overhead and sitting alert for our departure. When I finally caught his eyes, I searched for some meaning there, some clue as to whether he was showing restraint, or that his passions had cooled. I found none. Aloof or oblivious, he disembarked without fanfare, wishing me a hollow "so long" as he headed off to claim our precious cargo.

---

hree weeks without paint made my fingers itch. It was intolerable. Despite the mountain of work I had ahead of me in preparation for the start of the fall term, I headed to my studio.

My charcoal sketches of the bog were interesting, but hardly did the subject justice. "Good thing it's not an autumn scene," I mumbled to myself as I took inventory of my oils. My stash was devoid of warm tones, most likely lost to the desert I was so fond of painting. A trip to the art supply store that was my lifeline was out of the question so late in the summer, at least until my tenants showed up and paid their balance. Those tenants were expecting clean sheets and a stocked fridge, so luxuries would have to wait. I had enough of the dark, cool tones I needed, but still, the principle of the thing nagged.

I put my doubts about what would happen next year if I *didn't* get my professorship aside as I treated the largest canvas I had left, covering the surface in a pure black suffused with colder greens and blues. Working from the darkness up would produce a better result for what I envisioned, and I willingly lost myself in the broad, sweeping motions of my four-inch brush as I moved from one edge of the canvas to the other.

Painting had the incredible ability to clear my head, and as I offered the canvas the last of my strokes and cleansed the brush in paint thinner, I had a solid idea of what I needed from the store. Grabbing my shoes, I was tempted by my camera, lying coyly at the edge of my computer desk. Locked inside was the face that haunted me, the one that I had tried, unsatisfactorily, to copy from memory on the plane. I'd had nothing else to do, but sitting so close to someone for all those hours, especially Alex, distracted me, and I couldn't do my best work. I snuck a few minutes to plug my memory card into the computer and run off a few copies of the first images I had taken of Anglesey Man's face, his distinctive features cast in soft lantern light. For once, the printer cooperated, giving my high-resolution photos all the attention they deserved.

Feeling productive, I pulled four sets of bed linens and bath towels out of the closet and hoofed them down to the basement. I tossed the first load in with my last drop of OxyClean and cracked the windows in every bedroom before heading out. I came home with a car packed to the gills with laundry soap, dish soap, bath soap, and the ridiculously overpriced hand soap made with Turkish fig oil that Ravi specifically requested. I loaded up the kitchen with college staples—Red Bull, Ramen, rocky road ice cream, a good Shiraz, and cheesy poofs.

Two cans of all-purpose Pledge and a box of Swiffer was the bare minimum for exiling the dust congregating on every frame and artifact in the house. Dusting two floors of Egyptian antiquities and a sprawling basement library was a full-time job. I was dry-dusting an Anubis fetish when my mind found its way again to Anglesey Man. Leaving the ebony of the jackal god's torso gleaming, I slipped up to my room, and found my images spat onto the carpeted floor. I collected and ordered them with care, bringing them dutifully down the hallway to my parents' bedroom.

There had been no one to scold me for over a decade, but still I could not bring myself to transgress the door. I spoke quietly into the wood, painted white and flanked by sphinxes, their feathered wings outstretched over the upper lintel.

"I found one," I whispered in a trembling voice, fingering the pictures in my hands. "His name is Anglesey Man. He's incredible,

Daddy. You wouldn't believe how well something wet can be preserved. Skin, teeth, hair…"

I stopped, unsure. The door was unmoved. I selected the best image, and slipped it into the narrow, darkened space under the door.

"Wish you'd been there," I whispered, coming to sit with my legs folded on the hall runner. Suddenly the house felt very big, and very empty. I leaned my head on the door, and bawled like a child who'd been left behind, whose parents had moved to the other end of the world and had forgotten me, discarded along with all the lifeless objects it had become my duty to dust.

I allowed myself the time to expend my sorrow, and when my tears had again run dry, I picked myself up and shuffled back up the stairs to the top floor, entering my art haven, the circular room encased by the stone tower façade of our Victorian. It had been empty storage before, but skylights and the distance from the common areas made it an ideal workspace. I pinned the remaining photos I'd run off of Anglesey Man and Cerriglyn Bog, keeping the foliage I wished to invoke close to my easel.

I mixed colors between loads of laundry, looking for just the right collection of high- and low-lights to bring the bog back to life. I mixed, saw they modulated too bright in the sunshine, shut the lights, and mixed again. Stifled by the summer's last hurrah, I peeled the flannel shirt off my back as I readied myself for move-in day. Within four hours, my knuckles were cracked from alternately building on my palette and scrubbing my hands vigorously before applying pristine white linens to all four of the guest bedrooms.

I finally sat down to my canvas. Warm, moist air crept through the open window, gravitating toward the tips of my hair and causing them to crimp and curl around my ears. The black paint gleamed, stopping me from seeing colors and shapes as they should have been. The glare from the windows and the sun's swelter annoyed me, pulled me away from my art. I got up and pulled down the heavy shades, allowing only the smallest slit of light to escape.

"Okay, Google, play *Marche Slave* by Tchaikovsky," I called out, doubling down on creating the right headspace. Before the song's first movement met its brooding conclusion, darkness had swallowed up the room, my imagination of the tower in which I painted as high as any cathedral or castle. All that remained was my canvas and me as I poured my soul into it, my brush conquering the wintry blues, grays, and muddy greens of the fen's underbrush.

7

_I_ was woken by the unexpected vibration of my phone in my back pocket. I can't recall lumbering over to the black leather couch and falling asleep on it, but there I was, and there again was the droning noise on my ass that made me want to roll over murderously and keep snoring.

Perhaps I should have done that, instead of rubbing my hand over my face as the other one retrieved the text from Alex.

Body's in the lab. You coming or what?

I stumbled over to the bathroom, blitzing my skin with a cold shower. That did the trick. I donned a fresh shirt and comfy, beat-up sneakers and headed down to the kitchen. The deli meat and tomato wrap I assembled for myself wasn't half as tightly packed as the ones the cafeteria ladies excelled at, but this was a cheaper meal. I hoped the cheese wouldn't all melt away to oily nothingness and stink up my toaster as I trotted back upstairs, remembering my painting at last. It looked good both with and without overhead lighting, which pleased me. I nodded, grunting in self-approval on my way out, and thought to add a slight bit more detail in the front and push everything back another layer when I got home.

My wrap sucked, but I ate it, mainly because I didn't have another option. My stomach's growling turned my head again toward my dwindling cash flow. That I was heading to see Alex fused in my head with the reason I had broken it off in the first place. He'd asked me to pay for the hotel room in Wales, the one I never saw the inside of, and I'd made the fatal mistake of taking him into my financial confidence. He'd always complained about his wife being tight with her money, but that was the first time he'd let slip that he thought he could have mine. Or what he thought was mine. That was the last time I heard even the pretense of a divorce.

It had been months since that day, but it still stuck in my throat to be a small part of a bigger, if imagined, bargain, and I let myself fume in the car as I drove down the sloping roads to College Hill and parked outside Hayes Hall. Our undergrad assistants wouldn't be showing up for at least another week but being all business with Alex had become routine. Still, there had been smiles, furtive glances, the serendipitous grazing of hands and incendiary banter. The absence of those stolen seconds, especially in an otherwise abandoned lab, felt like the epitome of the cold shoulder. I'd made it clear I was done, and I meant it. But what girl doesn't at least want the guy to put up a fight?

This situation was of my own making, and I willed myself to take what I asked for and shut up about it when I entered the lab. All thoughts about how I was ever going to focus left my head at that moment. To the left of me, just inside the door, was a man-sized crate, propped up against the wall, and a half-dozen more crates lining the floor.

"I thought you'd be here to greet your boyfriend," Alex quipped, pulling a worn lab coat over an even more worn polo and pants.

"Excuse me?" I snapped back.

"You kept drawing him on the plane like a lovesick school girl."

Bile gurgled in my throat, and I could feel my cheeks flush a hot red. "Are you a scientist or a ten-year-old?" I barked, snapping gloves on my own hands and becoming quickly distracted by my own eagerness.

"Small boxes first?" Alex queried, the right corner of his mouth tugging upward as he dropped the attitude.

"Yeah, okay," I countered, pulling a long film of plastic out of a narrow drawer and tucking it under Anglesey Man's crate.

"Wouldn't it be easier to lay it flat?" Alex asked, standing peevishly stationary at my side.

"I want him upright," I said curtly, annoyed at myself for not keeping my own anger in check. "At least, for now," I added, more softly.

"Egyptian style, eh? Well, it's your show now." He grabbed a crowbar from his duffel.

"Careful," I said, seeing more solid layers of dirt snaking through the widening aperture at the base of the crate as Alex pried it apart.

"Any softer and it won't budge," Alex grunted, perspiring before several minutes had passed. The left seam popped, and the nails hung jaggedly from the cover. The far side was quick work, and we instinctively reached for opposing ends of the lid, pulling it away with great care. The full weight of it strained my hands as it perched there for the prolonged period it took for us to shuffle it gingerly to the side; the latex covering over my palm ripped open.

Relieved of the lid at last, we were met by a wall of peat. It was easier going to uncover Anglesey Man the second time, with the soil surrounding him shifting slightly in flight. That, and the fact that his angles had burned themselves into my psyche, so I knew instinctively where to dig.

"Put a few more layers down, so we can pull them away as we go." Alex gestured to the mud spilling forward at Anglesey Man's feet. I wordlessly complied, lining the floor with several smaller layers of plastic.

Anglesey Man's face reemerged first. Seeing it again lifted a great weight from me. I smiled in the conviction of having made the right choice. We worked silently for two hours. It was not the comfortable, concentrated silence that Jakob and I had shared under similar circumstances. The air was thick with restraint, the bog body between us a welcome distraction growing to obsession as I worked single-mindedly, tracing the curves of his bowed arm down to his elbow, sloping inward again to the hand and finding the hip, following it down to his toes. I stepped back and blinked, taking in all we had unearthed.

He was in complete possession of all his limbs and extremities, unlike any bog body ever. I reached instantly for the camera in my bag, ignoring Alex's snickering as I snapped away. They were not as moody as the ones taken in his resting place, but I captured more minute details of the whole and its many parts in the harsh, sterile light. Alex pulled up a stool.

"Don't forget the penis," he said gruffly, the starchy linen of his coat scratching against itself as he folded his arms impatiently. "To tell the truth I'm jealous of the guy, even in *this* state."

"That's inappropriate," I snapped, vicariously insulted for our vulnerable subject.

Alex let out a low chuckle, no doubt counting how many times I would have been justified in saying just that but welcomed it instead. He was secretly grateful for the interval of rest, I'm sure, and I left him to it.

Satisfied, I restored my camera to its place, and reached for a blank legal pad and pencil. Alex showed no signs of moving as I inched closer to the body, ready to begin in earnest. Inwardly, I shrugged. Like he said, it was my show. My fingers worked tirelessly to record every detail, seeing nothing as too minute to escape notice.

Aside from the wrinkling and tanning caused by the elevated acid levels of the peat, the skin was smooth. There was no tell-tale crisscrossing on the chest or arms, nor the hips or thighs, that would have indicated a woven fabric, long ago eaten by the same cold acids and bacteria that had preserved human flesh for thousands of years. He had been submerged, like so many other bog males, in nothing but his own skin.

The upright posture of his burial was remarkable in that it was unique to him and the other specimens found in Cerriglyn Bog. Tollund Man had lain curled in a semi-fetal position, as had Grauballe Man. I didn't believe that was insignificant and marked it on my pad in terms of cardinal directions, having a sense that a head pointed north might be worth investigating.

I'd already spent enough time studying his face, both in and out of the lab, but I made a note of his expression, that subtle, pained sleep that he had in common with Tollund Man, the most well-preserved bog head, with possibly the exception of the one currently before me. It was easy to see that he had been handsome—his straight nose, full, though now wrinkled, lips, and nicely shaped eyes were striking even in his death pose. He was well-groomed, with thick, well-kept brows but no rusted stubble to match the almost-shoulder-length hair that hung from his head. The coloration, too, was a function of the bog peat. He most likely had been dark-haired. His hands, held in front of him by a long rope, were also well cared for, the fingers and nails neat except for the earth packed tightly underneath. His shoulders were hunched now, and extensively wrinkled, but I could imagine the full breadth and muscular hulk that gave the body its now-shriveled appearance.

"His organs might be intact as well," I said over my shoulder to the superfluous lump sitting guard.

"The med school has an MRI we can probably use. Anything else?"

"I'll take care of it," I grumbled, going back to my subject as I plotted out in my head the multitude of different experts who might be able to shed light on Anglesey Man's final days, wondering if something useful like stomach contents could be determined without marring his unbroken skin.

The thought made me start, and my eyes quickly scanned Anglesey Man's form again. His skin was indeed unbroken. My brow furrowed.

"Something's not right."

The timbre of my voice lifted Alex from his perch, and he came to stand beside me.

"Not right?" he repeated.

"How did he die?" I asked, my stare not leaving the body.

Alex turned his attention from me to the Anglesey Man. After a moment's pause, he squinted. I wasn't imagining it.

"There are no gashes under the chin or over the heart," I continued. "And no signs of trauma to the head. The skull is intact."

"Fell into the bog, then?" Alex suggested.

"And he didn't struggle?" I retorted, infuriated by the sheer stupidity of it. "His muscles would be all contorted. He's docile and bound."

Alex puckered his lips and pushed them to one corner of his mouth, picking up the thin rope that circled Anglesey Man's neck. It was really two cords twisted together, with one end looped and knotted into an eyelet. The length was fed through the loop, wrapped once loosely around the shoulders and then down the back, ending in the front with the opposite length coiled around the wrists. There was significant slack around the neck, the cord not pulled taut into a proper noose.

"This cord," Alex said, deliberate in his words, "it's not even tight enough to restrain him. He won't have been strangled. Maybe hanged?"

"It didn't make an impression on the neck or chin," I concurred, putting tentative fingers into the peat to feel along the back of the neck. A thrill ran through me, and I closed my eyes as my gloved fingertips felt solid resistance beneath the leathered skin. The soil acids that so miraculously preserved skin and hair could, and often did, dissolve the bones if the levels were high enough. But the vertebrae were present, and intact. I shrugged at Alex and shook my head.

"His neck's not broken."

"The rope's not functional," he murmured.

"It's ceremonial," I pushed. He looked hard at me for a moment, then begrudgingly nodded. "There's something else," I added, teasing out the knot forming in my gut.

"His size?" Alex offered.

"Yes," I said, surprised that his brain hadn't shut down entirely.

Alex shook his head and grunted, working out the same problem that had nagged at the back of my mind.

"It's not normal to sacrifice the healthiest male. He would be indispensable. He committed some offense, perhaps? Offended the gods?"

I peered again at Anglesey Man's face. The expression that had once been pained and quiet now seemed inscrutable.

"Won't you speak to us?" I murmured, looking up at him with my hands curled around my hips. I stood stumped. "Poison?" I said at last.

"Did Druids poison their sacrifices?"

"No. At least, not that we know of, but it would explain the lack of slashes or cuts. Maybe he was forced to ingest something?"

"Or it was accidental. Could have died of food poisoning."

"The stomach contents should tell us something," I said, poring carefully over the torso. Maybe I'd missed something. Heaven knew his once-proud chest was folded enough in some places to hide a fatal wound in its depths. Propped up as he was, I had to crane my neck to observe his upper body, the muscles at the back of my head quickly becoming sore. I turned my neck quickly to the left and back again to crack the stiffened joints. In that flicker of a moment, a reflective glint caught my eye.

I inverted my perspective again. A metallic fragment shone dully back at me—the arc of a circle, wrought in gold. Carved into the metal was a wreath of laurels, encircling what looked like the talon of an eagle.

"Is that…?"

My query went unfinished, and I set myself instead to retrieving the precious object lodged in the leathered skin. It did not come freely. Seeking to wedge it out of its place without damaging the skin to which it had adhered, I dug my finger between the leathery folds of shrunken muscle, furrowing to the unseen edge. Something else solid obstructed my way, something that possessed the striated grain of wood.

"I can't get at it," I panted, attempting now to coax the concealing muscle to the side, relaxing its constriction enough to produce a clear path out into the open again.

"Can you see it?" Alex asked, hunching over me, but unable to see past me.

"It's…it's a stake," I said breathlessly, seeing its shape more with my fingers than my eyes.

"A stake?" Alex repeated incredulously.

"It's struck into him, over his heart. But there's something pinned to it—a gold ring."

The hand Alex had placed excitedly on my shoulder and which had lain there ignored, now asserted itself, pressing me to switch places with him so he might try.

"Here," he said, being less careful than I had been, but using enough force to dislodge the thing from its ancient mooring. As he did, a long, deep hiss emanated from the lifeless form, the sudden shuddering as an intake of breath.

My spine tingled. Tremors of shock raced up Alex's arm, the

contents in his hand clattering to the floor. He stepped into me, pushing us both back and grabbing my arm with terrific force. I held my breath.

Nothing else happened for several seconds. I don't know what I expected to happen next, but nothing did. Alex and I stood clasping each other, until my agitation got the better of me, and I scolded him.

"You were never this jumpy with the pharaohs," I cried.

"*They* had the decency to keep quiet!"

I released my iron grip on Alex's arm. "You scared me, you dolt," I chided, blaming Alex as I smoothed back my frazzled hair.

"I scared *you*? I think I pissed myself a little."

Our nervous laughter broke the horror of the moment, waking us from the impossible realm where something else *might* have happened. Settling down, I thought we were both grateful to continue working more amicably. But before kneeling down to retrieve what Alex had dropped in his terror, I scrutinized the death mask before me. It was as it had been before. I observed it closely, becoming increasingly frightened by its *lack* of movement. The fear of expectation in that moment was supreme. When my fright bored me, I picked up what lay at Anglesey Man's feet—a wooden stake, either oak or birch, and a thin, closed loop fashioned out of iron, from which hung an amber amulet. Encrusted in the amber was an insect, with long, spindly legs like that of a mosquito. Beside all this lay what had first seized my attention—a signet ring, bearing a Roman emblem, forged in gold.

"It's remarkable," Alex said, holding the piece up to the fluorescent light. "The details of the inscription are exquisite."

I took the ring back from him, turning it over in my fingers. I shot an astute glance at Anglesey Man, taking in the whole of his features once more.

"This is *his* ring," I said with excited conviction.

"We can't know that for sure. Men traditionally wear rings on their fingers, not staked to their chests. It was most likely scavenged."

"*Look* at him," I demanded. "The broad chest, the fine grooming, the straight nose."

Alex's expression transformed from one of scrutiny to awesome revelation. "By the gods, I think you're right."

"He was pegged as a Roman, literally," I said, pinching the ring between my fingers in demonstration. "His death was an act of war."

"Does our timeline jibe?" Alex asked, his voice upbeat, optimistic.

"Claudius outlawed Druidry in 54 A.C.E. Our soil samples were dating anywhere from

100 B.C.E. to 100 A.C.E."

"So, it's possible this man was involved in that campaign," Alex concluded.

"Very possible." I nodded, feeling the same surge of triumph at first finding Anglesey Man return in all its vigor.

"Do you know what that means?" Alex asked.

"That the only soft tissue remnants in existence of an ancient Roman are standing next to us," I answered, my heart pounding as all the implications of this discovery rained down upon me.

"This is absolutely incredible!" Alex shouted, his broad grin and electrified laughter contagious. We jumped at each other in jubilation. Our mouths pressed together, until I jolted myself free. Did I kiss him first, or did he kiss me? I didn't *think* I did. Damn.

I tried to step away, to let air pass once more between us, but he trapped me, the small of my back pinned against the edge of the narrow stainless-steel table. He pressed his hands on either side of me, caging me, keeping his face so close to mine that I could feel his warm breath in my face. His soft brown eyes pleaded with me.

"Won't you forgive me? We were so good together, Azi. So good…"

"Good for *whom*?"

His lips parted gently, inching closer to mine. I had just about reached the extent of my ability to curl my back away from him when his phone rang. His lips set in a thin hard line, and I knew it was his wife. He didn't immediately release me as he brought the phone to his ear, speaking gruffly into the receiver.

"What?" he growled.

A shrill, infuriated voice blared through, her words sufficiently stifled by Alex's cheek, reduced to an incensed braying.

"I said I was going to the lab, so I've come to the lab. It's just Azi. No," he continued, turning his back from me and pacing the room, "we're having dinner with the Whateleys *tomorrow* night...Go without me, then. We've found..."

Just Azi. I stood straight at my place, trying hard to control the look on my face. I did not betray a hint of mockery, or hatred, or pain. I did not feel.

I turned my head from Alex and shuddered. Anglesey Man looked bloated, the wrinkles of his face smoothing out. I drew nearer and peered hard. I perceived no movement. My earlier fright had turned my head silly, but—I had studied his angles—the lines of his brow, the curve of his nose and lips. The proportions were off. The removal of the stake might have caused his innards to fill with air, I reasoned, leading to putrefaction two thousand years too late. If we were going to preserve him, it had to be done quickly.

Trying to get Alex's attention was useless. By the time he'd restored his phone to his pocket, he was halfway out the door. The look on his face was jarring, like a man who'd been caught in a bald-faced lie. I suppose it was appropriate.

"I'm late already," he said. "Could you—?"

I nodded.

He pressed his lips together again, the way he did when he knew he was wrong, and either didn't know how or didn't care to fix it. When he curled his index finger under my chin, I promptly jerked my head away.

"See you tomorrow, kid," he murmured. With that, he was gone.

8

_I_ thought to take a few facial measurements, though I had nothing to compare them to. I would if I stayed long enough. The impulse to sketch Anglesey Man was so strong, especially if he wouldn't remain this way much longer. And it wasn't as if I was expected to continue without my advisor present. I pulled out the pad and charcoals left over from our trip, having never unpacked them, and flipped to a clean page. I started the way I usually did, but this time without the distractions of the airplane's droning engine or Alex's inquisitive eyes. The silence was punctured only by the insistent ticking of the clock on the wall and my own breath.

His nose took shape first, down to his lips and chin, tracing the jawline up to the cheeks. Next, I set the eyes into the face. I imagined his waxed hair falling downward, giving it life. I was struck again by his beautiful symmetry—his sleek profile, the shadows on his high cheekbones. I put my tools down, satisfied at last at having produced a good likeness.

"What happened to you?" I pondered into the stillness. No answer came. When I looked at the wall clock, I was surprised by how much time had passed. Yet, in all that time, Anglesey Man's face had not changed under my watch. It was late, and there was nothing else I could do without a supervisor. The rings, amber, and stake went into canisters I labeled quickly, saving the lengthier cataloging for tomorrow. I locked them away in the back room. I was washing the latex powder mixed with charcoal dust from my hands when I heard a crash from the room beyond that sent me running. Had the foot of Anglesey Man's box lost its purchase?

I rushed to the far side of the lab, where Anglesey Man lay crumpled. His back was smooth. The tanned, brittle leather was fraying and ripping, dimpling like elephant skin where it was renting itself open. The damage to the skin was much more severe than a fall out of his box could have accomplished. I bent down to examine the tears, and my heart stopped. He was moving. His chest heaved up, then exhaled again. My feet gave out underneath me and stumbled backward. I was paralyzed, unable to catch my breath, as the shrunken, twisted body lurched forward, uncurling his bent, collapsed form and groping his way toward me. He shed more of his skin with every painful, protracted movement; it deteriorated and drifted to the floor like a cloud of ash. My brain was shouting at my limbs to do something, but they remained unresponsive when Anglesey Man bent his neck upward to face me. Behind the leather, like a husk waiting to be shed, he opened his eyes, flashing the clearest blue I have ever seen.

I didn't hear my own screaming, but felt the mangled rawness of my throat. I scrambled away from him, away from the door. He crawled, stretching an arm out to me. A gurgling issued from his open mouth that froze my blood. I raced around the other side of the table, chancing that I could beat the thing to the door, but he was standing upright before I could reach the handle. He lumbered at me, pinning me to the wall to the right of the door frame. I screamed then. His fingers curled around my shoulder, the cracking sound resounding against my ear, dust collecting on my shirt and at my feet. I clawed at his wrist, shaking it violently to free myself. His skin shrugged off in my hands, crumbling away to the ground—I touched cold, pink flesh that sent a shockwave through me. I dared to look again at his face—the darkened hide was splitting like a mask, a man breaking out of his shell. His eyes were pleading, glassy. He vibrated with incoherent noise, his lips separated, but the dark slit of the preserved mouth above it did not quite rest on the proper seam. He stuttered the same sound over and over again.

"*A-a-a-adiuva!*"

I stared wide-eyed, my whole body trembling.

"You're...you're alive. Jesus Christ, you're alive," I murmured.

The panting that echoed through his skin was his only response. The leathered muscle tore at his shoulders and his hips as the living tissue underneath expanded, pushing itself free of this shrunken shell. I inched closer, risking my sanity as I peered again into his false face, trying to see past the corpse to the man underneath. His breath rattled in his throat, hoarse and wet. I lifted my hands to his cheeks, to test the bond of the tanned hide to his emerging face. Before my hands reached him, he shuddered and pivoted away—scared, or ashamed—I'm not sure which. His shoulders slumped under my relenting, unbelieving stare. I could not look away. I was afraid to close my eyes even for a second. If I opened them again and found nothing I shouldn't have, just a body in a box, I'd have to admit to myself that I'd finally gone insane. I took the chance and blinked. He was still there.

I didn't trust my eyes, didn't want to. Suddenly I wished that Alex hadn't left, just so he could wake me from this nightmare. Alex! He was never going to believe this, but when I *proved* it—my heart fell like a stone as soon as the shadow of the thought flickered across my mind. I knew exactly what he would do. He'd imprison the Roman—if he truly was—submit him to endless tests and inquiries and keep him in a sterilized cage like the Fiji Mermaid or the Last Yahi. That would be worse than whatever he had already been through.

"*Adiuva...*"

His desperate plea came again, weaker this time. He slumped forward and closed his eyes with such effort that, for a moment, it looked as if he might not open them again. When he did, his voice came a third time, barely a whisper.

"*Adiuva.*"

I couldn't tell Alex. I couldn't tell anyone. Responding only to the desperation in those brilliant blue orbs so close to mine, I yielded.

"Okay," I whispered. "Okay." I mustered the word "*etiam*"— yes in

Latin. My hands went up, a quick show of goodwill, then I pointed to the line of hooks next to the door that held the lab coats. He lifted off me slightly, his stance faltering as the adrenaline that had propelled him upright seemed to leave him. When I covered his body with a free lab coat, more dust shook off him. He stepped forward and covered the floor with a thick layer of human sediment.

"Shit," I cursed under my breath. He couldn't do that from here to my front door. He leaned his forehead on the wall, and I pulled harshly on the desiccated form covering his legs. A groan rumbled from his throat, but the skin beneath, from his ankles to the soles of his feet, was unbroken. I opened the door of the lab and poked by head into the hallway. No one was supposed to be here. The hallway was empty, thank the gods, so I stepped through the doorway and held it open for Anglesey Man to follow. The minute my body cleared the door frame, he shrank back, moaning and turning his face away from the fluorescent glare of the hallway lights.

Panic rushed in on me again. The longer he took, the higher the chances that someone—a janitor, a security guard, *anybody*—would find us. I walked back through the door and stood before the trembling, undead body. Without thinking, I got close enough to whisper, and was knocked back by the stench of a foul, damp grave. He'd borne no odor before, but now the seal of his preserved body was shattered. The mossy, rotten stench of millennia filled the room. My stomach contracted, my knees devolving into jelly. The abandoned voice of reason screamed between my ears. *Run. Run and don't ever look back.*

But his eyes kept me planted there. There was a living, breathing human under there, one I had discovered. Finding human remains was what my dad had always dreamed of—what I had always dreamed of. They were my responsibility, to handle with respect. The fact that the remains could stand on their own didn't lessen my responsibility. If anything, it was multiplied a hundredfold. I held my breath to stop the smell from creeping all the way up into my brain. I made a mental gathering of every Latin word I knew.

"I can get you out of here and keep you safe, but you have to trust me. Do you understand?"

When he dipped his head in acknowledgment, a layer of his neck disintegrated, scattered to dust across his broadening chest. We made it out the door unseen, but still I rushed him to my car as fast as he could shuffle. When my headlights blinked on to unlock, he trembled like a pile of dead leaves.

"It's okay," I said, unable to think of a Latin substitute. *Tutum*—safe— was the best I could do as I opened the back seat and gestured for him to lie down and stay hidden. I had never driven that fast, but those fifteen minutes felt like forever. Two-thirds of the way through, he started groaning louder, and I heard an ominous wet sound. I screeched to a halt, popped the passenger door open, and helped him crane his neck to the ground. Watching him vomit up wave after wave of peat was awful. I doubted anything in the ancient world could hit ninety miles an hour in a few seconds. He emptied his guts and probably even his lungs. The muck was too black to tell if any of it was blood. He swiped at his face with his hand, and the skin covering his jaw came off, leaving a gruesome veil covering the crown of his head down to the bridge of his nose. He was not happy to take his place again in the car.

He resisted when I gestured for him to lay his head back down so I could shut the door again. I was kneeling down to talk him into it when another car zoomed by, blinding us in its headlights and filling the night air with the blare of its horn.

Anglesey Man screamed. And screamed. When it seemed like he would never stop screaming, I closed my hands over my ears to block out his wails.

"*Stop!*" I've never screamed that loudly. I scared myself, and it pulled me out of my own frenzy. Silence reigned on this corner of the road, but I could hear the distant hum of another engine just over the next hill. I put my hand firmly on the door above his head.

"I'm sorry, but we can't stay here. A little bit more. Just a little bit more."

He ducked back in without another sound, and I slid into the driver's seat. I gripped the wheel more to stop my hands from shaking than to lead the way home. But I had to drive. All I could do was drive, because I had no idea what happened next, once I got to the driveway.

$\bigcirc$

I closed the door to my foyer behind us with a reassuring click. It was a quiet street, and neither Anglesey Man nor I made a sound as we exited the car and climbed up the steps to the front door. He kept his head tucked all the way up the grand staircase, focusing on one step at a time. Slowly we moved down the hallway to the bathroom. I ushered him into the bathtub and ripped off the two coats—tossing them behind him in the tub to contain his chaos. I kept the light off, starting to think of all the things that would frighten him, and how to ease him out of his suffering. I lit the aromatic candles at the edge of the sink and threw a pillowcase from the adjacent closet over the lamp sconces on either side of the mirror before turning them on. At least we could see each other. When I turned the shower on, he cried out.

"It's okay," I said again. *"Aqua."* He grimaced at the spray. I adjusted the water to just this side of lukewarm—his skin was still clammy and cold to the touch, what little I could feel of it. The bulk of him was covered in dried skin that was cracked, hanging loosely, waiting to come off. I reached into the shower, getting dizzy and nauseous as I put my hand on his matted scalp, rusted by peat acid, and slid it off his head, letting it slough onto the enamel tub with a sickeningly dull thump. The shell covering his chest followed, no longer having a claim on him. He stepped over his own corpse. I tried to guide him, to put his back to the shower. The water did little work on its own, leaving a thin film of dark, inky gunk and the smell of rotten vegetation behind. I hesitated to push the sediment collecting on the small of his back past the curve of his ass but sighed in resignation—there was nothing else for it. I chased the detritus away down past his calves, swollen in power, yet limp and shaken, like they had forgotten their own strength. I turned him again toward the stream, his face assailed by pressurized water. He didn't know how to breathe through it and got panicky. I tried to calm him, but it was tough work, reaching in to help him. I was soaked up to my elbows, the spray reaching the floor and getting all over my shirt anyway.

"What the hell?" I muttered, pulling my shirt over my head and shrugging out of my pants and shoes. We were in this together, it was happening to both of us. Maybe this would help to mitigate his shame. His eyes widened before he shut them firmly, turning his head away from me. Seeing the water pooling in my bra, I think it was the first time he realized I was a woman.

Calmer, he let me slide the muck off his shoulders, his hips, his face. He slowly participated, running his hands through his hair. At last, he was clean. He was whole. And he was magnificent. His eyes spoke volumes of pain, fear, and a humbled pride. They met mine again, the intensity of his stare at turns awesome and frightening. He lurched forward, not finding a steady grip on the slick tiles. I pressed my back against the wall, trying to give him space, but he leaned ever closer, on the verge of collapse. My breath came rapid and shallow, and I couldn't think. He stopped just short of crashing into me. Our foreheads touched, and we were surrounded by the hissing of the shower. He felt so weak, as if I might blow him over if I weren't careful. I inhaled sharply at his touch as he slid closer, the skins of our abdomens touching. My fear melted away under his anguished expression, replaced by an overwhelming compassion. I ran my hand tentatively through his dark hair as the water sluiced through it. He put his head on my shoulder and sobbed.

I stopped the shower in time with his tears. The steam quickly left us, and I reached behind me for a towel. I ran it over his head, his shoulders, and finally, keeping my gaze level with his eyes, wrapped the soft white linen around his waist. I stepped out after him, grabbing a second towel for myself, wrapping it under my armpits and squeezing my hair out at the nape of my neck. I gestured for him to sit and put my hands in front of me. I raced to my room, threw on a dry tank top and pajama pants, and padded barefoot to my parents' room. I danced awkwardly in front of the door for a minute, before remembering that they would be helping him themselves if they could.

"Sorry," I said under my breath as I burst into the room. Anglesey Man wasn't going to fit into any of my clothes. With his size, I'd be lucky to find anything of Dad's that fit. I absently looked for an oversized college shirt with Arkham's griffin mascot on it, for when he played touch football with the other faculty, or when he was being lazy and just looking to put his feet up with a cold beer in front of the TV.

This was the first time I'd been away from Anglesey Man. As I rummaged for clothes, shutting out the millions of memories carved into every corner, my mind raced to process the miracle. Suddenly all the things flying in my head organized themselves into unending lists— of what I'd have to buy (underwear, toothbrush, shoes), what I'd have to explain (airplanes, TV, computers, atomic bombs), how we would communicate...how I would explain what had happened to him. How *he* would explain it to *me*. For the thing that Alex and I had brought back from Britain was certainly dead. Yet the thing sitting patiently in my bathroom was not.

He had begged for my help, and I intended with all my soul to give it. Once he was settled for the night, I resolved to head out to the store for essentials, and to poke around a bit between here and the lab, make sure there wasn't a neat pile of peat moss pointing straight at my door.

I found what I wanted. The beaten pullover sweater rested in my limp fingers as my thoughts arrested my speed. I could smell my dad, a forgotten scent trapped in the fabric that rushed back to me in all its vividness, of days watching him play intramurals. I used it to wipe my tears. Instilled with a new sense of urgent worry, I hurried back to the bathroom. There he sat, exactly how I'd left him, poised like a marble statue with his hands on his knees, set apart enough to create a dark shadow between his legs that my eyesight thankfully could not penetrate.

He remained silent as I approached him, and I wondered how much of that was an effect of the condition of his throat—burnt by peat acid, or simply sore from disuse? He did not attempt to speak, though I was sure he had understood my sketchy, academic Latin. I was willing to be patient. Our nonverbal communication was all either of us required, for now.

He took the sweater from me warily, turning it over in his hands and inspecting it from each angle to which it turned. Of course. I clicked my tongue and mumbled an apology in English as I took it again from him, righted it, and pulled his head through the hole meant for his neck. Understanding came over his face, and both arms followed suit on their own.

I knelt in front of him, fixating my eyes on his feet, and only his feet, as I pushed his ankles through sweatpants. I wasn't giving him my dad's underwear. That I didn't have the courage to clear out my parents' things was bad enough. Being more used to a toga or a leather skirt, I didn't think he'd mind. That would have to wait. I kept my fingers at the waistband as I stood up. He stood with me and held my stare as I slipped the waistband under the towel until it rested comfortably on his hips. He removed the towel himself and presented it to me, his eyes soft and appreciative, but still wide from the shock. There were times when I observed his interest shooting quickly around the room, attempting to survey his surroundings, but each time his brow furrowed deeper, and his face returned to gaze intensely at me. Perhaps another human face was the only thing he could make sense of.

When I took the towel from him, I saw that the skin surrounding his knuckles was red, and cracking. The skin was new and needed all the moisture it could get. I motioned for him to sit again at the chair facing the marble vanity, and pumped lotion from a container on the edge of the sink into my hand. I looked at him for some expression as I worked the lotion into his fingers and palms, but he sat docile and patient. Intimidated by a blank stare, even one as peaceful as his, I kept my face to my work. That's when I noticed that his fingernails were still entrenched with peat, packed stubbornly underneath. I clicked my tongue again, reached into the cabinet above my head to the left, and pulled out a pair of nail clippers. I knelt in front of him again and shortened the nails enough to clean out the beds. As my task neared its end, I was consumed with worry. His stoicism might be shock, and I wouldn't know how to treat him by myself. As if in response to my thoughts, he squeezed my fingers tightly. I looked up to see him regarding me, his eyes shining again. He opened his mouth as if to speak, and my heart quickened with anticipation. He shuddered as he inhaled, choked with emotion. He closed his lips again with a smile and brought my hand to them, kissing my fingers in gratitude.

I pressed my open palm to his cheek, and he pulled me closer, tucking me between his legs and embracing me again. I rested my chin on his shoulder as he squeezed, surrounding me by his size even in his weakness. I pulled away, leaning on his forearms as I stood. I took him by the hand and led him out of the bathroom and down the darkened hallway to my bedroom. It would do until I could figure out where to keep him. All the spare bedrooms were booked up, and I wasn't going to sleep in my easy chair forever. I couldn't expect him to, either. I left his side to dim the light bulb next to my bed with a shirt, then led him in. His steps faltered as he neared the bed, and I knew he would not resist being put to sleep. I offered him a glass of water, which he took readily. He settled in quickly enough, and I bade him goodnight.

"Tomorrow," I whispered, grabbing my boots on my way out the door.

9

QUINTUS

*S*unlight sneaking into the room woke me. Everything was sore, my mouth most of all, and my chest felt like a dead weight imposing itself atop an empty stomach. My limbs screamed as I stretched, lifting my head to sit up. I rubbed my eyes, dizzied by the sense that, though I had slept soundly, for how long I knew not, it was nothing compared to the cold grip of death that had until then ensnared me.

I took in the room, but my gaze informed me of little as to where I was, only that I had not dreamed my waking out of that senseless deep. A blanket rustled and moaned to the right of me. I turned my head to see the face of my rescuer, that angel who had secreted me away to safety and made me whole again. I was surprised to find her there and took in my resting place more carefully. After all she had done to give me back a sense of my humanity, she had given me *her* bed. Her features scrunched in dismay as Helios heralded the morning across her eyelids, and she slunk behind the shadowy comfort of her blanket, tucking her knees even closer to her chest.

I rose slowly, letting my bare feet gain firm purchase on the rug. I gripped the arms of the chair in which my savior slept to steady myself and roused her gently with a soft tap on the shoulder. Her slumbering mind must have forgotten, for she flinched at the sight of me. Her quick fright was contagious, and I jumped back. It lasted only a moment, and she just as quickly collected herself, shaking herself awake.

I backed away, giving her space to rise. She gestured to a sitting area by the window and quit the room, looking at me in a way that I had come to recognize last night, that she would be returning presently. She came carrying plates full of bread, cheese, and fruit, some of which I'd never seen the likes of before. There were grapes, apples, and oranges, but nothing to help me place myself. I had seen enough only to know that I was not very near my cohort. After breaking my fast with my caretaker, I would have to bid her farewell and seek the direction back to my encampment, to tell, at last, what I had seen, to stir the men to action, and pull the others from the predicament from which I had been so recently extracted. She offered a warm, unfermented beverage. Though it did slide down my throat with ease, it left a bitter taste in my mouth that only many mouthfuls of clean water could wash away. When my lips puckered despite my attempt at gracious acceptance of all my hostess offered, she, ever with her gaze fixated on me, added a fine white powder to my drink, which made it infinitely more palatable. I smiled and nodded in consideration. She smiled in return, but I could see that our lack of conversation was vexing her. Her fingers fidgeted in her lap as we dined, as though she were impatient to get on with whatever exchange we were to have before I took my leave of her. Maybe, when the score against me was settled, I could come back. If I was welcome.

I felt guilty, having foisted my own horror upon her, sentencing her to a night full of dreadful, painstaking care of my person. It had uplifted my spirit out of the dank prison which had held me, yet I could see that the same event grated on her, the wariness in her eye a signal that her trouble, perhaps for harboring me, was just beginning.

There was a curious fruit on the end of the table, a slender yellow thing plump in its curvature. I inspected it and put it to my mouth. The outer skin was tough and unwieldy. Unsure of the rules of decorum in such a circumstance, I paused to consider whether to place it uneaten on my plate or simply bite harder. Before my opinion on the matter was fully formed, she grabbed it from me, and dug the nail of her thumb into the curve at its neck. From then she peeled away the outer layer, to reveal more tender flesh beneath.

I observed her carefully as she handed it back to me. Her cheeks had reddened, as though she felt it a mistake to serve me it in the first place. I tried to assuage the flush under her porcelain skin by partaking again, this time with greater success and a rewarding sweetness. As I downed the feast laid out for me, I considered my company with the utmost compassion, rising to meet her inquisitive, unrelenting stare.

She was no Briton; of that I was sure. Her finely sculpted features were unlike any of those who had surrounded me in those last moments, their leering, howling faces forever burned in my mind. I would not believe her to be even a rogue member of the vicious band who had shown its rebellion in such heinous fashion against Rome—against me. Her glossy, raven hair was cut short like a man's, yet it suited her, framing her slender chin. Only the longest, well-tended tresses dared to bounce at her shoulders. Against her creamy skin, her eyes were a deliciously warm, reassuring brown. She dug her teeth into the right corner of her lip repeatedly, and seemed almost skittish, nervous of me, perhaps of being alone with me.

I tried to restrain my observation of her to what lay above her neck, though her choice of clothing was airy and light, giving my eyes free rein of her generous curves. That her body was that of a woman's and not a girl's I knew very well. She had bared nearly all of her splendidness in that overflowing fountain, yet her clean, sweetly scented skin and fresh, young face were not those of a woman overly or ill-used. Her abode was clean, well-appointed, though strange, from what little I could discern in the dim sunlight. She carried herself as one well-bred. I cleared my throat, ready to make my introduction.

"I am Quintus."

She let out a sigh of great relief as I spoke. She placed her hand on her lovely throat as she replied, oddly unsure of how to identify herself.

"Azi. Asenath," she corrected. Then, with a confident finality, "Azi."

I followed the thin line of gold down her neck, daring a glance between the mounds of Venus and pointed to the charm she wore.

"Ra," I said, pointing at the talisman shaped as the eye of the deity.

"Hmm?" she questioned. Looking down, she clasped the eye in her hand, and understood.

"You're from the land of the pharaohs?" I asked.

She waggled her head. "By birth, not blood."

I nodded. "Azi," I repeated, putting my hand over my chest and bowing my head low in deep gratitude. "Thank you."

She became uneasy as I spoke. It perplexed me, and I inclined my head to her. It was plain she had something to say and was very anxious to say it. I pulled at the fabric covering my chest.

"Thank your—husband?" I ventured.

Azi shook her head. "Father," she corrected. Listening to her curt answer was a strain on my ears. Her words grated like broken glass. They had all the necessary components, but the cadence and emphasis were all wrong.

"I would like to thank him, if you please."

She took longer to respond, her eyes shifting to an indeterminate focus, trying to understand what I had said. A shadow passed over her face as she did, and she gave another short reply, aware of her own linguistic limitations.

"My parents are dead."

I offered my condolences. She sighed deeply then, turning her face away from me, curiously guilty. After a pause, her eyes returned to mine.

"When were you born?" she asked. Her voice was timid now, concerned I think over the propriety of her question. Her eyes, though sad, were focused, and I knew instinctively she asked with a purpose. I replied.

"I was born in the year of the consulship of Lentulus and Sabinus."

She nodded, as if I had confirmed something she already knew. She counted silently on her fingers then nodded to herself again. I was ready now, to attempt expressing my own wish.

"I need to report to my superiors. Can you show me the way to Mona?"

She tongued the inside of her cheek. Rather than answer, she posed another query. I watched her full, soft lips move as she asked, "Can you tell me...what happened to you?"

I shrank from answering. She had seen enough horrors from me already. I pursed my lips, and with closed eyes, shook my head quickly in the negative, to shut out the memory.

She understood readily and mumbled what I took for an apology. She reached for my clenched fist as it lay anxiously on the tabletop. I clasped it and repeated the one word she had spoken over and over again the night before, using it correctly, I judged, from the smile it produced.

"Okay."

Touching had the effect of melting the tension that built between us. She had been unwittingly roped into my curse and had chosen to stand with me, though it benefited her none and brought a stranger to her door. The warm concern of her touch quickened my heart. I tried my query again.

"Thank you, Azi, for all you have done. I am forever in your debt, but I must return now to my regiment. Can you show me the way? The way to Mona?"

She took another deep, worried breath, this time resolved to answer me. She pulled from her satchel a set of maps, keeping them carefully rolled up. She laid them facing me. A land whose shape I did not recognize stretched before me. I studied it carefully, but after no response from me, Azi pointed to a small island connected to a larger one by a thin strait.

"Mona," she said.

"Yes," I answered excitedly. I looked more carefully. The land was remarkably well-charted, showing some features that I instinctively knew, but the size of Britannia and its surrounding islands seemed disproportionate to my superiors' knowledge, as far as I was privy to their thoughts.

She rolled back the map, showing me another one, one I knew very well indeed.

"Rome," I said aloud in confirmation. I pointed to a place in the southern district. "My parents own a tavern on this road."

Azi licked her lips, daring not to breathe as she rolled it back, showing a third map. She kept a tight grip on the rolled edge to my left. I looked down, puzzled at what I saw. The scale of the map was unlike any I had ever seen. The features, lines, and colors of this intricate measuring meant nothing to me. Azi pointed to a darkened circle at the center of a light red parcel of land, positioned near the center of the map, with a long tail jutting into the sea.

"Rome," she said.

I looked again. I had never seen it drawn at such a distance, but pieces of my mind cobbled together the proportion of nearby territories and farther lands. Her words rang wondrously true. At a sign of my acknowledgment, she moved her finger farther to the left.

"Mona."

I nodded again, understanding the map's orientation. When her movements were arrested, I looked up at her, searching her face for the cause of her dismay. She seemed to be waiting for me, waiting for our eyes to meet so she might continue. She unfurled the rest of the map in her hand, revealing a broad ocean, and lands of obscene size to the west. My mouth gaped.

"America," she said, and pointed to its northeastern coast. "We are here."

I had no words. No memory of traveling such a distance. The absence of that alone frightened me. How could I have been removed so far from that wretched place, and yet been kept senseless? I had never heard of a place farther west than Britannia, and yet here I seemed to be.

"How did we get here?" I finally asked.

She quit her place, taking hold again of both my hands as she knelt in front of me.

"Quintus," she said, her voice breathless, "you have been...asleep... for two thousand years."

I pulled my hands quickly away.

"Witch!" I berated her, striding rapidly past her and into a long hallway, deaf to her wild cries as I burst out of the room. I was immediately blinded by a brilliant, dazzling white light. I felt as though I had stepped unwittingly into the sun and was being consumed by its rays. A horn sounded nearby, followed by a jumbled cacophony that poured like poison into my ears and rattled my skull. Roars and screeches charged through the open windows, crashing in upon me as a pack of hell-hounds.

I collapsed before I reached the landing down to the outer door, covering my ears to keep out my own screams. Nothing around me was familiar, nothing made sense...only Azi. Had she saved me from the depths, just to deceive? No, no, that was chaos! I screamed louder and could not for the world find solid footing for my thoughts.

Azi came upon me in seconds, garbling at me in horrific Latin that lacked nothing in vigor. "Quintus, Quintus, please trust me. I can help you. What happened to you is unspeakable, but it is the truth! Let me help you!"

I sank into her arms, knowing in my gut that she had not lied, that I had seen no deceit in her eyes when she told me where and *when* I was, that she was as pained to tell me as I was to hear it.

"M-my parents," I stammered. The thought of my mother and father, having believed their only son lost to them...that they were forever lost to me...

"I know," Azi wailed, tears flowing down her cheeks. "I know. I'm sorry, so sorry."

I clutched her, seeking the only comfort I had known for millennia. She held my hair, and sat crouched with me, shrouded in sorrow, for I knew not how long. When all my tears had run dry, I stood slowly. Daring the light, I gazed upward at its source. I squinted, using my hand as a shield.

"Electricity," she explained, and pushed a small protrusion in the wall, forcing a downward position. After its resounding click, the hallway was dark, save for the subdued light filtering in the windows from overcast clouds. Upwards she pushed it, and the light went on again. Then off. She left it that way and stretched her hand out to me. I took it and was led back into her sleeping chamber. I tested the artificial light myself, saving its strength as I sat down again, facing her. I looked closer at my surroundings. Objects of unknown materials and shapes lay everywhere, having been obscured only by the gloominess of the day. I realized the consideration Azi had shown in refraining from the artificial lights upon waking, trying carefully to bring me to the truth.

"Forgive me," I said as we sat down again at the table. "I should not have spoken to you as I did. I did not mean any of it."

"It is all right," she said in return.

"No, it is not all right. I was harsh with you, and for no cause." I reached for her hand, contrite.

"I accept your apology," she answered. "But really, Quintus. I understand. Nothing like this has ever happened before, and I do not believe in witches."

My face reddened at the recall of the vile label I falsely thrust upon her, but she continued.

"I do not believe in witches, or magic, or gods even, but," she shook her head, incredulous, "here you are."

I considered for a moment, relishing the soft touch of her fingers brushing against mine. Withdrawing her hand reluctantly, she bent down to retrieve a thin black slab with a lustrous obsidian face. It looked to be a finely polished stone, but could not have been, for she pulled an even thinner, flatter portion partly away from the base, and set it upright on the table. She was watching me carefully, gauging my response as she tapped the top of the slab with one finger. At her command, the face of the stone glowed from within. I jumped in my chair. She put her hands quickly in front of her, her open palms facing me.

"No magic. Only science," she said. Her eyes begged me for patience. "Please, Quintus," she whispered, eyes wide as two dark, glistening pools. I relented, still wary of what to all reason looked like a scrying board. She turned it to her for an instant, tapping it purposefully with the pads of her fingers, her eyes darting constantly back to me to see if I would run again. I did not. Whatever she was doing, I knew with an acute certainty that it was not her intention to harm.

In a moment, she returned the slab to its place. The surface now glowed a pure white. She spoke deliberately in her native tongue, in a crisp, clear voice. The words were unfamiliar, all, except one or two that sounded like a bastardized form of those among whom I was stationed.

She pointed at the stone. I turned my head, stunned. It was no longer blank. It read, in perfect Latin:

This will help us communicate, for now. It is not magic, it is not alive, and it will not hurt you. Speak, and it will translate what you say for me to read.

I stared at her in amazement. She gestured for me to try it. I considered what I should say, what we should do next.

"How did you find me?" I asked.

She laughed in a peculiar fashion, saying:

I was looking for you.

"For me?"

No, not you specifically, but bodies, yes. For study, she answered.

"You disturb the dead intentionally?"

The lines of her face grew long.

I am a student of science and history. Any human remains I find are treated with the utmost care. There is a great deal to be learned from the dead.

"Who was the man you were with before?" I asked.

Azi furrowed her brow and cocked her head in confusion. I pointed at the healed wound on the left side of my chest.

"The man who gave me back my breath."

Azi jerked her head back in astonishment. *You were aware of that?*

I closed my eyes, trying to tie the fragments of my memory together. "Very dimly." After a pause, I ventured a guess, based on nothing more than an obscure impression. "He is your lover?"

Her expression changed, and I flinched, realizing too late that certain rules about appropriate conversation had not changed. To her credit, she answered honestly.

He was. No longer.

I failed to suppress a smile.

We cannot tell Alex. We cannot tell anyone.

"Why?"

Alex only thinks of himself. If I were able to convince him of the truth, he would claim he had found a living person who had existed in the greatest empire the world has ever seen. Countless tests and inquiries would follow. You would never see the light of day again.

She spoke with such gravity, I was shaken by the prospect of revealing myself to anyone but her, whose belief was borne out of seeing the transformation of my unbelievable state.

No, Quintus, she finished, *you cannot tell anyone who you are. Alex will surely call me, as soon as the university realizes you are missing.*

"My remains belong to no one."

Especially now, she answered wryly.

I could see we were getting somewhere prickly, so I diverted the conversation. "What will I do? What *can* I do?"

I do not know. I can help you start over, build a new life.

"Can you take me home?" I asked. Her fingers trembled under mine. "To Rome?" I pressed.

That is more difficult than it seems, she answered.

"It stands?" I queried nervously. She nodded deeply. My heart slowed for a moment, eased by the thought that I might, in some way, find my way home again, to be part of Rome's future, whatever that might be.

Traveling between different states requires special documents, Azi explained. *Documents that, without being able to prove who you are, or where you are from, I cannot get.*

I squeezed her fingers again, drawing her eyes to mine. It was too much to bear. "Please, Azi."

Her sorrow reflected my own, and I saw the recesses of her mind set to work. Light and shadow played across her beautifully dark eyes as she hatched several ideas, dismissing them without giving them voice, and finally lighted upon a possibility that showed potential. Her gaze rested on me.

I will try, but it will take time.

I bent my head down, leaning across the table to kiss her hands again. She blushed and withdrew from me. I straightened my back.

During that time...there is so much I can show you, if you want.

"Okay," I said again, my repetition of her words stoking the fire under her creamy skin, adding to it a smile that encompassed her brilliant eyes. I rubbed my own lids, strained from the glow of the talking artifice.

"Enough," she said with finality, laying the sheet flat on the table. In my own tongue, she asked, "Would you like to go outside?"

"Please."

She led the way down the hall, out the stairs, and through the front door. The air was heavy and wet, charged with portentous clouds that hung low in the sky as we stepped out of Azi's home, and stood overlooking a city nestled into the valley below. She pointed to a cluster of tall structures of various styles, some with pointed roofs, others with familiar columns upholding the entryways.

"The university," she said, "where I study and work."

The food market and government houses were pointed out as well, before a damp chill caught in my feet. I turned my wary gaze skyward.

"Rain is coming," I said softly.

"It is," she replied, pointing up to the heavens. "The moon is still there, and the sun. It still rises in the East."

I drew her close to me, wrapping my arm around her. "It does," I whispered, feeling her stalwart presence lift me from my anguish. I was thankful to be awake and not alone. I pressed my lips to her hair. She swung her hips into me, turning to face me. There was something in her eyes, something that had sparked between us in those inexplicable hours that needed no words and pulled my thoughts downward to her lips. As my mouth neared hers, she hesitated. I could not but acquiesce to her wish. It was too soon, I knew, to give sway to such thoughts.

*a*zi led me back inside, providing a tour of her home. It had belonged to her parents, she explained. Its appointments were laid out with great care, even if the taste for Egyptian splendor was myopic. It was much too large a house for only Azi, with three levels and high, airy ceilings on each. No room felt cramped, for all the furniture adorning the place. The whole of my parents' home, including the business establishment, could fit inside the kitchen alone. All gleamed, all was well-tended. She brought me again to her private bathhouse, which spoke to me of great wealth, though the absence of servants suggested otherwise. It fascinated me immensely. Azi was explaining the necessity of "flushing" when a small talking artifice buzzed and chimed, pregnant with news from some unknowable source.

"A tenant," Azi said.

"You are a boarder," I said, smiling.

"They arrive tomorrow for the school year. They are family."

"My mother, also."

She put the flat side of the tablet to her face and spoke, presumably to someone else. Her voice rode a wave of surprise, unhappiness, and forced politeness. The words themselves were lost to me, but I knew what had transpired nevertheless, having heard that same conversation so many times before. She cursed, I gathered, from the sharpness of her tongue as the tablet was secreted away in her garments, and she pressed her hands to her hips.

"Lost one?" I asked.

Her gaze shifted quickly from the tile floor to me. Resigned to it, she guided me out again into the hallway on the upper floor and unlocked the second door to the right. When she gestured for me to enter, I knew she was giving me the room, at extreme cost to herself. The depths to which she was allowing my reawakening to crash in upon her knew no bounds.

"I cannot accept this. It is your livelihood," I protested.

"It cannot be helped."

"Can you not find another?"

"I let only to…advanced students. All are arranged now. This is good. It may be many months before you can travel to Rome."

"Thank you, but no, Azi. It is too much. After all you have done already."

"What would your mother do?"

I smiled then, for I knew she would have done the same, and more. She would kiss both of Azi's cheeks with tears in her eyes for taking such good care of me, if she could. She would have liked Azi very much.

"I'm sorry," she said, seeing, I think, my countenance grow melancholy as I sat on the bed. On *my* bed.

I smiled at her, pinching her chin in my fingers and reassuring her. "Thank you."

"Do you need anything?" she asked.

I took in the room at last. The linens on the bed were immaculate and possessed a clean, wonderful fragrance. At the base were primly folded towels for bathing. There was a wooden desk furnished with an individual lighting apparatus and shelves for books or possessions. I had neither. The walls were decorated with a handful of small, well-executed landscapes.

"This is more than enough," I said softly.

Azi stood awkwardly in the doorway, not fully in or out of the room.

I do not think she knew quite what to do with me in that moment. I certainly had no ideas to offer.

"I think I should go to the store," she said after a prolonged silence. I stood to go, but what she said next pulled me back down into my soft, unmoving seat. "I am not walking. Using...the chariot with no horses. From last night. I will return soon. I will bring food. What do you want?"

"I will eat whatever you cook," I said graciously.

"I am not cooking," she answered quickly. I was at a loss for a reply. It had been long enough since our breakfast for my appetite to grow, but what could I ask for? What would be easy?

"Meat?" she offered. I shook my head. "Rice? Wheat?"

"Wheat," I answered meekly, not knowing which choices would increase her burden.

"Vegetables? Fruits?"

"Please."

"Boiled, smoked, or fried?"

I narrowed my eyes at her, and my mouth twisted into a wry grin at her meticulous questioning. She flashed a wide smile in return, and I got the impression that nothing I could request would be outside the realm of possibility. I began to second-guess going with her, knowing that I would eventually have to brave that nauseating beast and feeling guilty at having so quickly shrunk from the possibility of it before.

"Will you be all right?" I asked. "Should I escort you?"

"I will be fine," she replied smartly. "Women do not require escorts. Will *you* be all right alone?"

I raised my right eyebrow. "Grown men do not require chaperones, either."

She feigned a laugh, followed by a genuine smile, then left.

I walked first to the small reflective glass set into the dark wooden wardrobe. The glass was impressively cut from a single piece, reaching down to the floor. The clothes Azi had provided were humble, but I was not entirely displeased by my countenance. I hoped Azi would forgive me for not appearing at my best. If anyone was to understand why, it would of course be her.

I ventured back into Azi's bedchamber to examine the talking artifice. I fiddled with the surface and its edges, but it did not respond to my touch the way it had to hers. Wandering to the common area of the main floor, I found much of interest, but all too delicate to touch. So, I retreated to my room and did what I was most comfortable with—I slept.

I had lain undisturbed for a little more than an hour when a gentle knock on the door roused me, and I joined Azi for a hearty meal of warm, spicy noodles, as she called them, assembled with finely cut vegetables and a crispy pocket of I-know-not-what dipped in a sweet, fruity jam.

Well-fed and in a pleasant mood under the circumstances, Azi ushered me outside again, walking a small stone path to the rear of her house. She owned a small plot of land, with space for a metal table and fire pit encased in stone. At the far end near the wooden boundary of the property was a patch of tilled dirt, laying ready for a new crop. Where the edge of the soil met finely manicured grasses lay a collection of small, smoothly polished stones in all colors, large flat tiles of a cool gray substance, and thicker, brick-like stones of white. There were also potted flowers, greenery, and, I believe, an orange tree still in its infancy.

She made a sweeping gesture at all that lay there. "I did not know... what you might want. I thought you would want to build something."

"Build something?" I repeated curiously.

"For your parents. In their memory. It is your custom to build memorials, no?" She crouched down, her fingers lightly touching upon one set of materials, then another. "I just did not know what you would..." She stopped herself, opened up a wide bin, and mixed a bit of the sand within with water that she drew from a nearby spout. It formed a paste, which acted as mortar to bind the stones. She opened another parcel, a miniature fountain, connecting it to her water supply and demonstrating its function for me.

"Here," she said finally, handing me two hand-shaped skeins of fabric. "Gloves. To cover your hands. Keep them clean." She looked up into my eyes, unsure of why I had kept my silence for so long, fearful perhaps of having done or said something wrong. I took the gloves she offered me and pulled her as close as I could. I ran my hands through her silky hair as she pressed her face to my chest.

"That you would think to..." My emotions conquered me, and I squeezed tighter. "I fear I shall never stop saying 'thank you.'"

I could feel her laughing against my skin as she parted from me. "I will be in that room," she said, pointing to the topmost window in the circular addition jutting from the main house.

Forgoing the gloves, I chose to dirty my hands in the work. I considered it a necessary inconvenience, not having done my duty to care for my parents, to tend to their illnesses, and finally, to bury them with all the honors they deserved. I hoped that the Empire had treated them well in exchange for their ultimate sacrifice. In exchange for me. I built a monument as high as I could with what was so magnanimously given to me, constructing a grotto of sorts, and setting the fountain into its deepest recess. My mother had loved the soft whisperings of the Tiber River. She and my father spent many peaceful afternoons there with me as a boy.

I laid a blanket of vibrant summer flowers at their feet, mingled the deeper pinks and violets with the lighter hues of sunshine, flanking the edges of the space with the long thin blades of greenery that hung low in their pots, and crept along the ground where I planted them, ushering in the serenity of the place. The perfect spot for the orange tree presented itself behind the east wall of the grotto—there I committed it to the ground. Azi had bought much more than I could use. I looked about me, trying to decide what to do with the unplanted blooms, when my mother's familiar voice echoed between my temples.

All these flowers, and you don't know what to do with them? Give them to the girl, dummy.

She paid for them, my thoughts countered.

So? Make them nice. You'll see.

I did as I imagined my mother would bid me, and used the thin red ribbon tied around the orange tree, picking individual blossoms at the height of perfection and wrapping them together. Satisfied, I laid them aside, and set to arranging the smaller polished stones into a pleasing pattern. The sun, bursting through those boastful, portentous clouds of the morning, beat down upon my back. Such warmth as the fabric on my back provided me would have been welcome in Britannia. Here, it stifled, and I sweat profusely. That, and the obstacles of finding a good design for the stones joined to confound me. Thinking to save Azi from washing it prematurely, I peeled the upper garment off and continued in my work, stymied by my lack of aesthetic. I had an eye for appreciation of the arts, but its creation was another thing entirely.

Azi came out again and found me thus. When I stood to face her, I could not help but notice her distraction at finding me only half-dressed. She tried hard not to stare as she offered me a liquid reprieve, but whenever her eyes turned guiltily again to my bare arms and chest, her face reddened. Flattered, my grin turned wolfish.

"It is beautiful," she said, assessing all I had done, and putting her mind to something other than me.

"I am not sure how to finish it," I said, pointing to the array of rounded glass at my feet. "I thought for the face of the arch, maybe."

Her gaze shifted back and forth between the stones and the intended surface. She crouched and began quickly rearranging them. I could not discern the method by which she reordered them, but the effect was dramatic, playing on the subtle undertones of each to give an impression of intentional gradation. At the same time, the clear outline of a winged bird emerged.

"Is this okay?" she asked, not bothering to translate.

"You have a great eye for color," I said, thoroughly impressed.

"I am told."

Tsk tsk, go on—a separate corner of my mind nudged me. I lifted the bouquet and placed it in her hands. Her face lit in pleasant surprise. *She took them, see? Now it is settled.* The echo of my mother's laughter faded, and I felt my eyes moisten.

"What?" Azi asked, finding my expression curious.

I shook my head as if to say "nothing" as she lifted the blossoms to her delicate nose.

11

*W*hen evening came, I went readily to sleep, my limbs happy in their exertion and my returning strength. They needed no prodding to rest.

In the stillness of that long night, the demons burst in upon me. Their hateful eyes cut through me like razors, the pain in my chest throbbed as the fire-headed wench, bathed in blood, drove her stake deeper. Their howls matched my own, and I started out of my bed with a shriek at the sudden pulling and tearing of my clothes, those countless claws from unseen hands dragging me down into the cold, murky depths.

Unbound as I had been before, I flailed wildly against my captors until my arm struck something solid, and two small, warm hands clamped down on my shoulders. I awoke screaming heedlessly into the night, causing Azi to shrink from me. She was panting, as was I. Her eyes bespoke the terror I had instilled in my agitated state. She ran her hand gently through my hair, and I pulled her to me for comfort. She hushed me, the clasp of her soft hands enough to calm my violently beating heart.

"Forgive me," I whispered against her shoulder as I embraced her.

"It's okay," she whispered back. "I am here."

I found relief in her nearness. Seeing me sufficiently calmed, she stood up to go. The instinct of a moment made me tighten my grip on her wrist and draw her back to me. Her eyes gleamed in the moonlight drifting softly through the window, glistening off her pale skin like porcelain edged with silver. The trembling in my legs eased as she crept into the bed, and I shifted closer to the window to make room for her. She hesitantly settled under the covers, finally deciding on indulging in the closeness that melted the fear in our veins and bound us together at every moment. Her hand spread itself across my bare stomach, her head coming to rest on my shoulder. Her shirt rode up around her waist, and I dared to feel her skin. She shivered but did not resist as I snaked my hand up her back. I moved closer, trying to swallow her up in my arms, and she let me. I could smell jasmine and warm spices in her hair, a delicious, soothing fragrance in that fine silk under my chin. I twirled my finger slowly around her gentle waves until I could feel her heart slow against my chest and slid back into sleep as she fell deeper into my arms.

I was not disturbed further until morning, when I felt the inquisitive fingers of her right hand tracing the line of the scar over my heart. I cannot imagine how it must have shaken her, to see a dead thing rejoin the living. There was a wild terror behind her eyes as my left hand scaled her arm, from the wrist up to her shoulder. Her body quaked against mine as my fingers clasped the back of her neck, and my thumb brushed against her supple lips. Her muscles drew taut, and she pressed her open palms onto my chest as if to push me away, arching her back and digging her belly closer to mine, the thin layer she wore almost as nothing between us.

"I am not dead," I insisted, our mouths barely apart. "I am not dead."

The resistance in her hands dissipated, her mouth opened, and my lips were met with a warm, sweet welcome. A shiver thrilled down my spine and settled in my hips as my tongue traced a path across the fullness of her lower lip. My hunger grew as her body shifted and relaxed beneath mine, and I felt her grip tighten on the back of my neck. The fire of our embrace inspired such a passion in my heart as none in my own time. When we separated for want of air, she opened her maddeningly deep eyes to me, and I saw my life's happiness.

We were content to rest, to bask in the warmth of our mingled slumber as we listened to the overdue rain as it battered down the window.

"Alex will call today," she sighed, as unwilling to rise as I was.

"What is his position?" I asked, only caring for the answer in the way in which a man studies a potential enemy.

"My tutor. Do not say it. I know."

My lips hardened; my pulse quickened. I did not like that she could not be free of him. "Can he make trouble for you?" I asked.

She grunted, left without proper words. She reached over me to grab the talking stone she had left on my desk and gave me an unbidden glimpse of heaven across my face as she stretched her torso. I fought the urge to bite her breasts as they swelled in their temptation. She returned to her place, seeming none the wiser at the effect her body had on me in its glory. After a moment, she handed me the stone, which read:

The completion of my training depends on him. If they think I took you, I can kiss my job, and this house, goodbye.

I would have been very worried about my ability to shield Azi from the dangers of an unknown world, except for the last line.

But I can make trouble for him too.

The tablet vibrated in my hand, and Azi took it quickly, motioning for me to keep silent. She accepted the communique from Alex. She feigned ignorance remarkably well, mostly repeating what he said and inflecting into a question, matching the surprise in his voice at the appropriate moment. I did not like the way he yelled at her.

"I must go," she said, severing the conversation. "I do not know for how long."

I nodded, understanding. "You will be…okay?" I asked.

She shook her head in the affirmative, and I bid her good luck as she left me, flitting away to dress. I allowed myself a lazy morning, still smelling Azi's skin on my pillow.

When my hunger demanded that I rise, I ventured into the kitchen, took two apples from the cold box, and thin cheese squares that tasted like wax, wrapped in a clear film that was inedible. A loaf of bread was similarly cut thin. I did not know how to procure something warm and sweet, which would have been a boon in the rain. The house was dry, but chilly, and the old wood of the walls and floors creaked in the wind. There was no wine to be found. It seemed that in two thousand years, humanity had lost the art of making something worth drinking. As I closed the cold box, a light flashed on the smooth surface. Beneath it lay a tongue of sorts. Upon inspection, it sprayed my feet with a cool liquid. Licking my fingers, I realized it was a fountain that only flowed on command. I wiped the floor with a rag from the counter and found and filled a clean cup with water. I sat at the high, backless chair at the kitchen table with my findings. After what I refused to call a meal, I made my way to the open common room. It was spacious, but longer than it was wide. The far wall was lined with wooden shelving, stacked high with books and Egyptian fetishes. Centered there was a large blank slab like the talking stone. I fingered the edges of it, seeking to understand how it operated, but was left at a loss. I reclined on the dyed leather sofa, leafing through the bound scrolls, studying the words. The alphabet I understood but pronouncing the words did not lead to great enlightenment. I saw much similarity in how the language of the Britons looked, if not how it sounded. I knew that I must acquire Azi's language to begin repaying my debt. I could not rely on her rough Latin and did not relish dependence on the talking sheet. I wanted to speak to her, to tell her what was in my heart, so she might understand.

She found me thus idle when she returned, shaking off her outer garments in the entry before stepping into the common room. She handed me a tall, covered cup.

"Hot."

I took it readily, but shocked my tongue with the liquid's intense heat, like melted silver.

"I said hot."

I took a long draught of water to cool my mouth, placing both beverages on the table. She sipped her own cup slowly, blowing across the small aperture in the lid's surface. I took her hand and pulled her down to my lap. She was very uncomfortable with this and made to sit next to me instead. I shifted my legs and held her waist gently. Azi finally accepted, and nuzzled her fine round ass on my thigh, causing my blood to run hotter than her drink. Her knees hung over mine as she faced me, holding my right shoulder to steady herself. Being close to her was the only thing that put my spirit at ease. I wanted to be as close to her as she would allow. We were very close now, our noses nearly touching if I did not sit upright.

"How did it go?" I asked.

She shifted and sought the small talking stone from within her clothes. Before she could use it, I relieved her of it, bending us both forward to place it on the table, and forcing her to tighten her grip on me to prevent falling. She stifled a laugh as we almost both went down together, but I righted us, and we found the comfort again of our proximity.

"Use your words, and I will listen."

She mumbled in protest, but I interjected.

"I will learn. Please. Talk to me."

She began slowly, with a single thought. More thoughts followed, and soon the anxiety of my understanding was forgotten. I listened with keen attention, rapt by the fluid movements of her lips and tongue. It sharpened my desire nearly to the point of distraction, but I could not turn away. The longer she spoke, the more words I caught that I understood. Her language seemed to be some cross between Germanic and Britannic.

Her speech slowed again then stopped. I had learned some but had not enough clues to know what had transpired on behalf of my disappearance. Her tone was troubled, but in the way that portended longer worries ahead, and none so dire or urgent. The die had not yet been cast. An errant curl brushed against her check. I moved delicately to sweep it behind her ear as I attempted an exploration of her soft cheek with my knuckles. She leaned against my touch, her head lifting upward. A soft sound escaped her lips. Her ivory throat, now exposed, proved too tempting. I ran my fingers through her hair, finding solid purchase at the back of her neck as my lips caressed her skin. Her pleasure was voiced louder. I covered her open mouth hungrily with mine, consumed by a fire that burned as brightly in my chest as it did in my sex. Gods, the way she dug her hips into me drove me to madness. I sought her fingers, burying them between us to the one part of me where they had not yet ventured. My lips broke from hers, and I growled as her fingers tightened on my growing lust. My gaze burned through her. Azi fit so comfortably on my lap. Taking her like that would be a great pleasure.

She regained her sanity before I did, jumping away from me and straightening her clothes, running her hands through her hair in disbelief, at herself, I think, at how quickly our mutual wish had rushed to the surface. She mumbled breathlessly to herself, staring wide-eyed at me as I sat perched at the edge of the couch, fingers curled tightly around its edge. If I had pounced on her in that moment, taken her again into my arms, she would have submitted. I could see it in her eyes. But she begged me.

"I need…I need time."

Too fast. It was too fast, what was happening between us. I knew but was in no position to be sensible. I meant to have her, but not just today. I wanted her forever. She tensed as I approached, hanging her head in shame for ruffling my feathers. I picked her chin up with the crook of my finger. She bent her forehead toward my chest, her shoulders sagging as though relieved, the highest she could reach standing toe to toe with me. She wrapped her arms around my waist, and my hands found their way into her hair. My lips grazed the top of her head. She stretched up and kissed me, telling me my desire was her own, and sending my heart spinning. I inclined my head to her in a tight embrace. That was enough.

"Are you hungry?" she asked.

"Starving," I answered, gripping her tighter. The wolfish gleam in my eyes made her blush.

"For food," she quipped, smiling wide.

"Same answer." I grinned back. Lighthearted, she led me back to the pantry. I stood by as she reached for two silver cylinders from behind a small wooden door and opened them with a sharp tool from a slimmer, wider compartment beneath the counter. She guided my fingers over the apparatus of the second container, gripping the handle of the tool in my left while twisting the cutting mechanism with my right. The result was two open containers holding a murky yellow liquid. I was skeptical.

She emptied the contents into a silver pot on a circular black coil. Fiddling with the face of the apparatus produced a small flame that she bent to her will with a turn of her wrist. The soup was bubbling as she took it off the heat and poured it into two plain ceramic bowls. The minute, squared vegetables did not lend the meal the impression of being hearty, but as an unpaid guest in her home for an indefinite period, I had no right to complain. It went down easy, for all that. We shared a comfortable silence as the broth warmed us down to our toes. I took her bowl as she spooned her last mouthful, bringing it to the metal basin, turning on the fountain, and scrubbing it dutifully the way my mother taught me.

"Thank you," she said, a phrase I readily understood without translation. I led her back to the common room, my curiosity whetted as my appetite subsided.

"Why do you have so many of these?" I asked and pointed to the blank slab in the center of the wall. "Why is this one so large?" I picked up the tablet she always carried with her from the table, to demonstrate my confusion. She furrowed her brow, searching for the right words, I suspect, to explain things for which there were no ready terms.

"Similar abilities, different purpose. Talking," she said, lifting the device in her hand. Pointing upward, indicating the middle-sized table we had first used, still on the upper floor, she said, "Working." When her finger pointed to the largest screen, the one to my left, mischief played across her lips. "Watching."

"Watching?"

"You like theater?" she asked.

"Yes," I answered, perplexed by the oddity of the question.

"This is a theater."

"Say it again?" I must have misunderstood, misheard the word. She read the doubt on my face, and in response grabbed the smaller tablet, and held it in front of her face.

"Speak," she requested.

"What?"

"Talk. Say something."

"I am talking."

"Wave."

"Why?" I asked, complying but not comprehending.

She moved the slab away from her face, tapped the screen deliberately several times, then came to stand beside me, showing me the tablet's face.

"Ready?" she asked.

"For what?"

"Do not be afraid."

I will admit I did jump halfway out of my skin when she tapped the center of the tablet, and I saw my very likeness *moving*, heard my own voice. And hers.

Talk. Say something.

I am talking.

I took the device from her, flipping it over in my hands to guard against a shrunken copy of me crawling out.

"How is this possible?" I asked, unable or unwilling to shield my amazement.

"Video. It is a record of light and sound."

I nodded, trying, but barely understanding.

"You are you, still?" she asked.

I shook my head more firmly, sure of that much at least.

"This is a copy. A farce. But you can see it."

I tried hard to absorb her reasoning.

"A play is a farce, yes?" she asked.

"Yes..."

She was getting more excited now, making progress in explaining how she had mimicked me, us. "Think of a record. Not of us...of actors. On a stage. A very large stage."

I closed my eyes, coming to some sort of understanding.

"We can watch, without the actors here. We can watch a play many times." She pointed again toward the large flat stone. "Theater."

I nodded again. That particular spot on the back of my neck was sore indeed, but there was nothing else for it, no other appropriate response. I pointed to the screen, wanting to see for myself.

"You want to watch something?"

"Please?"

"Yeah, okay." She was thrilled now, and hopped about the shelves near the watching glass, searching for suitable material.

"War?" she asked. "Love?"

"Both?" I challenged.

She was trying hard not to disappoint, weighing her options carefully. A choice had been made. She beckoned me to sit back on the leather sofa. After preparing the "video," she sat beside me, showing me the art accompanying what she had selected.

"Troy?" I spelled aloud.

She nodded. "Achilles."

"Ah! You know the Song of Ilium?!" The prospect of this artificial theater was improving rapidly.

"Everyone does." She snuggled close, lifting my arm and leaning against my chest, curling her knees up beside her. Sitting with me, a seemingly small gesture, elated her. I dared a kiss. The frenzied hunger that had met my lips before was replaced by a soulful contentedness. The sentiment was mutual. What happened next, as the video began, entranced me.

12

ASENATH

*I*t wasn't until I heard Josh Groban belting out the end credits that I realized I'd dozed off. I rested my head on Quintus's lap. He stroked my hair as he stared in awe at the screen, silently beckoning me to jump right back into bed with him. Tall and strong, with an ageless sentience behind those smoldering eyes that put my most intellectual friends to shame, that he couldn't stop touching me—it drove me to the end of my wits. Because I loved the way he touched me. His arms made me feel safe and reminded me that I wasn't alone in the burning rubble that was my life.

Just sitting with him—watching a movie, keeping warm on a rainy day—felt luxurious. His gaze pierced me to the core, his fingers in my hair strumming my heart strings. He didn't have somewhere else he was supposed to be, someone else who was expecting him. He didn't constantly check his phone or watch. He was just here. With me. I wanted to curl up inside his powerful arms and stay there forever. And I wanted what I knew *he* wanted—so badly. But my lust was tempered with doubt, and I needed to be sure that once his feet were firmly planted in this century, that they wouldn't lead him elsewhere.

He wanted me to take him to Rome. Dean was my best bet, if he could even do it. If he could...was I buying Quintus a one-way ticket?

Were his feelings just a grown man's abstinence of two millennia, now in the company of an unsupervised female? Or the emotional fallout of the circumstances that had thrown us together? Were mine? I'd have liked to think not. But if we—if I let him in, only to be gone again like the rest—I couldn't bear that. Not with him.

One thing was certain. Staying away from Alex was no longer going to be a chore. I was angry, having never felt so cheated. Only now did I understand how little Alex had given, and how much he had taken.

"That was wondrous," Quintus said, drawing my attention back to him. The rolling credits shined in his eyes.

"Are you crying?" I asked.

He swiped quickly at his face. "No."

"Yes, you are. It is common," I said. "Even among men."

"Are there more? Like this?" he asked eagerly. I smiled.

"Many, many more." I rose, stretching my arms until my shoulders almost came out of joint. I found myself caught in his quiet seduction, that sultry, inquisitive gaze that had led my hand to his dick a few hours before. Either he had no idea how crazy sexy he was, or he was toying with me, the way a fox might fondle a mouse before eating it alive. I was in a lot of trouble, living under the same roof as him. I stood before he could kiss me again, not ready to start what I had nearly killed myself to stop the last time. He recognized what I'd done, and looked confused, wounded. Then those shadows left his eyes, chased away by sincerity and understanding. I wanted to jump him even more. I very well might have, if not for my wretched phone buzzing on the table.

"Who calls?" Quintus asked.

"Dean. Felix. My tenants. They are close." Just looking at the rain battering down the windowpanes made me groan. What a shitty day to be moving in.

The honk of Felix's beat-up Chevy half an hour later made Quintus jump. When I opened the front door, I could barely see Felix's headlights crawling up the hill to the front door until he was right in front of us, hearing only "Sweet Child of Mine" blaring through the storm. The convertible's fabric top was taking a visible beating.

"Come up!" I shouted uselessly into the deluge, motioning for Felix to put it in reverse and pull it up close. He inched slowly, keeping his head twisted toward me as he inched his back tires up half the marble steps of the front entryway, shielding the trunk with the overhang from the porch roof.

"Whoa!" I called out, stopping him just before his bumper tapped the columns holding up the portico.

Watching Felix and Dean get out at the same time made me laugh. They were entirely different men. There's only one way to describe Dean's more collegiate style, his cultivated look of subdued power behind thick-rimmed glasses and a fair-haired do-curl. He was, in plain English, a hipster Clark Kent. Where Dean tried so hard, Felix's devil-may-care Euro-chic was effortless—a finely tailored white shirt, ripped jeans, and goddamn sexy leather shoes. His clean, full haircut was roughed up by two or three days' worth of stubble. Felix was faster, and caught me in his arms first, kissing both my cheeks exuberantly.

"Hola, Princesa!" Felix shouted, lifting me off the floor and spinning me in a quick circle. "What a beautiful day, huh?!"

"Fabulous." I laughed, my feet back on the marble floor that was rapidly growing slick. I turned to greet Dean and was met by a boyish eagerness.

"Hi, Azi," he said softly in my ear, making me suddenly uncomfortable with how close we were standing. It wasn't just me. Quintus chose that moment to step in-between us, wanting an introduction. Quintus caught my eyes for a second, but then we were both distracted by Felix.

"Let's meet and greet later, okay? Better we set everything here before we all get washed away," he suggested, gesticulating wildly at the floor.

"Yeah, yeah, yeah," I answered, grabbing my hoodie from the coat closet to the left. Before I could don it, Quintus stopped me. My eyes questioned him, but he simply smiled, and crooked his finger under my chin before following the boys out.

Through the next several hours of boxes being moved first from the car to the foyer then upstairs to the bedrooms, I was not permitted to lift a single crate. It was a sweet, grand gesture, and to be honest, it went faster with him on the job. It allowed me to keep the floor dry and concentrate on little details like chilling Coronas as Dean and Felix settled in.

Every time Dean passed me on the stairs, I had to feign being busier than I was just to avoid his meaningful, crushed stares. The disappointment that had flashed on his face at Quintus's open affection for me coiled a knot in my stomach. I'd been as straightforward as possible the night before he left for summer, proposing a one-time cure for my Alex-itis. It had only broken my habit for about a week; it had taken Jakob to really shake it, and *he'd* had two weeks straight. Dean had been cool with it, I thought. Apparently not. I'd approached Dean because I trusted him, and he wasn't the rogue Felix was. Maybe that was what I had needed. Felix would have fucked me, then been back to raiding my fridge the next day without a thought in his head, like it had never happened. He might have been the better man for the job.

But it amounted to only a few awkward seconds, nothing more. As the bustle was winding down, an expensive car horn blared outside. Ravi sauntered through the open front door, sporting thick sunglasses and a black raincoat and black pumps under a black umbrella. She looked like she was going to the funeral of the wealthiest man on earth. Her rich caramel skin glittered with a dozen gold bangles on each arm, rubies dangling from her ears. She jingled in time with the rain as she glided toward us, cracking into the first round in the kitchen.

"What do you need, a written invitation? Go out there and get my stuff," she commanded, ripping the bottle from Dean's lips and taking a long swig. She swatted the men away as Dean and Felix planted wet kisses on her cheeks. "Hello, dear," she said, hugging me tightly as the menfolk went about their work.

"Good Lord, he's a handsome one," Ravi said, taking off her shades to get a better look at Quintus. "What an ass."

"That ass is mine," I said, before thinking about it.

"No shit! And Alex?" she asked, her voice lowering as she spoke his name.

I clucked my tongue before raising a bottle again to my lips. "Fuck Alex."

"Not anymore." She laughed. I laughed with her.

"Amen, sister," I said, tapping the neck of her bottle with mine.

"Good riddance, I say. That man is pure poison. Where's Kyle?"

"He transferred to Cal Tech."

"Oh! Good for him."

"He sends his regrets."

"Mm, yes, I like this one better anyway," she said, raising her drink to Quintus as he led the line hauling Ravi's stuff up the stairs.

"Don't you feel just a little bit bad not helping?" I asked, leaning closer.

"No," she answered, mimicking the tone of my voice and coming so close our foreheads touched as we giggled. "If you feel so bad, you go help."

"Not allowed," I said, sitting upright in my chair.

"Oh, that's so sweet, I think I'll vomit on your floor," she joked. "Does he have money?"

"Not a dime."

Ravi laughed. "You can have him, then. I give you my permission."

"All finished, my fine ladies," Felix announced as the trio came downstairs. Dean pulled a second round from the fridge. I whipped out my phone for pizza. No one was looking when I grabbed Quintus's Corona and shoved the lime through the neck before he had time to question it. Once I hung up, Felix was ready with our habitual start-of-the-year toast.

"May the wind always be at your back, and the warm sun upon your face, until we meet again. *Salud!*"

"*Salud!*" we echoed, tapping the butts of our bottles against the marble counter before polishing them off in ritualistic fashion.

"Welcome home, fellas," I said, the golden liquid sliding down to my empty stomach.

"Thank you again for your assistance," Felix said, stretching his arm out to Quintus. Quintus took it, grasping Felix's hand up to his elbow. My heart almost stopped.

"Old school, eh? I like it," Felix said, gripping Quintus's arm more firmly. Thank the gods Felix was cool in *every* situation.

"Quintus," he announced himself.

"He doesn't speak English," I said, licking my lips and rolling my eyes back awkwardly.

"*Ah.* Felix," he answered matter-of-factly. I followed that with an introduction of Dean, then Ravi, to whom he made a low bow.

The household dispersed for potty breaks and dry clothes before food, leaving Quintus and me alone in the kitchen. He glistened with the day's efforts, his sweat carrying a heady sweetness. I licked my lips, imagining all the other things that might produce that musky fragrance.

"What is this?" he panted loudly, not recognizing the need for secrecy.

"Shh! Beer," I hissed.

"What is wrong?"

I inched closer, taking in more of his scent and wishing it on my own skin. "Latin is not spoken now. I only know it as part of my study. We must be careful."

His face turned contemplative. "I must learn quickly, then."

"Yes. I am sorry." I pursed my lips to the side. I didn't like having to push him. He had enough to deal with. But he hadn't shut himself into a dark corner of his room, or gone stark raving mad, when I might have expected that. He was resilient.

But that alone wouldn't be enough. He couldn't wear my father's sweatshirt forever, and the things that would help Quintus acquire English faster weren't cheap. There would be no more paint this month.

Quintus surprised me as the day drew to a close. He was so comfortable among people with whom he could not converse. Over pizza, Felix asked the questions I should have been prepared to answer.

"Azi, tell us about our new housemate. What does he study?"

The phrase "Ancient languages" jumped out of my throat.

"Just up your alley, huh?" Felix smiled brazenly.

I was angry at my face for getting red faster than I could control it. Dean tried badly to be distracted by the Horus behind him, and Quintus simply inched his seat closer to mine.

"I can translate," I said acridly, throwing a snarky look at Quintus. It was returned only by that innocent smile that wasn't so innocent.

"I am a musician and a poet," Felix said, smiling at Quintus and giving a courteous bow.

"Computer programming," Dean offered, following suit.

"Architectural engineering," Ravi chimed in. Quintus inched his head to me, and I translated in his ear the best I could. We shifted to the parlor, and Felix moved to his customary place at the piano.

"*Mierda.* Azi, I've told you to keep this tuned," he scolded.

"I would if I knew how," I replied apologetically.

"Ach, why you didn't say? Come!" He pulled me to the bench with him, and I watched as he tightened strings and loosened others in the housing. When every note sounded to his satisfaction, I rejoined Quintus on the sofa.

Felix played his own composition. Its opening was bright and witty, up-tempo, just like Felix. As he glided his fingers over the keys to the second movement, the tone grew languid, sated with joy, and digging into lower notes and longer silences for a more sonorous mood, the absence of musical light. I leaned back into Quintus's arms, closing my eyes and inhaling the melancholy harmony, hinting with nostalgia at the first movement. Felix finished quietly, and we issued our congratulations.

"*Gracias.*" He bowed in his seat. "If my advisory board is as kind as you, I should be done by Christmas."

"Already?" Ravi asked.

"I'm sure they'll want changes, but yes, I hope so."

I stayed silent, stung to lose another friend. And another tenant. The ice I trod was not merely thin. It was treacherous.

couldn't sleep. I wasn't as exhausted as was usual because of Quintus's help. My mind raced to do all I could before undergrad classes began in two weeks. I was in my room, trying to figure out just what I had left to work with, what I could cobble together into some kind of final thesis that wouldn't get laughed out of the department, and do *something* to prove I wasn't useless without Anglesey Man when the doorknob rattled. I stood to find Quintus on the other side of it.

"Come in," I said in Latin, realizing two seconds too late what I'd done. I slammed a textbook closed over the picture nearest me, the close-up of Quintus's tanned, wrinkled face, and stood stalwartly in front of my desk as Quintus tried to rip the picture from me.

"No," I said, bracing my muscles in the expectation that he might just lift me off the floor and toss me aside. He looked sternly at me; his eyes ringed in red.

"Azi," he said with force, "Give it to me."

"No," I said weakly, trying, and failing, to keep my composure. He moved closer, and I stifled a sob. It was the first time I'd felt menaced by him, since...since we'd met. My knees were at the point of buckling when he reached his arm behind me and took the picture from its place, his silent, watchful gaze ever on me.

A last-ditch effort, I put my hand to his wrist, but was no match for the determination I felt there. I did the only thing I could.

"I am sorry, Quintus, I have to look. You do not."

He swallowed hard and turned the image over in his hand to face him. I watched helplessly as the light left his eyes. His arm went limp, dropping the replica of his death mask on the floor. He stumbled backward and grasped at the last minute for the door frame. I lunged for him, catching him around his thick waist before he crumpled to the floor. He was so heavy my own legs almost gave way underneath me. But I stood firm.

"It's okay. You are here, Quintus. I am here."

He became sensible of me as I spoke and clasped desperately at my arm on his chest. He closed his eyes tight in a frightened expression, as if to open them would open the abyss under his feet and send the world spinning around him.

"Azi," he pleaded, as if searching restlessly for me.

"I am here," I repeated. "I am here."

"Are you?" he asked, his deep voice now nearly a whimper.

"Yes."

He opened his eyes to me, reaching for my face and drawing me to him, our foreheads touching. He shivered as if intensely cold.

"That is not you," I said firmly.

"For longer than you can imagine, it was." His reply made me shudder, as from an unseen, infernal wind.

"I am sorry, Quintus, I did not intend—"

"Shh, I know. I know you must. You were right, I should not have—forgive me."

"Please, let me," I said, moving slowly away from him to clear my research away and shuffle it under the bed. "It will not happen again," I promised, leading him to my bed to sit down. He laid his head on my stomach as I stood before him and gripped my hips. He kept his head hung low, as if he were ashamed. What he thought was a proper way for a man to deal with coming back from the dead, that I haven't the foggiest about. I stood patiently while he regained his composure. He seemed to like my fingers in his hair as much as I liked his in mine. He was on the verge of purring contentedly when he appeared to remember why he had come.

He pointed at the computer screen on my desk, beckoning to use it. I was relieved not to have to dig deeper into my Latin. I understood him fine most of the time, but my respondent vocabulary was rapidly nearing its limit without a dictionary. I couldn't shake the slamming headache I'd had all day. No amount of Tylenol could compete with my overwrought nerves of harboring a bog body come back to life and the stress of recalling enough Latin not to sound like an imbecile. I spent so much of my mental energy anticipating what would freak him out that I was the one going to pieces.

"Are you all right?" I asked, sitting at my desk and tilting the monitor in his direction.

He nodded. *I came because I was curious. Felix, Ravi, they have traveled far to come here? Their speech is different from yours.*

I laughed. "Are you a linguist?" It took him a moment to comprehend what I'd asked, but he indicated that he was, of a sort.

"Felix is from Barcelona. Err," I corrected, "south of Gaul."

And Ravi?

"Her parents are from Mumbai—India—but they live in New York. South of here. Most Americans are from somewhere else."

And you? Where are your parents from, originally?

"My father's family has been here for so long I don't remember. And my mother's people have always been here. Narragansett."

He grunted, and I sensed he was just getting to what he really came to ask.

How many years do you have? the screen read.

"How many—oh, how old am I? Twenty-four. You?"

Two thousand thirty-six.

His sense of humor was back. Always a good sign.

I ask because... he hesitated, then started again, taking a different approach. *Your parents left you when?* he asked.

"I was ten." He looked down at his borrowed shirt. Embarrassed, I tripped over my own words. "I just never…I never got rid of…"

He dismissed the thought. *I am sorry, my angel.*

The conflicting impulse to blush and cry at his words nearly choked me. "Drunk driver," I said simply. They might not have had cars in ancient Rome, but I'll bet at least one man behind the reins of a chariot had put away one too many. The grave look on his face reflected his understanding.

And after that, who raised you?

I shifted in my seat, not sure where this was going. But it wasn't some great secret. "My uncle, for a while. He moved in with his sons, because I threw a fit when they tried to make me leave. The doctors told them that—"

Doctors? Were you ill?

"No. Here," I said, putting my finger first to my temple, then over my heart. "Here. They suggested a slower transition, because I wasn't—" I turned my head to the side and swallowed hard, trying to tamp down on the memories that were banging at the gates. "I didn't handle it well."

Quintus nodded sympathetically, and I continued. "They'd left me more than enough money to take care of me for the rest of my life. But my uncle—"

Quintus closed his eyes in a solemn expression, knowing what I meant to say before I said it.

"It was almost all gone by the time my father's attorney realized what was happening. He fought to have me emancipated and arranged caretakers for me until I was eighteen."

The others—are they alone also? he asked, indicating the rest of the household, settling into their beds for the night.

"No, their parents are alive and well."

So, forgive me, but why do they live here?

"It's only during their education. Their parents live too far away."

Are they around your age?

"More or less."

Are none married?

That came as a surprise. "Do any of us look married?"

Pardon me, Azi. I meant no offense. Is that common, to be unmarried at your age?

"Yes, very common. Though *you're* pushing it, old man," I quipped.

Am I too old for you, Azi?

He asked in such earnest, I felt bad for having made the joke in poor taste. "No, Quintus. Not for me."

He stood, and I rose from my chair as he neared it. His knuckles brushed my cheek in that gentle, yearning way they had before, when I almost—

"Your father, did he...are you promised?"

I mumbled dreamily in the negative, forgetting completely that this was a bad idea.

"Who would I ask, Azi?"

I shrugged meekly under his touch, wishing for the warmth of his embrace.

"Me," I answered humbly. "Marriages are for...for..."

"For love," he said softly.

"Yes," I whispered, my face so close to his that I could smell his warm, sweet breath.

He nodded in quiet understanding, swallowing me in his gaze. I thought he would kiss me. I wished for it so badly, the wanting became a deep pain in my chest. He held me close, and I listened to his two-thousand-year-old heart, thumping confidently in his chest. Why I chose just then to test the waters, I'll never know.

"I will ask Dean tomorrow, about helping you get home," I said.

"I am deep in your debt. I will repay it. Good night, Asenath."

"Sleep well," I said as I watched him linger in the doorway. I bit my tongue to stop myself from asking him to stay. *He* could ask if he wanted to.

I could tell he wanted to—his eyes reflected that and nothing else. But in a full house, we both felt the constraints of propriety and discretion. I listened to his sad footsteps echo down the hallway.

I tried for the next hour to come up with a plan for my thesis. I went through all the notes that had gotten me to Wales in the first place, and all the photos still on my camera. It was surreal to see Quintus in his previous condition, and I thanked my lucky stars that my mind had begun disassociating the two from the minute he opened his eyes. Defense mechanism for madness though it might be, I was not prepared to question what came so naturally. But Quintus and Anglesey Man were not completely severed, indeed *could not* be. Something had been done to Quintus, against his will, and probably against his knowledge. And either in spite of it, or because of it, the bog had preserved him, alive.

No, that wasn't right. He *wasn't* alive, not when we found him. But he *was* alive now. How did a stake, a bit of amber, and a gold ring accomplish that? Did the person or persons responsible intend for this to happen, to keep him in suspended consciousness, or did they simply set to drown him? Was there more to the ritual he had undergone that hadn't survived? How could I know, without asking Quintus? Had similar tokens been found before? I'd have to go back over everything I knew about bog bodies, all the theories about how they'd been put there, and why. But even then, what could I say—what could I *prove* without revealing Quintus? If I used only what was recorded, would my whole thesis be junk science, or worse—a lie? What would my degree mean then?

It was enough to make my head spin, and I'd had enough of that for one day. I needed to unwind if I was ever going to clear my head and make sense of what had happened, what I would do, what I was feeling. I wasn't sleeping anyway, so, obscenely late as it now was, I headed up to the tower loft.

My finished canvas was there, brooding appropriately. I stared a long time, unsure of where to begin next. I put the canvas to the side and grabbed another. Regarding materials, I had nothing to work with unless I wanted two of the same painting. I looked to the first portrait of Anglesey Man, in soft lamplight, and pinned it up in the corner. I saw only Quintus's face as it had been, and as it was now. I roughed out the curve of Quintus's jaw, his straight, dignified nose, his smooth brow, and piercing, brilliant eyes, set in an intense stare.

14

I was beginning to loathe Alex, and, for the first time, to fear that there were no limits to his self-preservation. Our relationship fell away like a bad dream. He had kept his distance after he called me down to the lab. Easy enough, since it was packed with professors and police. The crime scene unit dusted and catalogued, and we stood against the wall, a cloud of confusion and helplessness hanging over all of us. As they went about their business, my gaze roamed over every square inch. I hadn't knocked anything over, hadn't done anything to make the officers suspect there had been a struggle. There was no need to mask my shock at the scene—it wasn't out of place, even if the reasons for my stoicism were entirely different.

I stared at the crumbled peat on the floor, at the impression in the wooden crate where a body had once been, at the intertwined willow branches that had weighed him down. I couldn't stop staring at the remnants, at all the things that proved a dead man had been here. That man had slept in my bed, had pressed his body, his lips to mine. That man was not dead. Not at all.

How? Why? These were questions I could not fathom. But I craved answers. His transformation was so real to me, yet so incredibly outside my comprehension. I couldn't conceive of his experience and remembering how his face had contorted when I made the slightest hint at it, I would never dare to ask again. Besides, the extent to which Quintus would have understood what was happening to him was minimal at best.

My thoughts were interrupted by Alex's ranting.

"This is an outrage! Who would steal a preserved body?"

"It happened to Black Hawk," I said absently. He turned on me.

"What?" he snapped.

"Black Hawk, chief of the Sac. It happened to him twice, actually."

"Is that right?" Dr. Magnusson, the head of Archaeology, asked.

"Yup." I nodded. "Right out of his grave."

"Huh."

Alex was not consoled. "This is a secure facility!"

"Why are you yelling at me?" I asked.

Alex was on the spot as all eyes turned on him.

"Cool it, Carew," Magnusson warned. "We're all upset by this. Take a deep breath."

He inhaled as he came one step closer to me and loomed over me. "The only footprints they found here are yours," he growled, his voice low.

"Well, I *was* here," I replied. "So were you."

"*I* didn't track dirt all over the floor."

I held my breath as I looked at the hastened prints pressed into the linoleum, from when I tried to circle back around the table. The peat must've caught in the tread of my sneakers. I still hadn't responded when Magnusson intervened.

"She couldn't carry him without your help, could she?" he countered. "Unless you're suggesting he just got up and walked out."

Breathe. Must breathe.

Alex stared hard at me, his eyes almost narrowing to slits.

"This bickering is useless and unproductive. Go home, both of you. The lab will be open again tomorrow," Magnusson said. "We'll schedule a meeting in a few days to sort through all this." With that, he left, the rest of the department following suit.

Alex inched closer. "How long?" he hissed.

"Excuse me?"

"How long were you here after I left?" he asked, out of earshot of the police.

"You left me to clean up," I snapped back. "That's what I did."

"Did you get somebody to help you?"

"Don't be an ass," I cried, louder than I meant to.

"Is everything all right?" the officer closest to us asked.

Alex shot him a snooty stare, which resulted in the man coming closer, strengthening his stance in the event of having to interfere.

"Are you all right, miss?" he asked again.

"Yes, thank you," I said, and turned to leave as fast as I could. I stopped for coffee when my phone rang with a number I didn't recognize.

"Hello?"

"Miss Hayes?"

"Yes?"

"It's Richard Pryce."

"Oh! Hi, Doctor Pryce."

"I'm so sorry, Miss Hayes. Magnusson just called me."

"Oh, yes…" My voice trailed off, unsure of what to say.

"It's terrible, just terrible."

"It is, but I took plenty of pictures, so…"

His laughter crackled through the line. "See? And your advisor thought you were just wasting time. Always trust your gut, Miss Hayes."

I grunted, still at a loss. I'd have to get better at having this conversation. I had the feeling I was going to have it a lot. Probably for the rest of my life.

"Well, thank God no one was hurt. I just wanted to make sure you were okay and let you know that if there's anything I can do for you, you need only ask."

"Thank you, I appreciate that."

"Okay. Take care, Miss Hayes. Oh, and Jakob sends his regards. He's taking it pretty rough too."

"It was his discovery," I reasoned. "Tell him I'm sorry for not taking better care of it."

Tell him he'd never believe what he found, and how it's changed my life. Tell him I wish I could share the truth with him. Tell him—

"Will do. Goodbye," he said.

"Bye."

As I sat in my car, it occurred to me that, had I ever been a smoker, now would have been an ideal time for a cigarette. I really did want to tell someone. I'd never been a secretive person. I'd never really had anyone to keep secrets from. Now I was hiding the biggest thing that had ever happened to me from everyone. So far, it had been simple, because the truth was just so unbelievable. But I had the sinking feeling it was going to get harder. I thought of Alex and his questions. How long could I dodge him without raising suspicion? Funny how he cared for Anglesey Man the most *after* he was missing. I took a long draught of coffee and drove home. Quintus was waiting.

○

The rest of the week was about picking up the pieces. The yellow tape was peeled away so we could get back to work. The janitorial crew had been given the okay to clean the debris from the floor where Quintus had crashed to the ground, his eyes piercing through the cracked slits of what had been his perfectly preserved face, a simultaneous image of sublime beauty and unspeakable horror.

I couldn't put my work on hold until the day I felt Quintus's secret —*our* secret—was safe. That day might never come. As I expected, nothing else had been disturbed. Quintus's ring, the iron loop attached to the amber amulet, and the stake were still in their plastic dishes, secured in a locker. I needed to understand everything that I could about these objects—the stake, the gold, the amber—a collection of Iron Age materials that struck me as being combined deliberately. I had a long job ahead of me, looking at countless works of alchemy, British lore, and arcana with fresh eyes as to the potential efficacy of these materials and their acclaimed mystical properties.

I took a midweek detour to the library, hoping for something I had overlooked the first time to leap out at me. But nothing tied all these things together, no historical record, dismissed as lunacy, that someone had succeeded in drawing such powers from the humble objects. It might have helped if I'd known the intentions of Quintus's enchanters. Then my search could have been more efficient, and perhaps more fruitful. Did they think they were killing him? Or did they truly mean to keep him in suspension? As a sacrifice to the gods, perhaps? *What* gods? What did they expect this malignant deity to do with such an offering?

Why Romans would have been targeted for such a practice was perfectly plain. If the malefactors were Druidic holdouts, then it was a political move. Though whether it was preemptive or revenge for the destruction of Mona I couldn't be sure. Only Quintus would know a detail like that—science was wonderful, but it couldn't be that accurate. Was Quintus a victim of circumstance, or was this done to him purposefully? For what? Murder? Rape? There would be blood on his hands, surely—he was a Roman soldier. Given his age, it was unlikely that Britain had been his first campaign. But combat and injustice were two very different things. I saw no malice in his eyes. If Quintus meant to rape me, he'd had plenty of opportunity. No, those strong, slender hands had never touched a woman in anger. No.

Still, there were too many variables for me to research effectively. Nothing of his situation rang any bells. I returned the last stack of archival boxes to the curator, who looked relieved when I didn't present him with a fresh pile of call slips that would send him back into the bowels of Arkham University's Special Collections. Over the course of the week, I'd called all the holdings I could think of that might have held some clue and came up empty.

"There are no other arcana in the collection? You're sure?" I inquired. The thin, middle-aged man stood at his full height, pushing his rimless spectacles up the bridge of his nose. His lips curled downward in a frown that exaggerated his long face.

"There are some Arab texts, but I'm not sure that's what *you're* looking for. Can't be too sure though."

My eyes shifted to the side, considering. When they darted quickly back to the curator's face, I caught him glaring at me with a dark, eager expression that crawled down my spine.

"No, I don't think so," I said, anxious to leave. "Thanks anyway."

He looked disappointed, like a hawk who'd failed to catch his dinner, but he said nothing as he turned his back to me to place the boxes on the metal rack behind him and pushed them away, the wheels on the cart squeaking shrilly into the dim, carpeted silence of the archival wing.

My skin prickled against the cool, sweet air of the evening, heralding the imminent arrival of autumn. I drew in long draughts of breath, relieved to be finally convinced that I possessed all the pertinent information I was going to get and would not have to venture back to that stifling room for some time, if ever. All week, I'd had the odd sense that the library would suck me into endless, fruitless research if I let it, and today I'd managed to avoid that. I had my pictures, I had my piles and piles of notes, and I had the objects we'd found with Quintus.

Relieved as I was to be rid of the archives, my disappointment at having no reward must have been plain, for Alex offered me words of encouragement when I finally arrived at the lab. That, or he was trying to raise his own spirits, which was likely.

"Keep working," he said. His tongue was sharp, like it pained him to stay positive. Or civil. "Maybe it was all just a stupid college-boy prank. He'll turn up, and we can all get back to our lives."

I couldn't let the absurdity of that show on my face. But he did have a point. I *did* have to figure out something, had to write something, somehow, or I'd be finished. I couldn't expect Alex to protect me if I dragged my feet. Most of the professors in my department had been colleagues of my father's, friends even. If the fallout landed on both of us, I hoped that history would be enough to tip the scales. Alex may not have been popular among his peers, but it was easier to move Heaven and Earth than to get an academic department to turn on one of its own, if he pointed the finger at me. That I knew, deep down, to expect that, did not improve my mood. He knew how high the stakes were for me, and I wasn't going to let him throw me to the wolves to save his own skin. *Always trust your gut,* Pryce had said. My gut told me to keep my work to myself and get something down on paper, something I could show Magnusson at the meeting, however preliminary it was, to show that I could do the work with or without Anglesey Man. Because that's what it was going to take to impress them, and prove I'd earned a spot in that building *without* relying on my dad's legacy. That's what it would take to afford tickets to Rome, without selling one of my parents' antiquities. Whether Quintus stayed there or not, I had to get him home. It's what they would have done.

15

QUINTUS

I was in my room, admiring the moderately sized painting that hung on the wall. The scene was a river at night, with the tombs of the pharaohs visible in the far distance. The Nile shone by moonlight cast in soft gold tones. Details and figures in the foreground were not distinct in their brushwork but gave the remarkable impression that they were. I stood observing the subtle coloration of the deepening night on the far riverbank when there was a light tapping on my door.

Felix was on the other side. He led me outdoors to his horseless chariot, which relied on an unseen power and moved with a speed that nearly choked me. Thank the gods for the conversation that kept my mind off my churning stomach.

"So," Felix said, guiding the chariot by a large helm that looked to require *two* hands, "Azi, eh?" I didn't catch his meaning. *"Azi,"* he repeated emphatically, and kissed his fingers to the sky. *"Bellissima, sí?"*

I inhaled sharply, sucking in the cool breeze to keep my illness at bay, and nodded in the affirmative.

He smiled approvingly. I understood the next question from the glint in his eye alone and narrowed mine to let him know I would not divulge anything of our intimacies. He shrugged it off, and we arrived at a sprawling complex that was a center of commerce, flanked by unattended chariots in ranks longer and wider than an entire legion. Felix handed me a pile of clean-cut linen, with all the markings of money. I lifted it in my hand, to ask what we were to buy.

"Clothes," he said, pulling on his garments. "Azi." He pointed at the pile of currency in my hands.

I shook my head and tried to give it back. "No, Felix," I said, but he wouldn't hear it. He clapped his hand on my shoulder and ushered me into the circuitous structure. The design of the inner space was sleek and impressive, with high ceilings closed off to the sky by panes of glass, from which sunlight poured. I heard metallic, bland music behind the din of patrons. Azi's home was in a peaceful plot above this market area and gave no indication of supporting a population of this magnitude. The sheer breadth of the crowds overwhelmed me. More confusing still, I could not discern any rules regarding appropriate dress for one of my admittedly undefined station. Or any station, for that matter. I recognized no patterns by which I could make order of what people wore, or why they wore it. My feet stood numb in awe of the sight, and Felix pulled me out of the way of a mother pushing two crying children in an oversized cart, who had shown absolutely no signs of slowing as we leaped out of her way. Felix extended his arms outward, offering me my choice of business. I was at a complete loss. I made no secret of it, and Felix issued his reassurances. In short order, we had cobbled together a respectable wardrobe of thin silks and linens of white, soft grays, and warmer layers of blue and black, with two pairs of shoes.

I did not much care for the second pair. The leather was tight, but Felix shook his head with such vigor, saying Azi's name over and over again. I could not imagine that she would want me to be uncomfortable, but I trusted Felix's exuberance was not for nothing.

The remainder of Azi's generosity fed our appetites. The bright yellow grains and vegetables were warm and tender. I could have eaten three times as much, in truth. My appetite was returning with all its force, kept in check only by the fact that, despite a collection of culinary apparatuses that would make my mother weep, Azi had barely cooked anything in all the time I had known her. But for one who slept, ate, and was now clad in her generosity, I was grateful for whatever she deigned to provide.

We made our way home, with the clothes Azi had first dressed me in folded neatly away among my purchases, but there was no immediate sign of Azi. I returned to my room, sounding out a book on the shelf in search of familiar words, when I heard Azi's voice beyond the door.

"Quintus?"

I opened the door and found a goddess. She wore a thin, fine black dress that flowed to the floor and floated behind her in the breeze from my open window. A gold ring set with blue faience adorned her graceful hand. Her hair's gentle waves were prim and glossy. She looked positively radiant. The Eye of Ra hung provocatively down her neck, resting in the shallows between her glorious breasts.

Her eyes sparkled as she took in the sight of me, dressed like a modern man. She settled her attention on my feet and emitted a phrase that could not have been anything other than "nice shoes." I bit back a laugh.

"You approve?" I asked, already seeing the answer reflected in her eyes. She nodded. "You look ravishing," I added. She blushed in acknowledgment. I welcomed her into the room, where she proceeded to place what she called her "working" tablet on my desk and fed a small, flat discus into a thin aperture at the base. The tablet reacted, and Azi settled it before gesturing to me.

"This will help you," she said.

"What is it?" I asked, peering at what she called the screen.

"A language tool. Online learning," she answered.

I made to sit down, eager to start making real progress in Azi's language, but she put her hand gently on my forearm.

"Not now. Will you come with me? To dinner?"

She escorted me to an establishment filled with well-dressed patrons, turning heads as we passed through the room. Azi was the youngest and most exquisite female in attendance. I had never had such a beauty on my arm in public, and my chest felt larger. I stood a little taller, and my heart raced. The attendant led the way to a circular table with a high upholstered back, in a cozy, warmly lit setting. Candles, apparently, are used now only in setting an intimate mood in the place of artificial lights.

Azi sat close to me, our thighs touching. She laid her phone in her lap beneath the table, brushing her nose against my ear as she spoke.

Classes begin soon. That will keep me very busy. I wanted to spend some time with you.

I leaned closer, putting my arm around her waist. The enticing scent of her hair filled my nose. My voice caught in my throat.

"May I visit you? I would like to see your university."

Of course. Next week, perhaps.

A gentleman filled the empty glasses on the table with water and provided freshly baked bread and a small bowl of oil. I did not wait for the server to give us a list of the kitchen's offerings before availing myself of the bread.

The wine—I suppose something from a Roman vineyard will suffice?

"Wine?" I nearly shouted in her ear.

We are not barbarians. I have a few bottles at home that you are welcome to, but beer tends to be the drink of choice for students. Cheaper.

"You have spent a lot of money on me, Azi. I thank you. Forgive me, but..." I grunted, loathe to bring it up. "Can you afford to be so generous?"

She nibbled on bread at that moment. I was bewitched by the tender motion of her lips as she chewed, the slick shine she licked away.

Let me worry about that.

I glided my palm over hers, our entangled fingers resting on my lap. "It is not my wish to burden you, Azi."

The wind puffing my chest left me. I had no position to offer her, no security, no means by which to lavish her with comfort or beautiful things. I was an unsuitable match for her. It pained me deeply, to have found a woman I would have as my wife, one whose splendor shined all the more brightly for her unending warmth of heart, for her sharp wit and keen mind, and in whom I had caught a glimpse of great, untapped passion. She had answered my initial overtures with open interest, even when her work kept her away from me longer than I liked. Azi exceeded my humble expectations for a partner. Yet I could not bind her to me. I lacked the resources to serve proudly as her husband. I needed not only to survive in Azi's world. I had to thrive in it.

That none of my worries were reflected in her sweet visage filled me with great hope.

"What do you want?" she asked, offering me a variety of meats and fish.

"Whatever you would like," I replied.

"No, I will have my own. What would *you* like?"

"Oh. How about that?" I asked, eyeing a plate piled high with rice. The intoxicating scent of jasmine filled the air. Azi stuck her nose up, spying the meal, and nodded in recognition just as the server approached again. She made her requests, then turned her attention back to me.

I talked to Dean, she said, her voice delving even further into secretive tones that were drowned out by the surrounding chatter. *He has a friend who might be able to furnish you with travel papers. It will be some weeks, though.*

"Is it costly?" I asked as the waiter brought the wine in a sealed bottle, making a big show of opening it and pouring the first glass before leaving it on the table. It was so splendid I nearly cried—I could taste the graceful aging of the vineyard from my time to hers.

Please stop asking me that.

"It is, then."

She let out a breathless laugh. *I am only forging the most sensitive kinds of documents, and if we get caught, the lot of us will be thrown in a rat hole we will not ever climb out of, so, yes. It is costly.*

I opened my mouth, but I was not permitted to speak.

And don't tell me to forget it, because it's too late now. I wouldn't anyway, because I know what it means to you, so shove it.

She downed the contents of her glass and promptly poured herself another. I chuckled under my breath, unable to suppress a grin.

"You're going to be a handful, aren't you?"

I'm a what, now?

"Never mind."

Shit—here comes trouble. Heads up.

A red-headed woman called out Azi's name and approached us. She was heavily made up, accentuating her maturity rather than hiding it. She was markedly thin, which made the slackening of her skin around her chin and neck all the more ghoulish. On her arm was a man who foamed at the sight of Azi. Or rather, at the sight of Azi with me.

Good evening, Mrs. Carew. Professor.

His eyes turned vicious when his wife looked to the waiter. Azi's eyes glimmered with smug satisfaction. Alex's wife returned her attention to us, making some glib remark that did not carry far enough to be translated by Azi's phone. The daggers the crone threw at Azi made such details unnecessary. When Azi seemed genuinely not to care, the woman's look became sharper, her voice crisper. But whether her husband's infidelity was known or only suspected, of that I could not be sure. That their conversation did not draw unwanted attention from our neighbors and evoked only a silent impatience from the man himself, seemed to suggest the latter.

I pushed the idea of that graying man grunting and sweating on top of Azi as far away as I could. She deserved more. The way she leaned into me as he glared filled me with pride. I could please her better than that rotting pile of bones. And I meant to.

I determined that I did not like him. Not out of jealousy, but rather, knowing the disadvantage Azi would have been in, embroiled with a man who had a wife, *and* served as her mentor. It was too easy to imagine the disparity, and unvirtuous men have always earned little regard with me.

He scrutinized my face, I dare say trying to place my likeness. It scared Azi and me both to be subjected to his stare, and she squeezed my fingers tighter. I lifted my arm and pressed my fingers into her shoulder, hoping to suggest it was privacy we sought. Her face showed not one iota of fear, but as I enveloped her, I felt her trembling.

When the professor spoke, it was directly to Azi. What he said drained her face of its color.

When? she responded.

He provided the answer, and she nodded.

I'll be there.

The couple turned their backs to us as our dinner was served. Azi finally allowed herself to breathe.

"I thought he would recognize me," I wondered.

He should have. But attention to detail was never his strength. She paused, lifting her fork pensively as she took me into her confidence. *The truth? He's a lazy scholar. Perfectly willing to take credit for* my *work.*

"You don't allow that, I hope?"

Never. My own reputation is too important. My dad never thought much of him as an assistant. The longer I know him, the more I see why.

"You've known him a long time?"

All my life.

"What did he say to you?"

There's a department meeting, Monday. There is no trace of the "missing body," and they want to see both of us. It was our research, our responsibility.

She bent her fingers up to her mouth, unable to keep still.

If I can't produce my research, I can't graduate. I won't find work, and I'll lose my house.

"It's bigger than you need," I offered. "Why don't you—"

That's my parents' house, she shot back. *Everything in it, we dug up together. Those are our discoveries, our memories.* Her eyes rimmed with tears, and she turned her face from me, unable to control her grief.

"Azi..." I squeezed her tighter, and she turned again to me, wiping her face harshly, ashamed of her own sadness, eager to be rid of it.

How can I sell that? She shuddered at the intake of her breath.

I took her hands away from her face and kissed her fingers. They were black around the edges. Clean, for the most part, but some stubborn pigment hid in the seams between her nails and her flesh. I wished to divert her soul from its sorrow.

"Are you an artist, Azi?"

She looked puzzled, as one does at a soothsayer successfully plying his trade. I showed her fingers to her.

"Oh." She withdrew them quickly, embarrassed.

"I had a friend who was a sculptor when I was young," I explained. "His hands were never truly free of the plaster."

She laughed, redirected. *An occupational hazard.*

"Tell me more," I requested, savoring the herbal headiness of the creamy grains laid before me. Even a bowl of rice was treated as a work of art, with small greenery deliberately placed, served individually to me. Azi had chosen a small bird with dried fruits resting atop a bed of greens that smelled delicious. We exchanged bites as I wondered at how eating out, since all had access to cooking at home, had transcended to an indulgence, rather than a necessity.

I do landscapes, mostly. In oils or charcoal. The one in your room, the Lower Nile's West Bank?

"*You* did that?"

She nodded humbly. *It was the view of the pyramids we had from our rooms there. It's older now. I should replace it.*

"No, I like it. Were you trained?"

No, not really. It started as...to manage my grief. It grew from there.

"Will you show me more of your work?"

She blushed inexplicably, digging her eyes into her meal to avoid mine.

Soon, she swallowed. Her fingers drummed the table nervously. *Do you mind if I—will you let me sketch you? Just something quick.*

I rested my fork, and turned to face her more fully, while she unfolded a simple white linen laid on the table and pulled a thin pencil from her bag. I watched her as she scrutinized me, her pupils flitting between my face and her canvas. Her vision followed the lines of my chin, investigated the angles of my nose and eyes, plumbed the depths of the shadow on my cheek as the house lights dimmed further. Her face glowed softly in the candlelight. Watching her fear and her pain fade from her face like exorcised demons was remarkable. She was entirely absorbed by her art, and long minutes passed her unnoticed. Where her studies brought hardship, in this she found peace. Watching her work was beautiful.

Her pencil lifted for the last time, and she reflected.

I can do better, with more time. She flipped it around to me. Down to every curve, I stared as if at a reflection in a pool.

"Any better, and you'll have my soul."

Yes, it's my masterpiece. Face on a napkin. Twenty million. I'm sorry I snapped at you. I just—

"I understand."

I know you do. That wound is still fresh for you.

"Yes. But I am not a child. You were."

She shrugged, looking down at her lap.

"You could sell the house, and not sell everything in it," I suggested gently. You don't need all that space. Especially in the kitchen."

She puckered her lips.

Are you complaining? She shot me a sultry stare that made my palms sweat.

"No."

That sounded like a complaint.

"I am only saying you do not need a kitchen that large."

Don't expect me to cook for you.

"Certainly not."

I take you out to a nice restaurant, and you want a home-cooked meal.

"I am having a grand time. You are lovely company."

Is that right? she said, looking up at me with eyes that flashed like fire and set my heart racing again.

"Mmhmm." I craned my neck and lowered my voice, letting my lips graze her cheek. "If you would let me, I would make love to you right here."

She inclined her head to me and let out a soft sigh. The candlelight flickered in her eyes as she considered taking me up on my offer. I kissed her hair and soaked in the sweet fragrance of her creamy skin.

The red-headed harpy shrieked across the room. Her husband had spilled his drink on the table. The flush on Azi's face must have distracted him. I could not help but grin in his direction.

Before Azi could speak, a final dish, a white sphere atop a darker cake, garnished with strawberries, was laid at our table. I tried the white pillow of food, inspecting the smooth texture with interest before tasting it. At the shock of it, I dropped my spoon with an unceremonious clink and clamped my hand over my mouth to suppress a laugh that would send it spilling back out again.

"What?" Azi cried, alarmed.

"It's cold!" I said finally, swallowing.

It's ice cream. It's supposed to be cold.

"I saw the smoke rising from it and expected something hot!"

We laughed, and she spooned a bit of the cake on my forgotten utensil. When she broke into it, the center oozed.

This is hot, she warned.

The flavor was deep and heady—bitter, but also provocatively sweet. A moan of satisfaction escaped my lips.

That, she explained, *is chocolate, the best thing to come from this side of the world. If I don't have at least a little bit every day, I go crazy. Now try them together, hot and cold.*

This last dish was easily my favorite. The pairing of divergent tastes, textures, and temperatures was masterful. There was great care in every aspect of our meal. I was thoroughly impressed with the sophistication of what we had been served and the well-crafted presentation, right down to the shape and color of the plates. It felt luxe.

The air was balmy and peaceful on our way home. A large bell tolled the late hour in a building to our right. A white cross gleamed from its roof.

"What is that?" I asked. Suspicion slid down my spine.

Azi's eyes followed my gaze, then came to rest on me. Mischief spread across her lips.

"What do you think it is?" she asked.

"It cannot be what *I* think it is."

"No? It is a house of worship. The Nazarene."

I stood amazed. "And you, do you give tribute there?" I asked. Azi shook her head.

"That was not my family's way. My mother believed a great spirit lives in all things." She smiled to herself, reminiscing. "My father, he—he hoped he might pass through the Twelve Gates, to test the virtue of his heart."

"Egypt was his great love."

"I haven't been there since..." Her voice trailed off, and she redirected herself away from the thought. "I went to Britain with Alex because...because I was afraid. I was afraid to go alone. To lose my way again inside the pyramids and not find them there."

"I am sure you would have the courage, but I cannot say it was the wrong choice."

She laughed, the sorrowful look in her eyes lifting away. "Me neither."

The serenity of the evening was broken only as we neared Azi's front door. We were greeted by boisterous mirth overflowing from within. The household was gathered in the common room, a large table set there in place of the usual, smaller one. On it was laid a board, painted in dark, brooding colors that suggested a condensed map of sorts, with large letters to indicate places. Mounted against every edge were decks of cards large and small, all with differing designs on the back. Azi's friends were exuberant as we entered. Dean foisted the largest deck on Azi—a blind choice. When she saw the face of the card she had chosen, she let fly what I assumed from her tone was appropriate only to soldiers and sailors.

Her audience moaned and cursed as she flapped it on the table, already defeated by a faceless man draped in yellow. Dean stood up and bared his hands to her throat in a mock strangle.

"I'm sorry, I'm sorry!" she pleaded. She offered me a place at the table. I nodded enthusiastically, though I had no idea what we were doing. I was content to be included. We were dealt in—I received a card with a face and information I could not read, a small pile of red and blue tokens, a mimic of money, and pictures of a dagger and a red stone.

"What's the game?" I whispered in her ear.

"A fight against evil gods. We win together or lose together."

"The strategy?" I asked. The preparation was more complicated than any game I had ever played, and I grew nervous of my ability to catch up.

"Based on the cards—a different game every time. It took me two weeks to learn. Relax, and follow me."

I observed keenly as each player brought their own skills to the battle, determined by the pretend objects with which they began the game, and what they were able to acquire. The pieces moved across the board based on general consensus, until the card dictating the acts of our opponent shifted our objectives. We were constantly foiled. A luminous blue star on the board was a step toward victory. We required seven. A great deal of the game's narrative made no sense, but our progress at each task was measured by a dice roll, which was simple enough. My token's abilities made him an ideal warrior, and without complaint, I deployed my one-man army against the most ferocious monsters, plucked from a red cloth bag. I amassed their little square corpses in front of me as trophies. It was deep into the evening, or dare I say the morning, when the game slowly turned in our favor.

Our momentum kept us from our beds longer than it should have, but Hastur and his legions would live to fight another day. Come tomorrow evening, we were to arrive fresh to battle with sharp minds and a conviction in our collective purpose sufficient to bring the campaign to a successful close, with enough time to spare for more restive amusement.

My bed linens sent a chill down my naked flesh as I lay my head down, and I yearned to warm myself in Azi's arms. The taste of her neck, the sweetness of her mouth—they lingered on my tongue. My languid muscles ached, restless in their solitude. My thoughts were filled with the memory of Azi's bare shoulders in her dress tonight, how delicately the fabric rested there, yielding to the gentlest of touches. I imagined her settling into sleep just down the hall. It was a short walk, one which I could do silently, but that silence would be short-lived. No, I must not do that. I laid my head down and dreamed of the day when I could share her bed and not leave it.

〇

*T*he academic calendar was set to begin anew in a few days' time. Azi and her housemates prepared for the return to their routines, without much mind for me. There had been times when I felt superfluous—I was not accustomed to not being of much use. Azi did not ignore me, but she was unavoidably occupied for the majority of the day, and even into most nights as she readied herself for the classes she was assigned to teach, while also furthering her own studies. For both our sakes, we agreed that she would not share what she had learned unless there was a pressing need for me to know. I admit, however, that I was curious to see what she could make of what had happened to me.

She was as industrious as any man her age in Rome would have been, working to make his way in the world. She showed such vigor for the intellectual work as I had never witnessed in the females whose acquaintances I had made. That may have simply been a function of opportunity for some, but not for all. Azi shone among her own peers, whose work ended upon their arrival home. Her work consumed her days and nights. So as not to become a shut-in, she worked in the common room, open to the occasional distraction of her friends and myself. Just as often, she became so absorbed in the workings of her mind that questions posed to her went unanswered. I do not think she heard them at all. Her friends teased at this, making crude faces at her or acting foolish to break her concentration. But her face was lovely when it was focused, except when something on the screen caused her to frown or curse, making me wish I could take it all away and carry her weight for her.

One night, Dean took his cajoling a little too far and sent a crumpled piece of paper flying toward her head. Before I could block it, she had caught it in her hand, without bothering to look up. She redirected its course and sent it careening into the bronze refuse bin in the corner of the room and marched silently up the stairs. The gesture set us all to silence. That an orphaned girl who had spent her childhood in the company of unfeeling books would have morose moods was perfectly understandable. Those moods were more profound for the lack of ire that failed to accompany them. There was no raging fury inside her—

only silence, a void where some part of her used to be, which had died along with her parents. It was on those days that I ached the most—not to ease *my* loneliness, but to dispel the solitude that weighed upon *her* spirit.

She was never unkind, toward me or anyone else, and when she emerged again, she was as she had been before—rueful, witty, and affectionate. Whatever storm brewed inside her in those dark hours, we never felt its power. Only her absence.

16

ASENATH

"*P*aper! For fuck's sake, don't any of you have any paper?"

I blew through the house like a tornado. I was ten pages short and hadn't realized. There was no time to go to the store, no time to stop at a computer lab. I was cutting it close already but wasn't going to arrive at a meeting that could decide my fate empty-handed.

"Here," Ravi shouted, flying from her room in silk pajamas. "The correct response is, 'Thank you!'" she said behind me as I ripped the paper out of her hands and raced back to my printer. I waited for the insidiously slow inkjets to print out the rest of my work and inserted the full-page images in their appropriate places. I could barely breathe.

"Are you well?" Quintus stood in the doorway; his brow deeply furrowed.

"I will be when this goddamned thing prints out!" I shouted in English, leaving him at a loss.

"You can't go in there like that," Dean said, coming to stand behind Quintus. I'd whipped myself into a frenzy, and it was contagious. I would have settled down if I could.

"Do you want a Zoloft? I have a few spares," Dean offered.

"No! I don't take that shit anymore," I spat.

"Stand aside—" Felix came out of his room at last, an oversized paper bag in each hand. From the tops poked several pre-stretched canvasses. "Here," he said, laying them at my feet. The bottoms of the bags were heavy with paint tubes in more than a dozen shades. "Only an artist can cure another artist. This is what you needed, *verdad?*"

I finally remembered to breathe. I did it a few times—drawing long, deep draughts into my lungs.

"*Sí,*" I said calmly, allowing the passing seconds to crawl over me.

"I saw you unraveling for a few days. I just didn't have the time to stop there. *Lo siento.*"

"Thank you, Felix."

"*De nada, princesa.*"

"And thank you, Ravi. You're a life-saver. I'm sorry. All of you. I'm sorry." I stood awkwardly, feeling bad about terrorizing everyone like a bat out of hell.

"Don't waste your time apologizing to us," Ravi said, her voice taking on a stern timber. "Go and kick his ass. Make us proud."

I nodded. The house dispersed, and I dashed to the door. In my haste, my outfit had undone itself. I smoothed my skirt and my wild hair and tucked my shirt back under my waist. Before crossing the threshold, Quintus caught hold of my arm from behind.

"Good luck. Be careful, Asenath."

I looked at all I had to protect, all I had to lose if I let my nerves get the better of me. It steeled my will. I gave him a confident glare and pressed my lips to his. His eyes shone at me as he shut the door.

Out of control nerves over accusations of stealing a bog body were the perfect cover for nerves about harboring said body come to life. There was no choice but to go with it. When I arrived in the chair's office in Hayes Hall, Alex was already there. So were the Graduate Director for Archaeology and the Vice Principal of Humanities. I'd been in plenty of rooms like this before, paneled in wood, save for loft windows, and made stiflingly warm with dense carpets, plush upholstery, and gilded, antique frames, packed with stiffening white men. But with all eyes on me as I took the empty seat beside Alex, I felt hideously out of place.

I resisted the urge to look to Alex for some sign of the room's mood and stared ahead at Magnusson. I sat straight as a rod.

"So far," Magnusson started, "the police haven't found any real leads on your body. Given that it's been almost a month, I doubt they ever will. And of course, in matters such as these, the university conducts its own investigation as well."

I dug my canine into the inside of my lip to stop myself from screaming or passing out. Both were equally possible.

"Miss Hayes?" he started.

"Yes?" I squeaked.

"You told the police officer on the scene you closed the lab at eight o'clock?"

"Yes, sir," I answered in my normal voice, pushing my fingernails into my palm.

"You locked up?"

I hadn't remembered until he asked—who had time to worry about such things when you're driving home the Mummy?

"N-no, I didn't," I stammered. "I didn't have the key."

Magnusson started in his chair, his eyes stabbing into Alex as he spoke to me. "You were there alone?"

Alex looked at me with eyes of steel.

"Just for a few minutes, professor."

"That's not what you told the police, Carew."

"I had a family emergency," he grumbled. "What difference does it make?"

"Students are not permitted in the labs without a faculty member present," Magnusson said sternly. "You left the lab unlocked and unguarded. That changes the entire aspect of the investigation."

A storm brewed behind Alex's eyes, but he said nothing. Vice Principal Booth cleared his throat from behind Magnusson's chair.

"I wouldn't classify the Whateleys' dinner party as a family emergency," he said simply. When you're up for tenure," he cleared his throat again, with menacing emphasis, "the least you could do is keep your lies straight."

The room was deathly still. I didn't know where to look and settled for the corner of a Napoleonic painting to the left of the window behind Magnusson. My gaze rested on the lower right corner of the frame, where the flourishes carved deep into the wood had accumulated a considerable amount of dust. Magnusson addressed me, snapping my eyes back into focus on his unyielding face.

"Is there anything else *you'd* like to tell us, Miss Hayes?"

I couldn't think, for having too much I *didn't* want to say. "I have a question," I ventured.

"Yes?"

"Um, what's going to happen to me?"

He leaned back into the pink, puckered upholstery in his chair, and folded his hands neatly in his lap.

"What do you think should happen to you?"

Tension erupted from my gut like a volcano. "*Why* would I steal him? He's *my* research—I can't learn anything without the lab, and now that he's gone, my whole future at this university is in jeopardy." My cheeks flushed hot.

I couldn't read Magnusson's face—the wrinkles around his brow and at the corner of his eyes and lips puckered into an unsettling cross between amusement and pride. The contortion gave way to mirth.

"Is *that* why you're wound as tight as a German cuckoo clock? We never thought *you* were to blame, Miss Hayes. As you said, you are the one with the most to lose, and nothing to gain."

I saw my opportunity.

"I've been working off the things we still have, along with the images of Anglesey Man that I took." I handed Magnusson the result of my labors. "Here's a revised prospectus for my thesis, based on preliminary analysis."

Magnusson was surprised by its weight. "You did all this since you came back?"

I nodded.

"You certainly don't waste any time, Miss Hayes," he said, clearly impressed.

"This is the first I'm hearing of this," Alex cried. "You didn't think it was necessary to show your advisor?"

"I sent you a copy on Friday. Check your email."

And I had, but I knew Alex only deigned to check his email on Wednesdays. Today was Monday.

Magnusson flipped immediately to the images of Anglesey Man and sighed, then began perusing the text. So far, I'd managed to emphasize the importance of the physical objects and believed mystical properties, and an assertion of Anglesey Man's identity as Roman. Without looking up, Magnusson spoke.

"And what are your conclusions, Carew?"

"Conclusions?" he asked, caught foolishly off-guard.

"*Conclusions,*" Magnusson repeated impatiently. "Your thoughts on Anglesey Man."

Exasperated, Alex balked at the question, finding it absurd. "What observations could I possibly make if the evidence has been stolen?"

"Quite a few, it seems," Magnusson answered, finally putting his fingers on the top page of my prospectus. "Thank you, Miss Hayes. I appreciate your determination to see this through. We're not giving up just yet," he said, standing as a sign of dismissal. "The find was spectacular, and to lose our body *is* devastating, but remember—he wasn't the only one."

I shuddered.

"In the meantime," he continued, "keep working."

Alex jumped out of his seat, annoyed that Magnusson had wasted his time.

"We're not through, Carew—I have another meeting now, but I want you back in here by four."

"You're not going to pin this on *me*, are you?"

"Save it. I've had all the excuses I can stomach from you this week." Again, my gaze wandered, gravitating to a floral curve in the ruby-tasseled rug.

Alex nearly bowled me over in the doorway as he made his exit.

"Alex..." I whispered under my breath, frozen in place as I watched his back thunder down the hallway. Magnusson stepped into the doorway behind me as I rubbed my shoulder.

"Asenath," he started, "do you mind if I call you that?"

"Of course not," I replied. My oldest memory of him was at my parents' holiday parties. People usually brought wine or champagne. He'd always brought *me* a gift. He'd never done anything to shake my kind impression of him. Even today.

"Do you think you could get a first draft ready before the Thanksgiving break?"

"A draft of the whole project?" I gaped.

"I know it's not a lot of time, and I certainly don't want to rush genius, but...could you do it, Asenath?"

Not sensing there was much of a choice, I told him that I could.

"There is a method to my madness, I promise. Also..." He coughed, less sure of himself now. "This thing is taking up more of my time than expected. Do you have room in your schedule for another class? Just Intro to Egyptology."

I hesitated. A complete draft *and* another class? It was lunacy, but it would help take the edge off of the missing rent—one less thing I'd have to sell. And I'd taught the class before.

"Sure, why not?" I answered.

"Thank you, Asenath. I don't trust anyone else with it. The rest of these stuffed shirts couldn't tell Horus from Hatshepsut." He laughed breathlessly at his own joke. I turned my head back down the now-empty hallway, staring at where Alex had been.

"Steer clear of him, Asenath," Magnusson said with an undertone of an occluded purpose. "Send your work directly to me."

I looked at him, puzzled. What he requested amounted to dropping my advisor.

"Dr. Magnusson?"

"His tenure is not secure." He spoke low, his hushed tones soaking into the wooden panels of the hallway, as if this were gossip. I knew full well he was in his tenure-year. But the process by which professors secured their positions was mostly ritual and formality.

"He knows," Magnusson continued when I simply stared in silent confusion, "that we only have the budget for one more Egyptologist. Whose idea was it that you go to Britain?"

I was crushed beneath the weight of what Magnusson said. Now that I was no longer seeing Alex with doe eyes, the chair's suggestion rang all too true. He'd steered me away from the Valley and made me think what he offered me was all I ever needed. He'd nearly taken everything from me, as if it were nothing. As if I were nothing. I'd never felt real hate burn inside of me before now.

I made my way numbly home, brought back to life by the scent of roasted cardamom and yogurt as I walked through the door. I found Ravi in the kitchen, supervising Quintus as he dug a spoon into a bowl of brightly colored chicken marinade. Hands occupied, they greeted me with smiles.

"What happened?" Ravi asked, sliding the knife in her hand down the length of a skinny but powerful red chili.

I shrugged, leaning over the pale marble counter to inhale the intoxicating perfume of the meal taking shape. "I have to haul ass on my doctorate, and Magnusson gave me another class."

"Oh, thank God!" she said, putting down her knife and squeezing me, keeping the deadly poison on her fingers crimped inside her palm. I simply stood, not having the mind to hug her back. I should have been happy, but my relief had been overshadowed by what had been spoken after. Whatever vestige of my old life I'd been holding on to, Alex knocked out of me with a shove. I felt an overwhelming sense of loneliness. Quintus furrowed his brow as I peered listlessly at him over Ravi's shoulder. Alex's treachery had only *threatened* my future. He had not destroyed it yet and Quintus would not be here without it. My rage left me, and the rims of my eyes burned with guilt. I fell deeper into confusion, my only truth in that moment the comfort of Quintus's nearness.

Ravi returned to her chili. I inched closer to Quintus, searching for my center. I put my arm around his muscular waist. When I traced my fingers to the invisible lines of his taut abdomen beneath his shirt, they trembled, sensing the narrowing leanness of his perfectly sculpted hips just beyond reach. He flinched, whether from being aroused or tickled, I couldn't tell.

"Quintus came food shopping with me today," Ravi told me, the bangles on her wrists jingling as she introduced the chili and chopped garlic to the oil she'd heated in a wide pan. She spoke over the sizzle. "He almost went into shock. Where exactly is he from?"

"A place without supermarkets," I answered blandly. "I'm not smelling something, and I *want* to smell it," I said.

"I haven't started the rice yet. Calm yourself," Ravi replied, wiping her hands on the plain cotton apron she wore over her blue silk tunic. Even the sleeves of her plain clothes were embroidered with rose petals on the hem and shone with gemstones set in the center of the blossoming buds. Her contradictions made me laugh. She was a genius in architecture and homemade cooking, and full of laughter. Being her friend was the easiest thing in the world, but on any day of the week, the first word that came to my mind when I thought of Ravi was "flashy."

I drummed my fingers on the counter, impatient for the fragrance of jasmine to permeate the air, the grain of the cupboards, and the fibers of my clothes. I reached for the open pinot noir on the counter.

"Are you using this?"

"All finished," Ravi said, stretching up to furnish me with a glass from the cupboard.

"Azi?"

Dean's voice came from so close behind me, I spun around with a start.

"Can I talk to you a minute?" he asked.

I swallowed hard. Pretending everything was normal hadn't worked, it seemed. He was intent on making this harder on both of us, wrenching the truth from me rather than taking a gentle hint.

"Sure," I answered. I watched him climb the stairs, and I knew I had to follow.

"What is the matter with that boy?" Ravi rasped quickly, leaning to me. "He's been moping about since he got here."

"I know," I said, choosing my words carefully. Our conversation may have been unintelligible to Quintus, but the curious look on his face suggested that he understood enough.

"*What* do you know?" Ravi pushed. "Did something happen?"

I flashed a hopeless smile, ignoring Ravi's gasp and the glass on the counter, downing a hearty draught straight from the bottle to steel me for the task ahead. I dared not look at Quintus as I headed upstairs.

The first door to the left was open a crack. I pushed it in farther to reveal Dean, sitting on his bed trying to remain cool, which did nothing but make his nervousness more pronounced. I wondered if that's what I had looked like only a few hours before, a frightened rabbit that couldn't play dead, because it was trembling too hard. When he spoke, I imagined I heard the sound of his teeth jittering.

"I know you said it was a one-time thing, but I've missed you, Azi." He paused. When I did not respond in kind, he went further. "I was hoping that maybe you'd changed your mind."

I breathed deeply as I sat next to him, careful not to let our thighs touch. "I'm sorry, Dean."

"We had a good time together," he protested. "At least, *I* thought we did."

I bit my lip, remembering with a pang of regret that even at the height of Dean's excitement, I'd been thinking about something else. *Someone* else. I shook my head. The thought repulsed me. Everything I'd given Alex, I'd given freely, hoping against the odds that things would have worked out the way I wanted them to. The way *he* had promised they would. I cursed myself for being so colossally stupid.

"It isn't that, Dean," I said, determined to stay in the moment. He deserved that much from me. "I'm sorry. I love you to death. I never wanted to hurt you. I just—" I looked at him, for the first time since he had come. Really looked at him, seeing all the gold and copper flecks in his gray-blue eyes. "I just didn't trust anybody else."

He smiled gently at me, sad, but graceful. He held my hands. "I'm glad you did," he whispered. "I'm sorry too, I guess. For wanting more. That wasn't part of our bargain."

"You don't have to be sorry about that. I wish I *could* give you what you want."

"But your heart doesn't belong to you anymore, does it?"

Guilt rushed to my cheeks.

Dean flinched. "Yeah, I guessed that. I see how you are together."

I hung my head, unable to console my friend, to deny what he said.

"Azi. You don't owe me anything. You're my friend, above everything. I just needed to know."

"So, we're cool?" I asked, humbled by how well he was taking it. We were together one night, and he cared more about me than Alex had in almost two years.

"We're cool, Azi," he said, nudging me reassuringly. We had always been close, and not having to avoid Dean brought me more relief than the green light Magnusson had given me to move forward. Whatever "forward" meant.

I was drawn downstairs by the sound of searing chicken, but I stopped in front of Quintus's door. It was closed, but I could hear him inside, talking into the computer's microphone as he held a conversation with a digital shopkeeper. I knocked.

He stood in the doorway as he opened it, seeming to deliberate on whether to let me in. His expression was inscrutable as he acquiesced, and I got the distinct impression that he understood more of what had happened between Dean and me than he cared to.

We sat in an awkward silence. He waited patiently for me to express my purpose in disturbing him, and I was unsure of how to begin. I concluded that trying to impart the values of female sexual liberation would be a lost cause. Frazzled by the day, my baser instincts won out, and I hit the speaker button on the computer to translate.

"I suppose *you've* never had any lonely nights, *soldier*?" He instantly colored, and I bit my tongue. "Quintus, I—"

"No. You're right."

I shifted uncomfortably in my chair. Seeing me squirm, his steely jaw slackened. He held his hand out to me, pulling me onto his lap. I leaned forward, and he reclined on the bed, carrying me with him. I curled into his warm embrace, finding complete solace in the crook of his shoulder. He clasped my hand on top of his chest and sighed deeply.

"Never at the same time," I added, hoping to dull his agitation. He raised a curious eyebrow. I clucked my tongue. "I mean—"

"I know," he said, smiling wryly. "I have never been with someone who loved me," Quintus added quietly.

"Me neither. Being with a man can be casual. As casual as shaking hands."

Quintus played with my fingers as I clasped his chest. His left arm caressed my back underneath my shirt. His warm hands felt so comfortable, like they belonged there.

"I don't want to shake your hand." The sapphire brilliance of his eyes captivated me, and I let my whole body feel the affection of his embrace.

"Me neither," I whispered.

We settled into each other, my eyelids lulled to dreaminess, when he spoke softly into my hair.

"What troubles you?"

"Alex," I said bitterly, his name a curse on my lips. "He made me feel small today."

"You should not be surprised by that."

I groaned in acknowledgment. He held me tighter, and I tucked my feet between his legs.

"That does not make it right. You are a remarkable woman, deserving of great honor. I would see this insult answered."

"That may be possible. He and I..." I struggled, my Latin migraine returning. He stroked my hair patiently as I searched for words that would carry the proper weight.

"We fight for the same position and I have the advantage."

"Good."

Something else gnawed at me.

"Quintus. There were others."

"Hmm?" he grunted.

"Other bodies. With you."

His entangled fingers froze in my hair.

"Were they asleep also?" he asked.

"I do not know."

"Were they Roman?"

"I do not think so. Locals, more likely."

I felt a shiver run through him. Quintus was quiet, shaken by what I had said. I saw it weighed heavily on his mind, but he remained taciturn, nestling deeper beside me, seeking the same comfort I found enveloped by his strong, reassuring chest. I looked up at him, wrapping my arms tighter around him and reaching up to tousle his wild hair. He lurched forward, hovering over me, and I swooned at his intense gaze. His warm, sweet breath fell on my neck, and he closed his mouth over mine. I fell feverishly deep into his kisses and minded not a jot when he slipped a hand under my shirt. His confident fingers were closing in on me just as Ravi shouted up the stairs that dinner was ready.

My mouth hung open, and I inhaled sharply as his hand stood poised over my bare breast. He kissed me fiercely, tugging on my lower lip with his teeth, then withdrew. I wailed in disbelief, my goose-pimpled skin shuddering as his hand left me. He stood up and extended his hand to me, smiling wickedly.

"I'll remember that," I said, curt but playful.

"Now we are even." He smirked.

"Not even close," I answered, letting my whole body brush against his as I walked past him. My breath caught in my throat when I felt his arm wrap around me and pull me back into the room. I cried out when my back slammed into the wall inside the door. His hot kisses on my neck sent a shudder through me, and I had to pull on his hair to stop myself from moaning louder. He lifted me in his arms, and almost by instinct, I wrapped my legs around his waist as he pressed his body ever closer.

"Maybe just a quick hello," I whispered breathlessly.

He laughed in a deep voice, as if he'd understood me.

"You up there! If you're going to make me your personal chef, you could at least eat it hot!"

I groaned, disappointed, and put my hands on Quintus's shoulders, my feet looking for the ground. But he held me there, his eyes wild. His whole frame shook.

"When are you going to let me love you the way you deserve?" he pleaded. My breath caught in my throat.

When I know I won't lose you, I thought.

He lowered me to the floor, still holding on tight. I bit into the left corner of my lip, having nothing to tell him.

17

*I*t was remarkably easier than I had expected, researching for my thesis and researching for myself at the same time. I was asking the same questions, for the most part, the difference in language easy to track—*believed* to do such and such, versus *did* do. I tucked separate sheaves of paper into my notebook with private conjectures, and any questions or conclusions that didn't fit. It was what any good scholar would do anyway.

I didn't know what Alex did all those hours in the lab. We rarely spoke. He cursed under his breath a lot, slammed a lot of fists on the counter with his face buried in his computer screen. I thought he might have been trying to do legitimate work, trying to prove he was still relevant. Except he'd never led his own research team, had never taken the initiative. I thought he realized what others had seen all along— somewhere along the line, he'd lost the head for it, if he'd ever had it to begin with.

I dove headlong into my own work, studying the iron loop and the amber, Quintus's ring, the stake hewn from oak, and the branches. I tried piecing together their relationships to each other, how their alleged mystical attributes had combined to produce such a miraculous result.

The staking of Quintus's body was the biggest commonality between Quintus and other bodies deposited into bogs both in Wales and elsewhere. In Denmark, bodies had been found with branches and twigs lain thickly over the chest, the way Jakob and I had found them overhead. In Danish folklore, the act of staking was a way to control evil or restless spirits, so long as the stakes remained in place. A female body had been pinned into Huldre Fen with stakes almost two feet long, hooked at the bottom to keep her from rising to the surface. It was similar to the stakes used deeper in the continent's interior to keep suspected vampires in their graves, but in those areas, ash or birch were used deliberately. Ash was thought to be the bane of evil spirits. Birch was a relative newcomer to Iron Age Britain, and the Druids deferred to the all-powerful oak, whose roots, they held, stretched down into the world beneath ours—the "underworld."

Gold had been of great metaphysical value for so-called sorcerers and alchemists through the history of Western traditions. What interested me in its use on Quintus was the seemingly contradictory nature of its purported properties, especially in relation to the amber. As an encasing material, the sap of the oak that oozed and then hardened, amber had been valued by the Druids for its ability to trap, and thus concentrate, the power of fertility. It was also an environmental cleanser. The iron of the loop was used to ground a thing, while enabling the transfer of souls to other people, and even other worlds, which comprises what is known about Druidic beliefs in the afterlife, mostly from records Julius Caesar made of his encounters in Gaul.

Here's where things got tricky. Suppose, for a moment, that the purpose of the amber was to keep Quintus trapped in the bog. The branches and the stake stayed his body, the amber, his soul. At the same time, it may have been an effort to rid Mona of the Roman pestilence, as the Druids saw them, and protect their stronghold. The dictates of magical sympathy would then provide a rationale for the inclusion of Quintus's sigil ring—an emblazoned symbol of the empire, and Quintus the unfortunate representative of that threat. But—the sigil was fashioned of gold—a magical enhancer, a revered healer, an opener of spiritual doors, and a *preventer of spiritual corrosion*. Had the purity of the gold counteracted the intentions of Quintus's captors? Was his survival of the spell and his suspension through the ages a fluke?

I felt uncomfortable in my own skin as I recorded these possibilities, my academic, analytical indifference replaced by the open-mindedness of a New Age supplicant, those Orientalist hucksters who uprooted the most sacred traditions of the world from their contexts and smashed them together to make themselves feel better about empty religions, forming some hideously meaningless mumbo-jumbo. Even those older lores and practices were, I thought, the workings of unenlightened, superstitious minds, except...except...

Writing about supernatural systems was not what was unusual—it was my specialty. After all, I'd been brought to the tombs of dead kings as a child. While my parents were off studying political successions, my young mind had fallen prey to the mysteries of the pyramids, drawn to the allure of cryptic incantations. That pull had matured into a study of Egyptian mystery cults, and demarcating the fine, almost invisible line between religion, magic, and darker practices. That such things were deliberately occluded as part of the ritual presented both the challenge and the appeal of such topics. Taking in all I had at my personal disposal —an impressive library and a sizable collection of artifacts—my mind wandered to the Coffin Texts, the manuals scrawled on countless pyramid walls and sarcophagi to prepare the royal spirits for their journeys. I had to consider the very real possibility that what had survived as evidence of Quintus's transformation did not constitute all; there may have been herbs, long eaten away by bog acids, or hidden deep inside Quintus's gut, now reabsorbed into his cells. There would have been words—whether a few or many—to summon the power of their gods, to make good their offering. Words and gestures were revered in most magical systems as an essential component. The ones that had brought Quintus to me were lost forever.

I considered this as I picked up the amber again in my gloved hand, exposing every angle to the harsh stare of the fluorescent lights above. I put it up to my nose, hoping against hope for a minute engraving, and became intrigued by the thing frozen within. A long, thin body tapered out to even thinner, longer legs. The mangled edges of torn, transparent wings flared from the ridge of the back. It resembled nothing if not a sinister cross between a mosquito and a daddy long-legs. It wasn't any insect I knew of, which wasn't saying much. But it was unlike anything on the lists I was able to find on species local to Britain. I made a note to contact the biology department in the hopes that we had at least one entomologist on staff who could tell me what this thing was, or if it was an ancestor to something more common now. Once I had a name for it, I could start to dig for any cultural significance. Every other object that Quintus had been stabbed with had a meaning—mystical, alchemical, or otherwise. I couldn't imagine that any part of the ritual was done without forethought.

Reaching for the magnifying glass, I inspected the proboscis. Flecks of vermilion stained the tip.

The fucking thing twitched.

I recoiled, stifling a scream as it crashed to the floor.

"Watch it!" Alex shouted. "We've lost enough. For Heaven's sake, let's not *break* anything."

I had a few choice words for him, too. But they died in my throat as I picked up the amber. It had impacted on an angle, and a smaller piece split from the whole. The creature inside was still encased entirely in the main stone, the iron loop undisturbed. An insect coated in amber would have been killed in the process, the liquid searing its brain before seeping into every cavity. But I didn't imagine it. I shuffled both pieces back into their plastic dish and locked them up, not ready to look at it again.

I pored through the information sent to me by Dr. Pryce about the other bodies, but they were only marginally useful. For someone who had a bigger team, a greater pool of undergraduate interns to utilize, and, you know, *actual* bodies to examine, his notes about the circumstances of each were surprisingly slim. Even the preliminary cataloguing appeared incomplete and haphazard—certainly not the caliber of work I had come to expect from him. I called a few times, to see if he could fill in the gaps, but I could never get a hold of him. Once, a woman picked up the phone.

"Yes?" a tinny voice answered. The word was clipped, cut off by the sharpness of her tone. The connection was so bad I could barely hear her, the noise coming from her end only like the impressions of sound amidst the static.

"Is Dr. Pryce there?" I asked.

"Who is asking?"

"It's Asenath Hayes. We collaborated on the dig together. Who are you?"

The woman hung up. I never got through again after that. It was curious.

The photos I had taken at the sites were better than what he'd sent me, but even that wasn't a complete record, and I had to rely on what my then-unwitting mind had thought relevant to capture. I compared what I could and found Quintus to be the only one with gold pinned to his person. The others had been weighted by branches, and there *were* amber stones found in proximity to the bodies, some containing insects, but not all, and none forcibly attached. The lack of a consistent pattern was academically troubling. It was hard to stay objective, forgoing the assumption that Anglesey Man's case was a special one, even though I knew it was. Whether or not the rest had also been Romans would be determined by DNA testing. Not until I had made the suggestion that they might have been born elsewhere did anyone think to question the ethnicity of *all* the bodies we'd found. Looking at Quintus's face frozen in death got harder and harder. It was no small mercy that the images of the bodies Pryce had kept did not have the same effect. If they had been submerged alive, the condition of the bodies, missing major limbs and organs, promised them a peaceful end now.

On some nights, I woke bathed in a cold sweat, forcing myself to remember that Quintus lived and breathed, and slept soundly just two doors down from me. When I dreamed, I was stranded in dust-covered corridors of obsidian. I ran headlong, left, then right, down, then left again, racing toward something and not finding it as the ancient labyrinth swallowed me up. My way became barred by mummies stiffened to attention and flanking me, choking the way forward. If I ventured too close, I saw their faces. I recognized my father's straight nose, my mother's sloped eyes and soft, now-wrinkled mouth. Beside them stood Quintus, his face hung low, puckered and shriveled in contours I knew too well. The walls shook with my screams.

On those nights, I quit my bed and crawled into his, tucking myself into a tight ball at his side, unfurling only in the morning when his body's heat had silenced the terrors of the dark. He never asked questions, never tested the waters with wandering hands. He just held me. I don't know if he understood, without my doing what my body screamed for daily, how much I loved him. But knowing him, only to be left by him, would inflict an irreparable mark upon my soul. I was afraid.

*C*olumbus Day couldn't come quickly enough. The whole house had been nose-deep in our private projects for weeks, and finally emerged with midterm grades submitted and our sanity intact. Even Quintus was single-minded. He was blowing through the software I'd given him, along with medieval manuscripts from my dad's library. They didn't bring him entirely up to date, but he could read them, and it helped make the centuries he'd missed a smoother discovery. By mid-October, we needed to milk the extended weekend for all it was worth, or we risked burnout, which none of us could afford. We were already coming apart at the seams.

"Just pick someplace already, even just so this conversation can be over," Felix pressed.

"I still say New York," Dean argued.

"I *can't* go to New York without visiting my parents," Ravi repeated. "They would disown me."

"So, go see them. Have lunch," Dean offered.

"That would defeat the purpose of a 'vacation,' wouldn't it?" Ravi countered. "Why don't you go spend the weekend with *your* parents?"

Dean closed his mouth, bested.

Ravi turned to me. "How about Miami?"

"Too far," I said.

"Not if we fly."

"Quintus *can't* fly," I replied. He turned his head to me at the sound of his name. I smiled back, mindful of his traveling limitations, but still wanting to advocate something he would appreciate. My cheeks grew hot as he put his arm around me. His touch still had the effect of a jolt of lightning. An idea finally came.

"How about D.C.?"

The room silently considered.

"Not too far," Ravi observed, "and we have a hotel there."

"So, we get a discount?" Dean asked.

Ravi laughed. "Discount. You're cute."

He shrugged. "I'm in, then."

"Good food, good nightlife, *perfecto!*" Felix cried.

We skipped town on Thursday. Quintus stood in awe at the platform for the train. That is, until it screeched its arrival, causing him to jump back. I linked my arm in his, and together we boarded the train, our small group muscling past a sluggish crowd trying to find open seats clustered together for all of us.

"What the hell did you bring?" Dean grunted, lugging Ravi's oversized bag behind him.

"Just the essentials."

"You know we're only going for the weekend, right?" he stammered, struggling to lift the designer duffel over his head into the upper storage bin.

Quintus took my half-empty overnight bag from my hand and stowed it away with minimal fuss, then turned to offer Dean a hand.

"I got it, thanks," he spat through gritted teeth. Quintus smirked and took his seat beside me.

I shrugged off my jacket, tucking it between my legs. Quintus's eyes widened at the serious amount of jewelry I'd bedecked myself with.

"What is all this?" he whispered in my ear, pulling on the multiple strands around my wrist.

"Wampum," I answered.

"That's an awful lot. What's the occasion?"

"Columbus Day commemorates the invasion of this continent, and the beginning of centuries of war and loss for native peoples everywhere. This is considered sacred," I said, pointing to the purple spot on the smooth ivory-colored beads. "If my mother could see me, ready to drink myself silly on this day, she would kill me. This way, I can honor her, and my ancestors, and still have fun." I smiled at the thought.

He studied the beads with a fascinated care. "They're beautiful," he said at last.

I removed a length of beads from my wrist and wrapped it around Quintus's. He smiled, folding our hands together.

Ravi's dad graciously put us up in one of his hotels, in the penthouse with plenty of beds to go around, and champagne coming out of the tap. I refrained from club-hopping at night—I needed to crash after the whirlwind tours I took Quintus on during the day. The government buildings styled after his own society filled him with an awesome pride. He marveled at the African elephants and the Bengal tiger in the zoo and smiled curiously at the throngs of people of every color, all under one flag. I'd like to believe that some part of him understood the logical progression from the empire he had helped to build to this.

His demeanor turned melancholy in the National Gallery. The crumbling columns and whitewashed sculptures saddened him. But the Renaissance wing moved him. He was attracted to the art and culture that had been born of the union between Rome, Naples, Venice, and Florence. As twilight crept upon us on the second day, he turned to me, confused.

"Our laws survived," he said. "Our art, our buildings, our culture, but where are our gods?"

That's how we ended up at the planetarium. We got lucky and happened to go on a day when you could actually *see* Mars. When the planet showed itself, he was visibly affected. Closing his eyes, bending them toward the heavens, he stood in silent prayer in the presence of the universe for a long while. I dared not interrupt him.

"Asenath," he turned to me, "what does it mean?"

"My name?" I asked. "It's the Egyptian form of Athena. Diana."

"Goddess of wisdom." He nodded. "Indeed, you are." He thanked me, kissing my hands the way he had done upon his awakening. "I could not have wished for a better guide in this world."

"My pleasure," I replied, squeezing his hands. He moved them to my face, cradling my chin as his lips took hold of mine. The warmth of his tongue made my heart flutter. I held him with all my might as he wrapped me in his strong arms and lifted me off the floor.

"Don't let me go," I whispered, losing my hands in the soft waves of his hair.

"Never, as I live and breathe. You're mine now, Asenath."

I closed my eyes and prayed, to whom or what I know not, that taking him home would not change his mind.

I worked furiously the rest of the month, feeling the oppression of the November break bearing down on me. Alex cornered me on a Friday.

"Show me what you have," he demanded.

"It's not ready yet," I answered firmly.

"Bullshit," he growled. "Are you proud of yourself, for that little stunt you pulled in front of Magnusson?" he asked, lowering his voice.

I narrowed my eyes. "Doing research is not a stunt. It's my *job*."

"*Your* job, huh?" He inched closer. Uncomfortably, menacingly close. "You think Anglesey Man can just magically show up one day, like he'd never been gone, and you can have your degree in hand the next? You won't. Not without me."

"Are you threatening me?" I cried, stretching my neck to peer down the hallway, hoping for someone, *anyone*, to pass by.

"You were the only other person in this room, and you know it," he insisted.

I wanted to leave. It was late enough in the day that I could leave. But to get past Alex, I would have had to push him. I wasn't that stupid. I simply scoffed, turning my head to the side and shifting on my feet. But he persisted.

"He's at your house, isn't he? Locked up with your father's books. You're doing this to get back at me, is that it?"

"You think that's what this is?" I cried.

"Then what is it?"

Fuck. I bit my tongue.

"What is it, Azi? *What* are you hiding?" He grabbed my arm and squeezed it hard.

"Get your hands off me."

"So that's how it is now, huh? Only a few months ago, you would have said otherwise."

The resounding clack of high heels on linoleum was my salvation. I spoke loudly, my words blasting in Alex's face.

"Let go, *professor*. I said stop!"

Alex backed away as a professor I didn't know pushed wide the door.

"Everything all right in here?" the gray-haired woman asked. She gave Alex the evil eye as he shrank back from me, his face contorted in disbelief.

"Would you like to make a report?" the woman asked me, waiting beside the opened door. I looked meaningfully at Alex.

"I'll think about it."

It was a low blow, and I wasn't proud of it. I wished I'd had a better way to defend myself. But the whole situation, *and* its escalation, had been of his making. And he *had* threatened me. I'd overheard worse, in the fierce competitions between archaeologists and the museums that subsidized them, between them and the Egyptian government. Alex had been forged in the battle for the pyramids and would fight to the death for his own survival.

Don't forget, I told myself. *So were you.*

I had to meet his challenge head-on. I came home with my hackles up, like a bear whose cubs had been harassed. A cold sweat raced down my back when I opened my notebook in the comfort of my room—it was empty. I flipped to the front of the notebook, then the back. I upended the whole thing, shaking it out toward the desk. Nothing. My heart leaped into my throat as I ducked my head under the desk, then lifted my chair off the floor. I spun around rapidly before racing down the steps, ripping my jacket off the hook as I sped out of the door.

Quintus called after me, but I ignored it as I pulled the door to my car nearly off its hinges and dove under the driver's seat. My breaths turned sharp as I repeated the process with the other seats. I jumped back as I stood up again and found Quintus's face not two feet from my own.

"Azi?" he queried. "What's wrong?"

I swallowed the bile rising in my throat. "My notes. The ones I keep for myself. They're missing."

His eyes grew wide with my own fear. If something terrible happened, if Quintus was hauled away, it would be my fault. I hadn't noticed I was shaking until Quintus closed his hands over mine.

Determined, Quintus opened the door again for me, and then hopped into the passenger side as I retraced my steps back to Arkham.

"Slow down," he pressed. "Even if you passed it, you wouldn't see it at this pace."

I pulled my foot back from the gas, compensating for it by squeezing my fingers against the steering wheel until my knuckles turned white. My eyes darted in every direction, looking for errant sheets of paper tumbling in the grass. But I knew it was hopeless.

"When did you see them last?"

"The last time I wrote on them," I answered lamely. I'd been so blindly infuriated by my confrontation with Alex that the rest of that day stretched away from me in a blur. "Alex and I argued, and—"

"What happened?" he asked sternly, though I knew his wrath was not building against *me*.

"He pushed me to share my work as I was coming home."

"Did he hurt you?"

"No. Someone else came by, and he backed off. I left quickly."

Quintus leaned back in his chair and drew in a deep breath, trying to calm his own nerves.

"What did they say?"

"I don't know...I don't know." I'd been looking at the branches again

—comparing the treatment of the ones used to weigh Quintus down with the encasements of full-fledged wicker men. Caesar had written of Celtic Druids burning such effigies, and the practices commonly linked British paganism to human sacrifice. Had I written Quintus's name? I pored over my legitimate notes in my mind, trying to recall what had been set aside.

"Quintus, I'm so—"

"Shh," he said, putting his hands over mine again.

I pulled up to the lot abutting the back of Hayes Hall and turned off the ignition. My lips formed the truth my mind already knew.

"He has them."

"You don't know that," Quintus said.

"Of course I do!" In my gut, I knew Alex had taken it, pulled it covertly out of my book when my back was turned. "Fuck!" I shouted, slamming my hand on the wheel.

"What will he do?" Quintus asked after a long pause.

My breathing was still shallow, but my rationalism came thankfully to the rescue. "I don't know what he could do. One little slip of paper is hardly proof of anything. But if Alex smells blood, he'll never let up."

Quintus puckered his lips. I could tell he was searching hard for a solution. He hated being helpless, especially when it came to defending me. He couldn't just walk up to the man and kill him, though it was clear he would have if I'd asked him. I wasn't prepared for another stand-off either. It would bring nothing but more trouble down on my head, but I knew there'd be no avoiding it come Monday—I wouldn't be able to contain my indignation. My rage. I had to get Alex out of the lab before he discovered any other secrets. And he had opened the way.

"All right," I said finally, "let's do this." I turned the key back in the ignition and circled around the campus, parking close to the Student Affairs building. It was clean and discreet, which you'd expect, given what they did. A middle-aged woman looked up at us through wire-rimmed spectacles as we walked in.

"Good day, darlin'," she greeted me. "What can I do for you today?"

I looked at Quintus, then back at the woman. I cleared my throat. "I'd like to make a report."

If the note was lying lazily under my work desk, I'd feel like a fool. A spiteful, vicious fool. Only Monday would tell. Focusing on anything else—Ravi's famous vindaloo, Felix's revised symphony, even Ray Harryhausen's skeleton warriors—did little to calm my nerves. In my despair, I may have had too much to drink.

18

QUINTUS

*A*zi's legs could not be relied upon in her state to transport her safely up the stairs, so I carried her. She went to bed without complaint, bending her knees docilely as I tucked her legs beneath the covers. As I brought my lips to her flushed cheek, she turned and sought my mouth. Her warm eyes called to me through heavy lids. She held my arm, keeping me close.

"Stay."

The sweet, fruity aroma of the wine on her breath hung in the air between us. By the gods, I lusted. But I knew not who beckoned me—Azi, or Bacchus. I intended to be sure.

She'd gone to work the next day agitated, but sufficiently sober. I had been pushing hard to complete my digital education of English and had nearly run the course of all Azi had given me. I could hold an intelligent conversation, but I was waiting for the right moment to speak to Azi in her own tongue. The masked bacchanal she had resolved to host at month's end suited my purpose. For now, I held my tongue and soldiered through. I'd become so absorbed that I hadn't noticed her come home, though the hour was late.

She was not in any of the rooms below. Dean saw the inquiring look on my face, and simply pointed upward. I climbed the stairs again and knocked on her bedroom door. No answer. I turned my head to the door at the end of the hallway, flanked by golden sphinxes with outstretched wings perched on the lintel. Trying the doorknob, I found it unlocked. The room was empty. I lingered in the doorway, my curiosity piqued. The sound of paper shuffled at my feet. The captured image of my horror still had the power to set me reeling, and I avoided it, actively pushed the knowledge of what Azi had seen to the back of my mind. I picked up the image without scrutinizing it and placed it on the bed.

The whole room was as a set for a stage play just ended, covered in a fine layer of dust that made everything sparkle in the warm glow shoving itself through the frosted glass of the windows, rays of light highlighting the chamber's details. The embellishment of a dress considered and discarded glittered on the bed. Pearls spilled out of their box. A gold pin was tucked in the bed's rumpled corner. Silk ties lay fallen from their perch in a heap. Dried, tacky perfume pooled on the mahogany dresser, never wiped clean. Bending my nose to it, I inhaled the subtlest hint of lush white flowers.

Specks of the past hung in the air, suspended in time, twinkling down from the firmament of stars painted on the inset ceiling. There were pictures—everywhere pictures, of a handsome couple in their wedding clothes, in the desert, nestling an infant girl. Azi had her father's features and her mother's hair. On the left wall hung a large photograph before a pyramid, yellowed with age. Betwixt mother and father stood a young Azi, her dark hair falling in gentle ringlets to her waist. Atop her head was a broad-brimmed linen hat, tied with a dark band of silk, pressed onto her petite head by her father's playful hand. She could have been no more than eight. She looked happy.

I quietly exited the room, fearing I'd be discovered in that hallowed place. Turning the doorknob silently in the latch, I heard the shuffle of movement on the floor above me. A narrow stairwell in the corner disguised as a closet led the way upward. I called out to Azi as I gained the landing but was ignored. Her ears were plugged in to a thin cord, producing a concert only for her. The shades on the windows were tightly drawn, and I peered into the darkness. My eyes adjusted and took in the room in shock.

Exquisite canvasses of all sizes and seasons were stacked in every corner. At the foremost of each pile were smaller studies—of hands, eyes, and noses, all too familiar. Azi sat dumb to me, encircled by wet pieces, all with the same subject. They were arranged to show the passing from night into day, the coloration and shadows on each slightly modulated as though I stood before a passing eclipse. To see myself so represented was unsettling and remarkable. I stared in awe at Azi's opus, executed with the obsessive exactitude of one in mad pursuit of true art. She was, in fact, intent on capturing my soul.

I moved not, nor made a sound. Only some preternatural sense alerted Azi to me. She spun round from her work, and gaped wide-eyed at me, her unsuspecting subject. She stood and pulled the wires from her ears. Her eyes darted around the room, finding nowhere to hide all that was laid bare.

"I—" She cleared her throat. "I don't have a lot of practice with portraits."

I stood mute.

"I should have asked," she said, hanging her head low. It occurred to me then, that even in her best moods, I had never seen a smile that so brightly matched that one captured in her youth, memorialized by her parents in their sanctum. It was this, her art, her private space away from that mausoleum of the floors below, that allowed her to exist apart from her grief, and gave her peace.

I walked steadily toward her. When my stride drew closer, she stepped back, unsure as I reached behind her for the stool I sought. I placed it in the appropriate position beyond her unfinished canvas and took up my place.

Silence reigned between us. Slowly, that stillness grew comfortable, as it had upon our first meeting. Nothing needed saying. For several hours I sat, admiring the passion that reflected in her eyes whenever she cast them back at me. My gaze took in more of the room, more of its simple, modern adornments and inspirations from older masters pinned to the walls. This space revealed her true self, unlike the wooden bones of the rest of the house, with so many memories haunting every stick of furniture, every floorboard and mantel. *This* was Azi, and I loved her for it.

○

*A*zi's bacchanal was drawing near, and I required a costume. I accompanied the men of the household to an establishment that carried all manner of disguises. Felix tried to goad me into a farce I absolutely could not abide.

"Come on! You're perfect for the Gladiator; you've got the build!" he pressed.

"Azi will absolutely lose her shit if you turn up looking like that," Dean added. He was no help.

"No," I insisted, sickened by the thought of playing at myself. The goal of the evening was to terrify only in jest. I suspected that the humor of it would be lost on both of us. Brilliantly decorated masks hung on a back wall, half-faces bejeweled in ivory and ebony, others a full mask, and some an elaborate band across the eyes. I reached for such a one, glittering gold on black, encrusted with small blue gemstones in its curling flourishes.

"Venetian carnival—very classy," Felix observed. That settled it. A feathered hat and cape of crushed velvet completed the ensemble. Felix had chosen an eye-covering as well, a simpler strip of fabric and a broad-brimmed hat embroidered with gold. A long thin blade emblazoned with a "Z" was his accompaniment. I didn't know what Dean was meant to be, in a suit of black and gray that was much too tight, with a black and yellow bird across his chest, and a horned mask. We arrived home to find the house overrun with fake cobwebs and mechanical ghosts that taunted as you passed them. I smashed half a dozen plastic spiders out of instinct over the course of the week, finding them in the unlikeliest of places. The day I woke screaming to one placed on my pillow was the day I started plotting my revenge. It was sweet when it came—hearing the sound of Azi's blood curdle in her veins when a tarantula the size of her face found its way into her shower. The creature was returned to the pet-shop, unharmed. I cannot say the same for Asenath.

Night fell on All Hallow's Eve. As the house thronged with people eager to commence their drunken merrymaking, I waited for Azi to appear. I had caught the unwanted attentions of a girl who looked, as Felix indelicately put it, "barely legal," covered by the blue and white fabric of a police officer in only the necessary places—and very poorly, at that.

I wished I hadn't understood her senseless chatter, and pretended, in fact, that I didn't, as she batted unnaturally long eyelashes at me. As I stood gripping my wine glass, seeking a way to extract myself politely, my eye caught the glint of gold at the top of the stair.

There stood the last of the pharaohs. Her hair's normal wave was made straight, forming a sharp, blunt line woven with golden threads across her cheek that graced her elegant, bare shoulders. Her skin gleamed, adorned with the gold and blue of kings. The broad circlet of beads covering her throat was no costume. Those stones were real, as was the ring of faience that always graced her finger. A dress of gold exquisitely draped caressed every curve, a golden asp with ruby eyes coiled around her wrist. Her lips were a bright vermilion, her eyes outlined in deep charcoal in the eastern style. She winked at me, and I almost dropped my glass to the floor, struck by her glory. It was easy to see how Azi's spiritual ancestor had felled Romans of the highest caliber.

Gasps throughout the packed lower floor told me my reaction was not entirely unique. Azi was stunning in her finery, and I was utterly captivated as she approached me, her eyes never leaving mine for a second. It was she who came so amusingly to my rescue.

"Oh hi, Azi, *great* party," my captor twittered on. "I was just telling Quintus how much—"

"Mm-hmm—now run along."

I nearly choked on the wine in my mouth and had to put my mind elsewhere to focus on swallowing. Azi had made remarkably easy work of closing the girl's mouth—at least momentarily. When the stun wore off, she continued.

"I was just—"

"I know what you were just," Azi interrupted again, her chin perked up high. "Just don't."

"What's the matter? Afraid of a little competition?"

I'd never heard Azi laugh so haughtily, a high tone with a deeper, sincere underpinning.

"Honey, there *is* no competition, but if you're looking for a guy who'll take what he can get, I believe you'll do better with the crowd in the kitchen." Azi grinned devilishly, her malice sending my heart aflutter.

The girl, whose name I never heard, looked to me for the final decision. I shrugged, unable to stop the smirk rising at the corner of my mouth. The child left in a huff. Azi mixed herself a martini from the sideboard at her hip, and we raised our glasses to the evening.

"Shame on you," Ravi said, sidling up to us.

"What?" Azi inquired. I'd never seen anyone feigning innocence look so wicked. She finally turned and saw Ravi in all her splendor. "Good God, Ravi!"

"You like?" she replied, stroking the pearls that dripped from every inch of her skin, even her hair. Her fingers and hands were stained a dark umber in intricate designs.

"What are you supposed to be?" Azi asked.

"Tataka, the demoness who relishes the favors of men before she eats them."

"You were supposed to come in *costume*," a deep voice echoed behind her. A dark-skinned man, with sleek dark hair pulled away from his face, put his hand on Ravi's shoulder. He wore an ivory jacket embroidered with gold, a curved sword at his hip encrusted with emeralds, and a magnificent tasseled headdress. Whether it was a farce or his true nature, he looked for all the world like a Persian prince.

"Lively party," he said to Azi, bowing gracefully before leading Ravi away. She turned to look at Azi, who shook her hand in the air as if it were on fire. Ravi's teeth gleamed back in joy.

Azi turned her attention back to me. She put her hand on my forearm, nearly climbing into my arms as her lips reached for my ear.

"I need to talk with my guests. Try not to lose yourself between some girl's legs."

"I make no promises," I countered, feeling my palms sweat uncontrollably before she left me. The evening passed gaily, and after a time I spied Azi standing alone outside, leaning her elbows over the edge of the porch, staring out at the stars. I saw my opportunity. Approaching her silently from behind, I alerted her to my presence only when my arms slipped around her waist. I removed my mask and brushed my cheek against hers as she leaned her head backward against my shoulder. My heart's pace quickened as I began to speak in English.

"Lovely evening, isn't it?"

She turned her eyes slyly to me, and my grin widened.

"How long were you waiting to do that?" she asked.

"I wanted to surprise you, without stumbling."

She nodded.

"Can you tell me how your work is going?" I asked.

"Fine, I suppose," she sighed. "I'm trying to understand how—how you're able to be here."

"Has Alex been bothering you?"

"No, not since the last time. He's not allowed in the lab while the investigation is open."

"Have you found your private notes?"

"No," she answered. She shuddered as if from a chill wind, only letting her arm muscles go lax at the touch of my hands. "If he did take it, he might be waiting to collect more information, which he can't do right now. Or he might have dismissed it as garbage." She took in short breaths, becoming increasingly unsure. "How can I know that it isn't? I'm guessing at what happened to you, but I can't be sure. I'm hoping that what I can share with the faculty will be enough."

The time had come.

"I can answer your question now," I said tentatively. She turned her head to me, confused. "What you asked me in the beginning. About what was done to me." Her smoldering eyes creased with worry.

"You don't have to think about that, not anymore. Not for *my* sake."

"Please," I said softly, tightening my grip on her and folding our fingers together, passing her a folded sheet of paper I had worked over many times. "I need you to know."

*H*er name was Hedra. She led me down into the bog's unseen depths to a watery hell, through a gaping maw, a wide space with walls too wet and insubstantial to stand upright. I shivered in my nakedness. The red-headed enchantress set an insidious creature upon me. Its long legs like pincers dug into my muscles as it crawled over me. I felt the pain of countless little teeth, wrenching from me my life force. It emitted a horrendous buzzing, leaving behind fire in my veins. I tried to swat it away, to crush it in my hands, but my limbs rebelled. Terror filled my mind, but a heavy stubbornness took hold of my limbs. My body became my tomb, and I was helpless to stop the creature from feasting on me. It fell to the floor in a wet flop, glutted. I imagined I could see my life racing through it as its metallic body shimmered in the reflection of the dark fathomless pool over which I stood bound. Blood dripped down the sides of her naked body, cloaked only in a fresh hide of white. Betwixt the stag horns protruding from her crown was a riot of feathers, also speckled white. Her scant garments, and those of her accomplices, were stained with blood and the dank waters of that unholy temple. The beast couldn't struggle as the witch plucked its wings with her hand. It could only produce an ungodly screech.

"So, you'll never stray too far," she said, her eyes glowing in the darkness. The witch placed the mangled creature in a mold, and poured amber over it, shouting in a strange tongue, not that of the locals. Holding the hot, malleable amber in her hand as it took its shape, she plunged it into the eye of the bog before me, where the coolness of its depths solidified it. She dangled it tantalizingly on her finger by the iron ring.

"Thank you, Roman, for offering your life to the gods of the deep, in return for all that you have stolen," she said to the gathering of devils, more than to me. "Rome will tremble in fear of our gods, driven from this hallowed place. Their blood will soak the ground, a feast for the mighty Dagda!" she shouted among fiendish howling.

She ripped my ring off my unresponsive finger. I fought hard to clench my fingers in my mind, to lash out at her. I could do nothing but watch the *mocking, jeering faces of those demons as she slid my ring behind the talisman and pierced me with it, pinning them to my chest. Her pupils dilated, drinking in the light until they were only two pools as dark as the chasm before which I knelt. She commanded me to step into that abyss, and I did. I wanted to scream, but my lips stayed closed, as if sewn shut. I couldn't break the invisible bonds that held me, couldn't turn on my tormentor and squeeze the breath from her throat. She held me fast, her spell unbreakable. The cold seized up the air in my lungs as I sank farther, their wickedness closed upon me, chanting as they layered branches upon my head, submerging my face:*

"I enter in and reappear through you, I grow in you, I cover the earth, and I am not destroyed." At the last, I only remember the darkness as it invaded my nose, my throat, my eyes. Then I remember no more. The water rippled and vibrated with the frenzied chanting of acolytes as I sank.

*M*y soul felt lighter, having shared at last the extent of my ordeal. Azi closed her eyes, brushing away the wetness on her lashes.

"I fought, Azi," I said quietly. "I fought with all my soul. And I was helpless."

"I know those words," she said, escaping my arms, and tugging me back through the party and grabbing her keys. A door on the main hallway I'd never used opened to a stairway leading down. She unlocked the singular door at the base of the stairwell, and we were blasted by a chill wind that emanated from within. The space was high and wide, as wide as the whole structure of the house, and dimly lit. Everywhere I looked were ancient treasures encased in glass: an ornately crafted chair, a casement of jewels with one neckpiece conspicuously missing, a richly decorated coffin plated in gold and painted red and blue. The air was thick with Egyptian dust. Statues of gods and goddesses stretched to the ceiling though the deities were seated, roped off on their marble pedestals. Beneath the stone tablets and hanging papyri on the far wall stood a locked case of books. Just beyond them was a long worktable, with lamps gentle enough to illuminate such precious texts without subjecting them to harm. It was the bookcase which Azi unlocked before fingering the volumes and pulling out a trio of tomes.

"What are you looking for?" I asked, unable to conceal my wonder as my eyes scanned the space.

"The words you used, just now, telling me what that woman said— were those her exact words?"

"Yes. I shall never forget them."

"I've heard that before. I know I have," she said, putting the first book aside and opening to the center of the next. She flipped frantically through the pages, as if the words might escape if she did not catch them now.

"There!" she said, thumping her finger down on the page before her. "I enter in and reappear through you, I decay in you, I grow in you, I fall down in you, I fall upon my side.

"The gods are living in me for I live and grow in the corn that sustains the Honored Ones. I cover the earth, whether I live or die. I am Barley. I am not destroyed. I have entered the Order, I rely upon the Order, I become Master of the Order. Spell number 330."

I looked to where she pointed but could make nothing of the language of birds and suns she had read aloud so effortlessly.

"What is it?" I asked, her sense of urgency transferred to me, now that she had found a recorded link to my experience.

"It's part of the Coffin Texts," she explained. "It's a series of spells and prayers inscribed on the sarcophagus. See?" She left the table and pointed out the symbols etched deep in the casket encased in glass. "Many are repeated over and over again across centuries, with new concepts introduced here and there." She came back to the table, scanning its contents again.

"The Coffin Texts are about four thousand years old. The 'I' in this spell is Osiris, the resurrected god. That sentiment of 'undying' coincides with my theories about the amber's meaning—an interpretation of eternity."

"How is that possible? That something from so far away could be spoken on Mona?"

"The Wiltshire Grave," she said. "Beads of Egyptian faience were found in a Bronze Age burial mound, dating roughly four thousand years ago. It is proof that trade over that expanse occurred on some level. The Celts were migratory, correct? Julius Caesar first encountered them in Gaul."

"And drove them out, forcing them into their stronghold at Mona," I added. "General Paulinus crushed them there. I was sent in the aftermath, to help keep the peace. I failed."

She rose, her eyes gazing earnestly up at me. "Hedra's the one who failed. Rome occupied Britain for four hundred years...and your ring, what she hoped would banish Rome from Britain's shores? I think it saved your life."

At that moment, she produced the ring from the folds of her gown gathered at the shoulder. I was overcome with surprise as I reached tentatively for it.

"But how did you—"

"Don't ask. And *don't* wear it that way in public," she replied, taking my fingers in hers and slipping the ring on, twisting the signet to the underside of my hand. "At least, not for a while," she added softly.

"Thank you," I said, threading my fingers through her hair and pulling her close. The smell of jasmine was intoxicating, and I reveled in it.

"It's yours. You should have it." She shrugged, blushing under my touch.

The chill of the room vanished from my veins as I pressed my lips to hers. Her kisses were hungry and urgent, but the sound of raucous laughter from the floors above broke the spell drawing us together. Our mouths separated, but our embrace lingered.

"You're safe now, Quintus. Your fight is over." Her body pressed to mine was all the comfort I needed.

○

I was in the living room several days later when Alex barged in with a small military force behind him.

"Check the closets and any loose floorboards," Alex barked.

"Don't you take one single step in this house, or my lawyer will have *all* your jobs," Ravi said, jumping up from the sofa and barring the path of one officer past the entryway. She was flanked by Felix, coming to stand with his phone before him to record any transgression. Dean rushed up the stairs to get Azi, oblivious in her studio.

Alex's ire was not cooled by our resistance. I could see his greedy, indignant eyes roving over all the appointments of the house, all he believed should have been his. He glared at me, and still he did not know me, the very man he sought. His small mind simply could not conceive of it. Tense moments passed, then Azi appeared, descending the stairs like a raging bull.

"You have no right to be here. Now get your fucking muddy shoes out of my foyer!"

"We have reason to believe you're hiding university property," the bulkiest man said, standing beside Alex.

"This is *private* property, not a university house. You're not getting in here without a search warrant."

The henchman hesitated, looking to Alex.

"Is *he* your boss now?" Azi chided. "You work for Arkham, whether he caught you sleeping in his office or not."

The man reddened like a tomato. "Come on, professor. Let's go," he said, tucking his tail between his legs.

"I have proof!" he cried, yanking his elbow from the policeman's grip and waving a crumpled piece of paper in the air. Faster than he could blink, Azi ripped it from him, read its contents, and laughed.

"Now you're reduced to stealing notes from students?" She tossed it back at him. "You can keep that—I think I'll leave that bit *out* of my novel. Mummy stories are so trite, don't you think?"

"A *novel*, professor?" the policeman cried.

I smelled mutiny.

"If you're itching to arrest a thief," Azi pressed, "the professor here has something that belongs to me. A set of canopic jars."

"Those are *mine!*"

"Funny how you only displayed them after my parents were gone." She turned her head to the tomato. "The set of four from KV 5, built for the sons of Ramesses II, retrieved in the March excavation, 1999. He keeps them on the top left shelf behind his desk. You know the ones."

"I do." He again sought to lead Alex out by the arm. But Alex broke away from them, charging at Azi. I stepped in front of her, stopping his momentum with a forceful shove.

"Leave. *Now.*"

Hate burned in his eyes, overtaken by fear. He didn't resist being led out the third time. The officer Azi had so promptly felled tipped his hat to her and apologized for the disturbance before closing the door behind him. I turned to hug her, and she nearly collapsed into me.

"You're a little too good at bluffing," I whispered in her ear. Her reply came muffled, spoken into my shirt.

"When your life depends on it, you do what you have to. And *you,*" she shouted over my shoulder as Dean crept down the stairs, "what closet were you hiding in?"

"Are they gone?" he asked in a subdued voice.

"Yes, it's safe now," she jeered. "What are you so frightened about?"

"I thought they were here for me," he said.

Azi erupted in nervous laughter. "Whatever for?"

"For *this*, you numbnut, or did you forget?"

He slapped a small leather-bound booklet in her hand. She opened it, then handed it over to me, her mouth agape. I twisted it in my hands, righting a picture of myself pinned to the top corner of a shimmering surface, covered in letters and numbers. "Quintus Sabatella" was all I could read. The rest appeared to be encoded.

"What is this?" I asked.

"Your ticket home," she answered reluctantly. I restrained my jubilation, to prevent the tears I saw welling in Azi's eyes from falling.

19

*A*fter all she had already done, the weight of Azi having to pay my passage and lodging abroad was too much.

As comfortable as I was with my working English, I continued to be wary of proper decorum, and so I required a guide into the workforce.

"Ravi?" I called, knocking quietly on her chamber door.

"Yes?"

"It's Quintus. May I speak to you a moment?"

She opened the door wide. "Come in, come in."

"Thank you," I replied, wondering how Azi might feel if she knew Ravi had received me in her bedchamber. Since the lady in question lent it no import, I tried my utmost to do likewise.

"What is it you need?" Ravi asked.

"Have I been of good help to you, in the kitchen?" I asked.

"Oh, yes, you make my life very easy."

"I thank you," I answered humbly. "Do you think my skills are sufficient to earn me pay?"

"You want me to *pay* you?"

"No, no, you misunderstand. I apologize. I only ask your opinion as to whether I would be of value in an establishment."

"I don't see why not. Many chefs have started with less in my father's business."

She had unwittingly cut to the point.

"Ah," she recognized. "Are you legal?"

"Excuse me?"

"Do you have a visa? Working papers?"

The complications were growing by the minute. Acquiring such proofs would only deepen Azi's debts, and I would not suffer her to shoulder that as well. My hopes to uplift her out of the monetary morass my appearance had caused were quashed before they were even fully formed. Ravi must have seen the distraught look on my face and taken pity, for she waved my cares away with a smile.

"Don't worry, dear, you wouldn't be the first. But you're sure you want to work in the kitchen? You're well-mannered, and that goes over well with big clients. And a sexy accent never hurt anyone. You could have a desk job."

I shifted in my chair and chose to ignore her compliment. "What would be the difference?"

"Between the jobs?" she asked. "Better pay."

I considered carefully.

"You'd prefer cooking, wouldn't you?" she probed.

"You are very perceptive, Ravi, but my ultimate concern is assisting Asenath."

She smiled warmly. "She would prefer to see you happy. Surely you know that much by now."

"Yes," I half-whispered, moved by the truth of it.

"It may be a modest start, but there's room to advance. Go down to the Cardamom Café on Friday and ask for Thomas. I'll let him know you're coming."

I bowed my head as I turned to leave. "Thank you. I am very grateful."

"It's just an interview, mind you. You'll have to earn the spot on your own. Hope you're good at taking orders."

I grinned widely. Within the week, I was satisfactorily employed during the hours when Azi was otherwise occupied, giving me leave to divulge my improved situation when it was fortuitous.

But Ravi had spoken the truth—my earnings were meager. It was a fine start, but a remedy for the more immediate concern of travel was to sell something. Everything I had belonged to Azi, save for the painting she had gifted me. I hated to part with it, but, reminding myself of how much my goddess had already forsaken, I consented.

Assuring the best price, I could readily do. My father had taken me to market days as part of my youth's education, and he prided himself on his silver tongue. It kept my mother from taking in less reputable, less reliable boarders out of desperation should the house not be full. He might not ever have afforded to supply her regularly with oil for her hands, cracked and sore from long hours in soapy water or the oven's heat, but he did afford her the luxury of a discerning house.

Finding the forum that would fetch the highest price—that was the tricky bit. I enlisted Felix to my cause, and together we made our way downtown to the art gallery where an old friend of his family's acted as auctioneer for finer works. Removing the simple brown paper wrapping in the gentleman's office, the spindly pole of a man considered Azi's brushwork silently.

"Okay," he said after a long, uncertain pause. "I can add it to the end of today's catalogue. At sixty percent commission."

"Absolutely not," I shot back. I could see Felix squirming in discomfort out of the corner of my eye, but I was determined to prove myself a worthy partner to Azi, not to enrich *this* man on her labor, or my sacrifice. I pushed him down to thirty-five. He could go no lower. With the particulars settled, the auctioneer led us down a hallway to a quiet, carpeted room with half-walls set at odd angles, showcasing the pieces available. He hung Azi's landscape on a north-facing wall, which I took as a good sign, and tacked a number underneath. I considered it for the last time, alongside the other selections. It was vibrant and immediate, with a carefully chosen palette—it showed a mastery of color. The scene evoked more power and intensity than the posed human figures or fruit and flower bowls it hung beside. Still other canvasses had no obvious subject—displaying only aberrant shapes or random paint splatters in shades too bold, too garish, and not mixed with Azi's deft hand.

It garnered some attention. Several potential bidders passed by it more than once, not daring to linger for fear of discovery by their competition. Perhaps I was slightly biased, but I felt confident as Felix and I took our seats in a separate room designed for the auction itself. The air was thickened by the dark, heavy drapes that hung lifelessly from shuttered windows. I filled a paper triangle with water from the corner fountain several times but could not banish the flush from my skin. I longed to be gone from this place, and pulled on my collar, letting a cool breeze drift down my neck.

"Don't move a muscle," Felix warned. "The slightest movement can signal a bid."

We waited in silence until Azi's piece was finally perched on the golden easel that had seen the rest come and go. Every piece had gone for higher than the starting bid, though not by much for some. I dreaded being at the mercy of a stingy crowd when the bidding opened.

"*The West Bank*. Asenath Hayes. The piece is signed by the artist, based right here in Providence. Shall we start at six hundred?"

We were in the second row to the front, and thus unable to see the hands that went up, driving the price into the thousands. The room had pinched its collective purse all evening—now they were let loose.

"Five, seven. Do I hear seven and a half, eight, eight thousand. Ten. Twelve. Thirteen five. Fifteen—"

I tugged on my ear to goad two bidders on when the game got too rich for a third.

"What are you doing?!" Felix hissed in my ear.

I ignored him, hearing the auctioneer call higher and higher increments. There was a pause at nineteen thousand five. I held my breath and tugged one more time on my ear.

"Twenty thousand. Do I hear twenty thousand five?"

Silence reigned. Felix clutched my hand.

"Twenty-five thousand," came the definitive call from the far-right corner. My heart resumed its duties in my chest, and with no further bids, the auction came to a close. Felix grabbed me, kissing both my cheeks.

"*Magnifico*! You crazy genius!"

"Is it enough?" I asked. He laughed.

"Quintus, you could fly her to Rome on a magic carpet with that and have enough left over to buy me a sandwich. All this competition stirs a man's stomach!"

We exhaled our excitement as the auctioneer stepped off his block and approached us.

"Well done, gentlemen. Tell the artist that if she has any other works, we'd be happy to represent her here."

Felix smiled wryly. "Other works? She could *fill* your *galleria, Señor*."

"Splendid. Come again next week, and we'll set a date."

"A date?" I asked.

"For her own show. If she's willing."

I laughed to myself. Azi had held the answer to her problems in her own hands all along. I returned cheerfully home, the diamond bracelet I had purchased on my way dangling in my pocket. Azi was in her room, glaring at her computer's screen. There was an intensity in her stare, sharpened by the books and papers stacked around her.

"Where were you?" she asked but didn't give me time to answer as she pulled me down to her and closed the door. "I started researching Spell 330 and didn't find anything useful. But when I typed in just the words," she said, pointing at her computer, "this came up."

The screen projected a painting—a coven of women, all naked except for the stag hides upon their backs. One wore a skin of hideous, speckled white. They moved obscenely before a fire in a forest clearing, forming a circle around the head of a white bull staked to a post at the center of the inferno. I gripped the back of Azi's chair to steady myself.

"It was painted in the eighteenth century, by a Danish master, Frederik Lund. *The Master of the Order*. The caption translates to 'I enter in, I decay, I grow, I cover the earth, in you. I am not destroyed.' It's the first link I've found between these words and magic, *not* the Coffin Texts. No one ever put them together before." She turned to look at me and stood up, noticing for the first time how I was affected. "Quintus are you all right?"

Sweat poured down my back, and I struggled to breathe. I pointed at the image on screen, my eyes not having the courage to meet it again. Though constituting only paint, those eyes seared my soul, *seeing* me, that sinister, knowing curl at the corner of her mouth. Smirking. Mocking.

My voice rattled in my throat. "That's her," I choked out. "That's the one who bewitched me."

Her head snapped back to the painting. "Which one?"

"The woman in white," I said, seeing the carpet slowly start to spin beneath my feet.

"Sit, sit," she said, seeing me waver on my own legs. She shut the computer and pulled a long, hard-bound book from the bed, flipping it open on her lap, away from me.

"Born in 1705, Lund lived his whole life in Copenhagen, started his painting career at age sixteen. He was initially unsuccessful. He painted cityscapes and was unable to secure a patron."

"He must not have had your talent." I chuckled, drawing breath from my gut as my world stabilized.

"No, his early work is total crap. Look." She turned the book around to face me. It was amateurish, the sky a muddy brown, the angles of the buildings hemming in on each other. She turned the book back to herself and flipped the page. "Then in 1734, relatives and colleagues noticed a marked change in his temperament, and he began to produce works of an entirely different character, focusing on darker subjects, especially witchcraft." She flipped through several pages, and I saw her eyes widen.

"Quintus," she said somberly, "she's in every one of these."

Bile rose in my gut as she leafed through the book to another passage.

"He conducted a tumultuous affair with one of his models—"

"Guess which one."

"And in 1737, he was committed to a madhouse. He had become violent and set his studio on fire in an attempt to kill his lover."

"*Did* he?"

"It doesn't say. He continued to paint while in captivity. These are…"

She paused, visibly disturbed.

"I don't even know what I'm looking at," she said, her pitch rising nervously. She turned the pages forcefully, to shut out whatever she had seen in the paint. "He killed himself a year later—ingested the paint thinner." She closed the volume with finality, and I came to sit beside her on the bed.

"I'll keep looking," she said, narrowing her beautiful eyes in determination. "There must be more about him somewhere. Or maybe…maybe she worked for other painters, and I can track her down that way."

I put my arm around her and kissed her head, unable to give her the answers she sought.

"I didn't mean to upset you," she said, leaning her head on me.

"You couldn't have known," I reassured her. "And whatever it means, *I* am still here."

She curled her arm around my waist and squeezed. I took hold of her wrist, kissing her skin before pulling the bracelet out of my pocket and slipping it on.

"What's this?" she cried, genuinely surprised.

"The first of many gifts, and only a small measure of all you deserve."

She turned my head to her and pressed her lips firmly to mine. It set my head spinning all over again. I didn't mind.

"Thank you, Quintus, but where'd you get the money for this?" she asked, her eyes lost in the glittering fire of the stones on her wrist.

I smiled proudly. "From you."

"From *me?*" she repeated, incredulous.

"I sold the painting in my room."

She absorbed what I had said.

"My painting—sold for enough to buy *this?*"

My smile widened. "No. Your painting sold for that, and *this*," I said, laying the remainder in her lap.

She snatched up the bills, counting them rapidly. Her wild eyes turned to me. "Are you serious?"

I tucked an errant curl behind her ear. "You are immensely talented, Azi. Now the world knows it. You're been invited to host your works at Peaselee's, at your convenience."

"Uh…yeah. Yeah, okay." She laughed. "Wow." She made to hand the money back to me, but I refused.

"After everything you've done? No, Azi, that belongs to you."

"The painting was yours," she countered. "Everything I have given, I gave because I wanted to."

"Let me help you, for once," I pleaded. "We can travel in the best of comfort to Rome."

"*We?*"

I started. "Yes, of course 'we.' Why wouldn't you come?"

She shrugged and turned her eyes downward. "I didn't know you'd want me to."

"Why ever not? With your permission," I continued, lifting the money from her lap, "I'll make the arrangements."

"Okay," she said after a curious pause.

In a few weeks' time, as we readied to depart, I dared a final visit into her parents' bedchamber, staring into the unseeing eyes of her father's portrait.

"I wish I had known you," I murmured, "that you could have known me. And her. I swear on my soul I will be a good husband. She has been good to me, and for no reason," I said, pushing back the hard lump forming in my throat. "Azi said I should ask *her*, and I'm sure you would say the same. All the world will tell me I need only her consent. But I would have your blessing." Bracing my hands against the wall, I pressed my head to the glass.

○

"*W*ill you stop?"

"Stop what? What am I doing?" she asked.

I swiped her hands away from her mouth before she gnawed her fingers to the bone.

"Enough already."

She jammed her hands in her pockets as we shuffled through security at the airport. "And take that thing off your head," I said, pulling at the billed hat she wore, sporting team colors she didn't know. "You look like a boy."

"Do you have the slightest comprehension of what you're doing?"

"What *we're* doing," I corrected, roping her close to me as we neared the front of the line. I craned my neck to whisper in her ear. "We're going to walk through those doors like everyone else, if you'll only just calm down. Pretend you're traveling with me because you want to."

"I *do* want to," she said, pressing her lips to mine.

"Then what's the problem?"

"No problem," she said, calmer than she'd been all day.

"That's my girl."

"Next, please!"

We were ushered through without any fuss and made our way to the end of the corridor to await our vessel.

"Remind me to thank Dean, for making this possible," I said, laying down my bag to stand near the window as planes moved slowly toward the building, another becoming airborne in the distance. "Do they ever fall out of the sky?" I asked, perplexed by the technology that defied all reason.

"Not often."

Such a comfort. As her apprehension had waned upon our admission to the gate, so did mine wax upon embarking. Being led into something so large where everything in it appeared so small was disconcerting. I spoke to Azi to distract myself.

"Your term is almost over, yes?"

"This is just another four-day weekend, for another holiday I don't celebrate. I'll get a break from teaching at the start of the new year. I gave Magnusson the draft he wanted. Now I just have to wait and see what he thinks. I can't imagine he knows about Alex's outbursts, or he would have spoken to me."

"Forget about him," I said, flashing a flirty smile as she moved her arms across my hips and down my waist. I ran my fingers through her hair and sought her lips again.

"It's just a seat belt," she said. "Don't get too excited."

The vibrations from deep inside the beast's belly unsettled me. "Are you sure we can't just book passage on a ship? That seems much safer than this metal bird."

"Relax, Quintus. We'll be there in a few hours—most of which we'll probably sleep through."

"If you say so." The small lights above our heads flickered on as the interior of the craft went dark. I reached for Azi, my guiding light in this world. I breathed easier when she took my hand in hers without complaint or derision. She had never once chided me for my bewilderment at modern science, never made me feel less of a man for my fear.

Fear was replaced quickly by wonder, as we drifted through wispy clouds in an otherwise clear night sky. When we had reached the proper height in the heavens, we were served something. I hesitated to call it food. In this sentiment, I was not alone.

"Where do they get this stuff?" she wailed, wiping the broad side of her tongue with a napkin. "This is worse than *my* cooking."

I laughed. "I wouldn't know. You never cook for me."

"We're on *this* again?"

She reached between her legs for the bag of food we'd bought while waiting to embark on our journey, offering me a share of her M&Ms.

"You never learned?" I asked, allowing the sweets to melt on my tongue.

She turned her head downward. "I didn't have anyone to teach me, did I?"

"That was stupid of me."

She shrugged. "Cook for yourself. You seem to like it enough."

"My mother was a good cook. I've learned quite a few things from Ravi, too." I leaned over, looking out at the moon's reflection on the still, shimmering water far below. Once off the ground, our passage was surprisingly smooth and quiet, save for the errant snores and rustling of books of our fellow passengers. "I wouldn't mind spending my days like that." In truth, I had been rather enjoying just that. My proficiency at modern techniques was improving, but I had much to learn. I relished the challenge.

"Cooking is a good profession," Azi observed.

I wasn't looking to merely provide Azi with a good life. The quality of her parents' house showed what they had intended to provide. It was exceptional. She deserved at least that, if not better.

"What about my own restaurant? Is that profitable?"

She smiled. "Ask Ravi's dad. That's how his hotel business started. But for *that* kind of success, you'd need some business classes, at the minimum."

I drew my lips closed. Training meant money. She smiled.

"If that's what you want, Quintus, I'll help you."

"You're very predictable in that way."

"I won't help you then. *Predictable.* That's like the kiss of death."

"Would you rather be wild?"

"It's more fun that way, isn't it?"

"I wouldn't know. You haven't done *that* for me yet, either." I relished the fire in her eyes.

We rested comfortably throughout the flight, woken hours later by the sunrise at my window. It was beautiful to see up close, and the sun shone gloriously on the city as the nose of the craft angled gently downward to reach it.

I thought I would feel at home the minute my feet touched Roman soil, but to see how the new was built upon the old produced a malaise that made me feel permanently out of place. Azi was my only home. I held her by her enticingly slender waist as we rode the public bus to our hotel, intent on lightening our burden before venturing into the city in earnest.

"Room 204," the landlord said, handing me the key.

"204?" I asked. "There should be two rooms."

He looked again at his record book and shook his head. "Sorry, *Signore.* Only one room reserved."

I looked helplessly at Azi. "Felix," I cursed, embarrassed. Sharing a bed would be nice, but I did not presume, and I certainly had not arranged it.

"We have another free, if you like."

I dug into my pocket, then felt Azi's hand on my wrist. My skin tingled.

"It's not necessary. We'll manage."

"*Bene,*" the man said, and came around the desk to take our bags. He led the way up a tight, winding staircase to the fifth story. At his age, the practiced ease with which he managed the stairs with the extra weight was surprising. I became concerned about being in cramped quarters as we ascended, but to my relief the door the gentleman opened led into an airy, modern space with plentiful sunshine.

"*Grazie,*" the man bowed as he left us alone, tip in hand.

I immediately grabbed the blanket folded on the end of the luxuriously tempting bed, draping it on the sofa. Azi said nothing as I did this, only relieved herself of whatever she carried on her person that she no longer required. It was silly, I suppose, thinking she would stop me, or tell me that that was also unnecessary, that the awkwardness of Felix's assumption was mutual. She was inscrutable in the matter. When I found the courage to face her at last, she appeared jittery, eager to be gone. Her eyes had not been so glassy, a moment before.

"Is something the matter?" I asked.

"Where do you want to go?" she replied, shifting her weight from her left foot to her right. Whatever ate at her sense of well-being, she was unwilling to share. I knew it was not the confusion of the sleeping arrangement, but I knew nothing further, and resolved not to pry into unwelcome subjects. She pressed me again, determined to distract her thoughts from whatever oppressed them, and I yielded to her impatience to begin our tour of the city.

I floated adrift in this unseemly place, meandering through old pathways that weaved and disappeared into unfamiliar streets, the shops and offices a mirage settled permanently over my memory, hazy as a distant dream imperfectly recalled. The harder I tried to orient myself, the more lost I became. The city's layout was dizzying, and as we reached a central plaza, I was paralyzed with confusion. In whichever direction I turned, there was something there that should not be. The city felt wrong. I felt wrong.

We walked at a slow, steady pace toward the Coliseum, the ultimate farce. I felt the leering faces of the gladiators as they preyed on eager passersby burn on my cheeks. In our own house we were mocked, reduced to sly references and bawdy jokes.

Azi's reticence offered little solace. She kept a curious silence, her exhaustion growing visible with every passing hour. We lunched on the Tiber's bank, at Azi's suggestion. The river itself had changed little, and it quietened my anxious heart, which was no doubt her intention. Our makeshift meal consumed, Azi set about capturing a flock of ducks on the opposite shore on paper but broke off shortly after beginning.

"What's wrong?" I inquired, eager to solve her difficulties.

"I can't concentrate," she answered simply, secreting away her supplies in frustration.

"Is it the show?" Her art had always been for her own sake; anxiety about the change in circumstances was understandable.

"Partly," she said, dangling her legs over the bank, daring to create small ripples in the afternoon stillness with her delicate fingers.

When I inquired after the other part, she turned away from me. I placed my hand under her chin so she might face me. As this morning, she was on the verge of tears, with no discernible cause.

"Azi?"

"Please, Quintus. Just leave it alone."

She pulled her cheek reluctantly from my palm and stared into the watery depths of the Tiber. Her scrutiny of the water's surface intensified, and she leaned farther over, retreated back again, and took up her brushes. She spent an eternity mixing her pigments, her eyes dancing back and forth as she produced a range of blues, greens, grays, yellows, whites, and even purples. Those surprised me, until she applied them on the small square canvas she'd packed with her. The scene she replicated did, in fact, contain hints of purple in the shadows cast by the stone pine providing us shade. She captured the sunlight flitting on the water's surface, darting toward the shadow then away from it again. The finished product was brilliant and ephemeral. She was pleased. I was awestruck.

"This is good for the show, right?" she asked finally, slipping it carefully into a case that allowed it space to dry undisturbed.

"It's lovely," I said sadly. Her ears pricked at the melancholy of my tone. I cleared my throat at her inquisitive glance. "I sold the one you gave me."

"You want this one?"

"It would remind me of this day. Of this moment."

She hesitated but acquiesced in the end. "It's yours," she said, rising to her feet and yawning.

"Are you well?" I asked.

"Tired."

"We can rest, if you wish."

"No, I'll be all right. I can only stay a few days anyway."

I didn't like the shadow that passed over her face when she said that. She was determined to push through, feeling the shortness of time.

"Please," I insisted, "I won't impose on you more than I've already done."

"It's been no trouble," she said, the pain in her voice stifling. I furrowed my brow. Was her intention to leave me here, and this her goodbye? I shuttered out the thought, and instinctively reached for her. Her initial response was cold, but I persisted, put on anxious alert by her forced aloofness. As we turned the corner to a thoroughfare leading to our lodgings, her restraint wavered, and I felt the reassuring weight of her hips fall more relaxed into the curve of my arm.

She fell quickly asleep upon our return. I sat at the small, wrought-iron table appointing our slim terrace, overlooking the alleyway below. I retrieved the map of the modern city from my pocket, unfolding it carefully. If I let my mind be pulled to those things that were recognizable, the cacophony of the ages that had passed me by fell away. From the markers that remained, I might judge the distance to my home from its proximal relationships. My fingers traced the lines down defunct streets and nonexistent avenues, until they found their destination. They pressed on the area south of us, undeveloped save for the ruins that moldered there. It was possible that what I sought might still be hidden in the rubble. I circled my goal with the nub of a nearby pencil and returned the map to my pocket.

Within, Azi slept restfully. I would lose the daylight soon, and with it my hope that this sojourn had not been made entirely in error. I kissed Azi's forehead and slipped quietly out of the room.

◯

*W*ending my way through the streets, I avoided the fluorescent lure of bars and discos as I remembered masques, bacchanals, and the honor of a culture turned vulgar. I was not under any illusions of the lack of these elements in my native society— being my parents' son ensured my education in more worldly habits— but still, the aspiration to valor, to civility, and the optimistic pride of the citizenry had turned cynical, lax, decadent. The baser strain of sentiment dominated, and it disgusted me.

I came close to my destination, and the present fell away as I came upon the shells of my neighbor's houses, a once neat line now laid low, the foundation stones exposed to the crisp night air. Streetlamps winked on as the sun dipped below the horizon, casting the stones in a pale, unseemly glow shrouded in ancient shadows. The frail, ghostly light set my hair on end. The dull thrumming of neighbors at their daily activities echoed in my head, wispy shadows drifted by in predictable patterns as they wound their way through the day. Voices resounded dimly through the open spaces between as they prepared food, swept doorways, exchanged gossip. The sight of my mother standing tired in the doorway arrested my steps. The wrinkles about her eyes and mouth were set deeper than I remembered. She looked right at me, *saw* me.

"*Mammam*," I called, my breath puffing white, quickly dissipating clouds into the night like the phantoms that surrounded me. I called again, but she only smiled sadly, and hung her head, deaf to me. When she ambled inside, I followed, leaning my hand against the invisible door frame, losing my balance as the impression failed to support my solid weight. My mother was not there. I blinked, and the night's spell crashed over me as a glass ceiling shatters. I stood alone in the wreckage, the right wall humbled, coming no higher than my knee. I reached for the third stone up from the ground, unremarkable except for its lack of supporting mortar. My eyes gleamed in the moonlight as my fingers pulled at the false face and felt the familiar grain of the plain wooden box where my mother kept her wedding ring, not bearing to part with it, but prepared to do so if circumstances absolutely required it. That it was still there, slumbering peacefully, contented my racing heart. In my absence, the empire I had defended provided for them. It was no small comfort. I took the ring and left the box, offering a silent prayer for my parents and our neighbors.

"Thank you, *Mammam*," I whispered as I left the space. A cold wind kissed my cheek, and my eyes stung with tears.

My feet took note of every stone and curve of the road, my ears committed to memory the song of the larks overhead, and my lungs drunk deep of the air, for I knew I would not come here again. The path behind me closed forever, for that way lay phantoms. I carried my love of my parents in my breast as my feet carried me to my future. To Azi. The fountain of Neptune and his maidens across the street beckoned me with its twinkling melody as the water rushed and bubbled over its slick surface. I sat on the marbled edge, rinsing ages of disuse out from between the gemstones, admiring its returned brilliance as I heard the clatter of someone running down the emptied cobblestone street. I stood, concealing the ring as the runner came into view.

"Azi?"

"Where the *fuck* have you been?" she panted. She proceeded to harangue me in a frenzied pitch. She gesticulated wildly, shouting too quickly for me to catch every word. She had panicked at the thought of me alone in this haunted city. She'd thought I'd gone for good, without a word of parting. She was furious and heartbroken. My own heart pounded all the louder. We'd shared the same fear. *This* had been the pall cast over her all day. Waking up to an empty room had confirmed her deepest dread.

I was a fool. I had complied with her request for time from the first, but now I saw. After all we had shared, she did not know, because I had not shown her, that my heart and soul were bound to her.

My silent, curious smile angered her further, and she railed at me, her passion squelched only by the interruption of a fierce kiss. Her rage muted, coiling into silence and wracking her with sobs against my chest. Her tear-streaked face dared a piercing stare into mine.

"I've got nothing left," she pleaded. "I can't lose you too." I lifted her off her feet, cradling her in my arms. It was time our claims on each other were declared in skin and sweat.

20

ASENATH

*N*o man ever made love to me before. I had known men in their drunken, post-adolescent frenzies, or the rushed rutting of a man who feared every moment, chancing to be where he should not, complaining of stolen minutes as they ticked away.

Quintus lived only for me. Every touch was sacred, every new intimacy precious, drawing us deeper into each other. The night hours stretched decadently before us, until there was nothing left of me that did not bear a trace of him—the weight of his chest on mine, crushing me with untold fervor, his ragged breath collected on my shoulder, his hands in my hair as I pressed into him, close enough to feel his heaving abdomen brush against mine, his soft, inquisitive tongue that explored and savored, the fingers that grazed every curve as they gave up their secrets at his gentle, insistent beckoning. Our bodies sang until my legs quaked, my fingers were numb, my mind hazy. Our cries of passion mingled with the coolness of the morning, until I could bear no more.

I quivered as the cold air of the dawn licked across my back. I inched closer to Quintus, breathing in the sweet fragrance of his exhausted limbs as he warmed me. The Bacchus stirred, his large hand tugging on my hip.

"Again?" I moaned weekly.

A wicked, raspy laugh bubbled low in his throat. "Again, and again, and again..."

I squirmed in protest as he climbed farther on top of me, but his thumb crossed roughly over my nipple, and I was at his mercy. He bit into my shoulder, sending a shock rippling through me as he attempted to turn me on my back.

"I want to see you," he growled, sliding his tongue across my skin.

"Nn-ngnh—you do the work." I sighed. Our fingers folded together as he preyed upon me, my muscles heavy and languid as we collided. His lust grew almost too powerful, leaving me breathless when he sat up, sending a stark breeze between us as he swung my leg around and pivoted me. He clawed at my thighs, lifting me onto his lap. I dug my nails into the nape of his neck as I screamed at our rapid reunion. His moans at the height of his pleasure crashed over me in a tumultuous wave, and we drifted slowly down to the lush satin pillows. A tremor took hold of me from the tips of my hair down to my toes, and I prayed he would let me eat before he ravished me further.

I settled my cheek on his broad, fine chest, my temples throbbing in time with his racing heart. It grew calm, and my lids drew heavily closed until I sensed its pace hasten again.

"You know what I think?" he asked, wrapping my hair around his finger.

"You can think?" I moaned. His abdomen trembled with mirth beneath me.

"I think I was meant for that bog." I raised my head and saw tears in his ferociously blue eyes. "If not for that, how could I be here with you?" He grazed my cheek with his thumb. "*Te amo.* I love you, Asenath."

Blissful tears spilled down my face. I had not heard those words since I was a child. I reciprocated, my voice scarcely a whisper on my lips.

He reached for his long-forgotten pants and withdrew an enormous pearl set in gold. Nestled against its side was a flowering burst of rubies. He opened my palm and laid it there.

"This was my mother's," he said. "I would see it on my wife."

My breath stopped, and I swooned head-first into those twin gemstone pools that were his eyes.

"I will be devoted entirely to you, my body and my blood pledged to your protection, and to lavishing you with every happiness in this life." When I did not speak, for lack of words, he kissed my hands, and turned his suppliant eyes to mine. "Will you grant me the honor of being your husband?"

I picked up the ring from my left palm and slipped it on my finger. It fit beautifully. "*Ego autem.* I will."

*O*ur engagement was met with jubilation upon our return. The last days of the year passed quickly in small preparations, for all those I would have witness our union lived in the same house. Classes wound down, and I breezed through student finals. Time for wine and a movie came easily and regularly when we were not in pursuit of the Elder Gods. Ravi came shopping with me, gifting me my dress and enough gold jewelry to weight me to the floor. I chose a sleek, striking gown that would have made Cleopatra green with envy. We had nothing to wait for, so in less than a month's time we stood before a judge in the most lavish hotel I'd ever been to, nestled in the Catskill Mountains. Quintus was devastatingly gorgeous in his suit, his hair neatly trimmed and glossy. Having no attachment to the surname on his passport, he took mine, and became Mr. Hayes. The historic resort was set aglow in the romantic twinkle of white Christmas lights bedecking the entire estate. We celebrated with champagne and an expensive, unforgettably extravagant meal, Quintus's gift to me from his success with my painting. Felix bestowed on us sweet, joyous music on the inn's piano, and our celebrations lasted deep into the evening.

We woke as man and wife for the first time to a thin blanket of fresh white powder, giving the hotel a dreamlike appearance of Christmases long gone. When I was not set upon by the tiger that was my bridegroom, I painted, and by week's end, I had the difficult task of choosing which would join the proud works that would represent me in my first art show. As it was, my studio was filled with enough for two more. I hadn't meant to hoard them, but my circle of friends was limited, and I could not fathom discarding them. Now they would settle Quintus and me nicely for a while and support his formal education.

All the paintings I had chosen to include were weeks, if not years, old, yet when the time came, I still didn't feel ready. The gallery did a great job of displaying them and organizing the swanky silent auction that would hopefully clear out some studio space and get me the cash I needed for what I was planning—*if* I could only bring myself to do it. But I couldn't live in my parents' shadow forever. With Quintus, I didn't have to.

He was so proud, even of the ruddiest little paintings.

"What about this one?" he pleaded.

"*No,*" I insisted, smiling into my glass of Bourdeaux. "You're not allowed to bid. It's against the rules. Please don't pout like that in public, where I can't do anything about it."

"I was the one who discovered you, and I only have a single painting."

"*What* single painting? There are twice as many at home still. We decided on these together." Moving closer, I spoke low in his ear. "Your favorites are safe at home."

He grunted.

"Quintus. They were just sitting around before. Now people will enjoy them."

More grunts. He slid his hand across my back again, stretching his fingers out to cover as much of my daringly bare dress as he could.

"Please stop that. Are you my husband or my chaperone?"

"It's too open; I told you. I can almost see your ass."

"You cannot."

"I must be dreaming of it, then."

"Must be. It's fine, Quintus. Perfectly acceptable, and I look good in it."

He kissed the back of my neck and removed his hand. "Yes, you do. And just like your best paintings, you're all mine."

It really was hard not to spoil it—that the painting he had sold had only been a practice piece—what I'd always considered a crude prototype for the same subject that had taken me much longer to paint. The details were more nuanced, the color and strokes more sophisticated. It had all been painted from memories of Hani's. It was the piece I was most proud of. I'd kept it hidden well. I wanted him to see it on a permanent hanging—the question was where. Neither of the rooms we alternately occupied were fit for a married couple. And the house *was* more than I needed. One way or the other, the sphinxes would have to go. Quintus hadn't chosen that—neither had some hypothetical buyer—though in *this* town, you never knew.

I still hadn't made up my mind, when Felix stalked up behind me with Dean and Ravi in tow.

"*Princesa*, you are now my richest friend!" He laughed, kissing my cheeks.

"Am I?" I asked, shifting my weight from one leg to the other and sipping my drink in an effort to look casual.

"Have you not been looking at the sheets?" Dean asked.

"No. I've been afraid to."

"You've sold almost everything," Ravi answered. "And people are still walking around."

"Hey, where's that maharajah I saw you with at Halloween?" I asked, looking over my best friend's shoulder to see that yes, in fact, people were actively bidding on all the things I'd kept stacked in corners for so long.

"Amir? I'm sorry love, I couldn't convince him to come. He is a complete Neanderthal when it comes to art. I'll have to train him."

"Ohh-kay," I said, laughing.

"How can you *train* a man to appreciate art?" Felix interjected. "It must take root and blossom in a man's soul!"

"Well said, Felix. *Salud*," I replied, raising my almost-empty glass. Felix evened it out with wine from his own glass. It didn't matter that I was drinking red and he had white.

"*Salud, princesa*. We are two pods in a pea."

"Peas in a pod," I said, smiling.

"Yes, as you say," he said.

"How would you have—" Dean started, trying to fathom Felix's words. "How could you think it was two pods in a *pea*? How does that even work?"

"*Callate*, you! Azi, dear—"

"Yes?" I giggled, the attention drawn back to me.

"Could you perhaps find it in your gracious heart to extend my stay under your roof?"

"Excuse me?"

"You are looking at the new pianist for the Providence Symphony," he said with a gleaming smile and a grand bow. Our little circle erupted in congratulations. "Thank you, one and all. And so, I will be staying in this city indefinitely. Is there room for me as your housemate?"

"Wait a minute now," Ravi cried, waving her hands. "If this is an option, I'm staying too. Where else am I going to find a kitchen like yours in the city? I would bankrupt my father for a room smaller than your cupboard. No, I won't do it."

I looked to Quintus. He was beaming.

"Well," I turned to Dean, "are you in?"

He hooked the passing waiter by the arm, sweeping away our emptied glasses and filling our hands with fizzling champagne flutes. "May the wind always be at your back, and the warm sun upon your face, until we meet again!"

The master bedroom it was, then.

○

I was running out of excuses to keep Quintus from the house when I was supposed to be working. But every time he was escorted someplace—the mall, the movies, the museum—I was left home alone, and I couldn't bring myself to empty my parents' bedroom. Every time I tried, my heart twisted itself in knots, like I was going to get in trouble. I'd bought everything, had everything installed that I could without being present—new paint, new floors, new furniture, all just waiting. Waiting for me. I stood again at the sphinxes, brush in hand, dipped in a paint can that was opened and closed more times that it should have been.

I stared hard at the winged lions that barred the way. As a child, I'd feared them, guarding the forbidden space. Today, they frightened me slightly less than they had yesterday. I closed my eyes and felt the hot sting of tears behind my lids.

"They aren't coming home," I whispered to myself. I climbed the stepladder, gripping my brush so hard I embedded tiny wooden teeth into my palm. Imagining their approval had failed to motivate me, and only brought more water to my eyes. I thought of Quintus—I dreamed of lying next to him in the room I envisioned as ours, and my forearm moved, passing over the mural in long, wide strokes. A few minutes and it was done. The wall above the door looked the same as the rest of the hallway, and the molding had a fresh coat of white. The sphinxes were still there—their eyes forever fixed on me. No amount of paint, however dark the shade, would stop me from seeing them there. I thought of the false doors common to Egyptian antechambers, the ones painted in a dubiously continuous pattern to obscure the treasure beyond, and allowed myself a furtive smile.

Not having to sort through everything, having even that done for me and shuffled in a corner, made emptying the room go quicker. The warm brown of the new flooring looked luxe against the cool, slate gray of the walls. I stowed all the portraits in my memory box, except for the one of us at Giza, and replaced them with photos of Quintus and me in D.C., at Halloween, at our wedding. Dad's cufflinks, a string of pearls, and other small luxuries I tucked in the back of a new chest of drawers. I hung Quintus's shirts in a mahogany wardrobe and perched the real *West Bank* over the bed; on the nightstand, I placed an ivory vase full of lavender. Light burst through the new French doors leading out to the private terrace, where I set bright cushions on wicker chairs and set out a porcelain tea set and a bowl of oranges on a silver tray. The window dressings were light and airy, the linens were plush, and the comfy upholstered chairs flanking the fireplace were livened up by the plum-colored Persian rug beneath them. That and the potted fern warmed up the cool palette. I scoured the retiled en suite, leaving it smelling like mountain air and lemons. On the edge of the clawfoot tub, I set down two champagne flutes and a bottle of Dom Perignon on ice. I stepped back, making sure I hadn't missed anything. I didn't feel bad, seeing it finished. I was actually looking forward to using the space, when Dean gave me the warning text that they were minutes away.

I barely had enough time to shower the dust and cleaners off my skin. I was still shaking the water from my hair when I heard the door open downstairs. I rushed to meet them, and quickly shooed the others away, taking Quintus by the hand.

"Do you mean to send me out again tomorrow on some useless errand because—"

"No," I interrupted him. "Come with me." I practically dragged him up to the top of the stairs. As he made the landing he paused, looking between me and the fresh paint at the end of the hallway. He turned to me, and I placed a key to the front door in his hands.

"Welcome home, Mr. Hayes." I gestured for him to open the door at the end of the hall, to the master suite. His eyes glimmered as he took in the space, his head turning to every corner, seeing all the little details and considerations that would make this ours, as the *new* masters of the house. He floated through the room as if on a breeze, pulling open the double-doors to the terrace and taking in the snow-capped view of the climbing hills behind, sneaking a peak at the barely-there lingerie I'd hung effortlessly on the bathroom door, and finally, coming to stand before the bed, musing at the breadth of the painting he thought lost to him forever. I stood on my toes behind him and wrapped my arms around his shoulders, feeling his chest heaving in my hands.

"I know how hard this was for you," he whispered, trying to choke back his emotions. I kissed the back of his shoulder.

"I never would have done it without you."

"It's perfect, Azi," he said, turning to me and cradling my face in his hands.

"You gave me a wonderful wedding." I shrugged. "I wanted to give you something."

He inspected the drawers, finding all his things neatly folded and organized. When he reached for the jewelry box at the back, I held my breath. He pulled out my mother's pearls, presented them to me, and clasped them around my neck.

"They lose their luster, if they are not worn," he said, his sweet breath caressing the skin behind my ear. "She would have wanted you to have them."

"They do match my ring," I said tentatively.

"They're beautiful, just like you."

I'll never get tired of his kisses. I nearly sobbed when he pulled away, taking my breath with him.

"What about our old rooms?" he asked.

I smiled. "When we're ready, I'm sure we can find a way to fill them."

With a meaningful grin and a swift move, he pulled me off my feet. The mattress was so plush it was like making love on a cloud. Perfect choice.

21

The spring semester was starting in less than a week, and I hadn't been given any assignments. Money-wise, I was more than fine. The art show had been a great success, but I hadn't heard back from Magnusson, and that worried me. I tried to keep my mind off it and used my free time to compile my private notes, including Quintus's account of what he had seen, the words he claimed were spoken over him—an Egyptian incantation meant to invoke a Druidic god—and the paintings of the woman Hedra, as he called her.

He was so sure of her face, convinced it was the same woman. And why not? If she had entombed Quintus, suspended his life, it was plausible she could extend her own—that *was* the seeming purpose of the spell itself. When I believed I had created as complete a record of these miraculous events as possible, and could take my research no further, a dark thought crept up from the bowels of my consciousness and frightened me. It was unreasonable to think Quintus had been the witch's first, or *last*, victim. If Quintus was indeed right, and she had been the very woman to drive the painter Lund mad, then she had survived through several centuries. Wasn't it possible, then, that she still lived?

When those thoughts became too much, I put them aside and thus could not avoid the anxiety that compelled me to call Magnusson.

"You must have ESP," he said nonchalantly, picking up on the first ring.

"Excuse me?"

"I had the receiver in my hand, ready to call you. Are you free today for a meeting in my office?"

You know I am. You didn't give me any classes, I thought. The ritualistic formality of the conversation shredded my nerves. I mustered a polite response.

"Of course."

"Good. Say, three o'clock?"

"That's fine. I'll see you then."

When I arrived, the room was filled with the same faculty members who had been present at the last meeting I had attended in Magnusson's office, with one glaring exception: Alex was not there.

My ass barely touched the cushion of the chair when I was bombarded with questions about my research. I fielded their inquiries as best I could, drawing on every piece of legitimate, archaeological evidence that I had amassed since even before Anglesey Man. My blood screeched in my veins at such a pitch that I dodged risky subjects that had so recently clouded my mind. I surprised myself at how plausible it all sounded. *All* of them had read my work—that much was obvious. Their queries were thorough, and I found myself elaborating on context, comparative analyses, my methodology. I felt a migraine coming on, having to bring all my intellectual power to bear, but I pushed back the pain. These were serious questions, the kind you didn't ask of a first draft. Rather, the validity of my entire project was at stake.

My tongue had run dry by the time their inquisition waned, and they shot sideways looks at each other. I tried to rally the little spit I had left in my parched mouth for a second volley and cast an absent glance at the grandfather clock in the corner. How had it been only two hours? I felt as if I'd been born in this room, only to answer ceaseless questions about the meaning of my own existence, my relevance as a scientist.

"This was your first draft, you say?" Magnusson concluded, a curious smirk pulling at the right corner of his mouth.

"Yes, professor, but I did work over some of the parts a few times. To give you something worth reading."

A chuckle emanated from his gaunt belly, rattling his clothes in a way that threatened to shatter the ribs beneath. The clothes would then collapse upon him, leaving nothing but a heap of shirred wool and argyle.

"Best foot forward," he concurred. "You *are* your father's daughter."

I bowed my head in gratitude.

"This is remarkable work, the best we've seen come out of this department since…" He didn't finish the thought, but rather jumped to another, outstretching his hand to me as he stood at his place.

"Congratulations, Doctor Hayes."

"What?" I rasped, ready to implode.

"Why do you think I asked for your work so soon?"

"I had no idea why you asked. You didn't really give me time to think about that, though, did you?" I said, feeling more comfortable in my own skin as I shook his hand heartily.

He laughed again. "No, I suppose I didn't. The *real* reason for the crunch," he explained, "is because Aarhaus University has an opening for a post-doc in their Archaeology Department. They need help with the other bodies. Dr. Pryce inquired after your progress, knowing how much you were affected by the loss here. I told him that under no circumstances should he appoint anyone else, so long as you had attained the essential titular requirements."

In one spectacular moment, I was shocked, honored, excited—and terrified. These warring factions stole my breath and prevented me from forming words.

"There's a healthy stipend, lasting from beginning of their semester next week until the beginning of the fall term." He stepped slightly closer, his eyes conspiratorial, but inclusive. "We can do your interviews via computer, but, as long as you want it, there's a seat here waiting for you."

"I do." I beamed.

"We expect to see this in publication soon, and you'll have to hit the ground running for grants, you know. The Egyptologist on staff should, as you can imagine, study in Egypt? You seem dumbstruck, Asenath. Have you got any questions?"

"Just one. Can I bring my husband?"

tried to contribute to the gourmet-caliber offerings planned for the dinner party, but Quintus shooed me out of the kitchen, and relegated me to the foolproof task of setting the table. Magnusson and the others were sorry at having missed our celebration. When I told Quintus, he insisted on hosting them. The rest of the household went out for drinks. I fully assumed we'd be joining them after.

Our guests arrived just as I was pouring a robust merlot into a decanter. I smoothed my hair and my dress and opened the door. At the sound of my greetings and the reception of gifts and a bottle of port, Quintus rushed from the kitchen, ditching his apron and welcoming the faculty with great gusto, ushering them to their seats in the formal dining room off the common area, which I never used, except for the occasional candlelit surprise by Quintus.

"Welcome, welcome," he said enthusiastically. "Please sit. Can we offer you a drink?"

Once everyone was settled and nibbling on the charcuterie platter Quintus had ordered me to set out, he scurried back into the kitchen to nurse a sauce that smelled like heaven.

"My goodness, Asenath," Magnusson said, his eyes drifting first to the crystal chandelier above the table, then to the fetishes in their built-in nooks. "This place looks just as I remembered it. Your parents used to host the most brilliant parties. At Christmas, this whole place was lit up. I used to look forward to it all year."

I breathed easy. They had taken Quintus's introduction in stride; not a one had indicated for a second that they knew him for what he had been. Other than I, no one had seen Anglesey Man in the flesh. A rational mind could not be expected to connect that corpse with him—tall, strong, with all the sophistication of a modern man, his ageless vigor reserved for me alone.

"I keep the place dusted." I shrugged.

Vice Principal Booth laughed. "That's quite a job, I'm sure. I'm surprised you've left it this way and haven't put your own stamp on it."

"It grows on you," I replied. "But we have made some changes on the upper floors, including a studio."

"Yes, I heard about that," Dr. Bard, the Graduate Director and Professor of Classical Studies, said. "I was sorry to have missed such a display of student work. How did it go?"

"Better than I expected," I said.

"You *have* been busy. Well done," Magnusson said.

"Thank you. And thank all of you, again, for…for appreciating a project like mine. And for the doctorate. *And* the job."

"It was clear the amount of work that went into it," Magnusson replied. "No one deserves it more, but the job part is still unofficial until all your paperwork goes through—just a formality."

Quintus emerged with a roast of veal stuffed with bacon, mushrooms, and Swiss chard. Roasted garlic potatoes and a divine cream sauce were all served on silverware I'd forgotten we had, polished to perfection. Quintus beamed with pride as he carved and served. His audience was salivating, myself included.

"Not to worry, Doctor Hayes," Dr. Bard said before sinking his fork into a tender potato. "The spot is yours, just don't go shouting it from the bell tower just yet."

Booth grunted. "Carew's already having a fit."

"He was not present today?" Quintus asked. In my excitement at the outcome, the details had fallen away entirely. Even the questions I'd had to answer were as inconsequential as a dream.

"He's been dismissed," Magnusson said. "We were deeply distressed to hear of his sad display at your door."

I bowed my head. "I never thought of being in competition with my mentor until he made it so."

"What will happen to him now?" Quintus asked, finally seating himself. I filled his glass.

"Not much, I'm afraid. He'll sink deep into his wife's millions, and I wouldn't be surprised if he resurfaced with an administrative post at her father's hospital, sooner or later," Magnusson answered.

"I can't see being dismissed for theft and gross misconduct going over well with anyone. And her social circles never really intersected much with his, anyway," Bard observed.

I was truly free of him, whatever happened next.

"He deserves whatever he gets," Quintus said, his voice tight. He spoke to no one in particular, though all heads nodded, their mouths stuffed.

"This is an exquisite meal," Dr. Booth said, helping himself to another dollop of cream sauce.

"Watch your gut," Bard warned, half-serious. "Your wife would have a fit if she saw you packing it in like that."

"A pox upon my wife," Booth growled, putting even more cream on his plate for spite.

"Your wives were *more* than welcome at our table," Quintus offered, clearly distressed.

"Oh, we know, Mr. Hayes," Magnusson said.

"Welcome by *you*, maybe," Bard said. "Trust me; this is nicer."

"Shame on you, Dr. Bard," I chided. But I couldn't hold back a laugh.

Magnusson smiled. "Really, Mr. Hayes, this is spectacular."

"Thank you, and call me Quintus, if you please."

"Quintus. Are you a chef?" Bard asked.

"Not officially, but I am leaning in that direction."

"Mm. Follow your calling," he said, wiping his mouth with a napkin.

"If you ever need a taste-tester, I'm your man," Booth said, swiping the end of his bread through his plate.

I laughed. "Waste not, professor?"

"Indeed." He chuckled. "I'd lick it if I thought that was acceptable."

"It's not," Magnusson assured him.

"So, Quintus," Bard said, "ready to follow the Mrs. to the farthest corners of the Earth?"

"She has not led me astray yet," he said, reaching for my fingers across the table and stroking them. He cast a glance at me that made my cheeks flush pink.

"It's only been a few weeks," Booth retorted. "And Erik here had her all twisted up with work."

Magnusson waved his hand in Booth's face dismissively. "Tell me, have you ever been to Britain?"

I winced.

After another glass of wine and a strawberry soufflé I couldn't enjoy, we said our goodnights, closing the front door after our guests. When Quintus turned to face me, a shiver ran down my spine. He grabbed my hand and pulled me up the stairs like I was a child about to be scolded. Only after he'd closed the door to our bedroom did he unleash his fury, and his fear.

"No, no, no!"

"Quintus. I *have* to finish this."

"You have to do no such thing!"

"And tell them what? Thanks for pulling all these strings for me, but my resurrected husband is afraid of having his life stolen again?"

"*More* than that!" he shouted, gripping me nervously by the shoulders. "I fear *your* life being stolen!"

"The last record of her, *if* you're right, is in Denmark. What are the odds?"

"Too high."

"She wasn't there the first time." He had no answer for that. "Maybe *you* should stay home," I mused.

He squeezed me tighter, almost lifting me off the floor. "I *cannot* let you go to that horrid place unprotected."

"I'll be fine," I insisted. "But what about you?"

"What about *me*?!" His eyes flashed wide in indignation.

"Even if she is there, which I highly doubt, she'll recognize *you*. And if that happens, she could try to put you back."

"This time, I know what I'm fighting. I won't be taken for a fool again!"

"It's *not* foolishness, when you can barely stand before a portrait of her."

He scowled, embarrassed.

"There's no shame in that," I reassured him, softening my tone. "But what happened to you *wasn't* by trickery. It was...something else." I hesitated to say more. No matter how true it was to me every day, I could not bring myself to say that this woman possessed an indescribable power.

"And if I'm right?" he pressed. "What's to stop her from setting her sights on you? I won't take that chance."

There was a warning and a challenge in his eyes. I remained silent, but firm. Several long moments passed. Quintus puckered his lips and blew out a gust of exasperation.

"And I'm supposed to *let* you go, so what happened to me might happen to you?" His fingers released my shoulders, sinking down to my waist. "I forbid it."

I sighed, falling deep into his embrace. "I didn't make a vow of obedience. Only love."

"I know. But now, whatever happens, it'll be *your* fault."

*T*he silent gloom that made its permanent home over Wales filled me with a pronounced dread. Quintus and I settled into the fellowship house, on the opposite side of the campus from Pryce's lab. It was an improvement over the dorm I'd semi-occupied on my last trip. We fought about little things, tiny quirks and details, getting on each other's nerves in the search for distractions from our more ominous thoughts, until we were at each other's throats, our bad humors soothed only after expending our mutual fury on the bed, the sofa, and the kitchen counter. In the dark hours of the morning, Quintus had slipped out, coming back just as I was readying myself to leave for my first day.

"Where'd you go so early?" I asked.

"There's a fishing store at the bottom of the ridge, near the lake's edge. I saw it on our way up."

"You're going *fishing*, now? What happened to staying put?"

He pulled out a hunter's knife and presented it to me. Its edge was finely honed to a menacing curve. I swallowed hard, fearful of its presence.

"I don't want that," I said, and backed away.

"If I can't be with you all day, you need *some* protection, at least."

I looked into his eyes, and saw my own wariness reflected there. I refrained from needling him.

"I don't know how to use it," I answered in a small voice.

He stood up, put the blade's handle firmly in my palm, and pointed at his own abdomen. "Kidneys. Dig in, and up, as hard as you can—it's a kill spot and won't get stuck in the ribs."

"So is this," I said, aiming it at his neck.

He smirked. "And how much do you have to stretch your toes for that?" he asked, pushing me backward with a deliberate shove to my right collarbone. My ass collided with the edge of the coffee table, and the knife clattered to the tile floor. He helped me to my feet and rubbed my rear lovingly.

"Weak stance, weak grip," he said, his voice sharp, putting the blade again in my hand, the point at his flesh. "In, and up," he repeated. "Call on me, if anything… Promise?" he asked, pulling his new phone from his pocket.

I looked down and puckered my lips. Taking the phone from him, I turned it on before returning it to his pocket, my fingers lingering in a place that threatened to keep me from my work.

"Promise," I said. The firm insistence of his kiss tempted me to stay. Our mouths parted, though neither of us wanted to, and he saw me to the door.

As I crossed the threshold, he grabbed me again, the fear raw in his eyes.

"It's not safe," he urged.

"I'll be *fine*, Quintus. I was fine before, and I'm fine now."

He grunted, unsatisfied, but he released his grip on me.

"I love you. I'll see you later," I assured him.

"I love you," he replied, closing the door with a heavy click.

I picked my way along the slick cobbled paths across campus between the fellowship house and the university's lab. I did not feel alone on my short walk, and I was perturbed by the sensation that there was someone always just outside the edges of my vision, no matter how far to the side I casually stretched my neck. I would try to forget it as I walked along, until the short hairs on the back of my neck stood at unwarranted attention. This cycle of craning my neck and casting furtive glances over my shoulder agitated me. I pressed my fingers into the cross-hatched grip of the knife in my pocket for comfort. I cursed myself for becoming superstitious overnight and determined to keep my eyes pointed forward as I trudged between forgotten buildings and emptied courtyards on the cusp of the academic body's return, and with it, life.

I meandered through the January fog, observing small patches of snow left over on the mud, and felt the wet promise in the air of more to come. The clouds and sky were married together in a pale, colorless expanse. It was not ominous or brooding, just an empty nothingness.

I was relieved to be inside when Dr. Pryce greeted me at the lab's outer doors.

"So good to see you again, Miss Hayes!"

"You too, Dr. Pryce. Thanks so much for inviting me back."

He swatted at the air with his hand. "I never wanted you to leave—I'm just glad you're still interested, after all that's happened."

That made two of us.

"Magnusson told me about your thesis," Pryce continued. "It's really remarkable what you've done, and in so short a time. I have so many questions, just…incredible. I hope to have many more clues to the fate of Anglesey Man here waiting."

Pryce was as happy as ever, but gaunter. Not like a man trying to get healthy and stave off the inevitable effect of fatty English foods, but rather like a man who was being starved.

"Are you well?" I ventured.

"Well? Yes, yes…" The jubilance of his reply was offset by his obvious signs of weariness—shortness of breath, and the rapid wiping of his brow with a blue silk handkerchief from his blazer pocket that looked like it had become routine. "Yes, quite, it's just…there's so much work to do still around here that it's hard to take it all in." As the double doors to the lab came into view at the end of the hallway, I attempted to steel myself for the sight of the other bodies and promised myself not to retch or faint at the grim reminders of how my path had first crossed with Quintus's. I had been secretly dreading this moment, and wondered how I was to manage a cool, focused head surrounded by this marshy, fen death in the coming weeks. At the same time, another part of my psyche itched to see them, to look deeper than their photographs allowed into the possibility that even one of them had undergone the same ritual that had almost captured Quintus's spirit in senselessness. But no amount of meditation or preparation could have prepared me for when Pryce opened the door. There, in a prim white lab coat and blue latex gloves, stood the red-headed demon.

22

"*T*his is Hedra, my new assistant," Pryce said, introducing the creature nuzzling her nose against his arm, and digging her nails into his sweater like a cat. "Hedra, this is Asenath Hayes. *Doctor* Asenath Hayes," he said proudly. "This whole thing was her idea."

"Hmm," was the creature's only reply. She glared at me, but said nothing, continuing to preen herself on Pryce's shirt.

"She's been my only companion since Jakob and the others left."

"Jakob's gone?" I asked, relieved.

"Not *gone* gone. But he needed the money, so I sent him to intern for Dublin University. It'll do the boy good."

Jakob is no boy, I thought. Still, he was safe, and I was grateful.

"But Hedra here," he said, planting a kiss on her fiery hair, "she's been doing all this just for the simple reward of knowledge."

I'll bet.

I didn't know how to act, for fear of recognition—which was silly. She wouldn't recognize *me*, only my husband. I didn't like her looking at me. I felt that she would peer into my soul and find Quintus there. Running wasn't an option. Was staying? She did not act as if she understood that I knew her for what she was. I was not a threat, just a nuisance. Not appreciating my paralyzing fear of her, she did her utmost to make me uncomfortable in her and Pryce's presence, to let me know where I stood. He was drawn to her—she touched and kissed him coyly, directing his thoughts and movements, and he scarcely knew it. I understood what Quintus had described to me as her "double" face—her features were in turn beautiful and hideous depending on the angle. From certain perspectives I saw both simultaneously, which jarred me, spurring me to avoid her face altogether.

Her skin was so pale and stretched so thin in places it appeared translucent—the veins underneath gave her a sickly blue complexion. She had a smooth forehead, marred by thick, pronounced eyebrows, hovering wildly over eyes as large and sinister as an owl's, set too far apart. Her pallid flesh sloped between them, ending abruptly in a nose that hooked at the end. Thin, colorless lips were disproportionately long when she smiled. I saw all the way back to her molars. It was like a shark smiling, the whole lower half of her jaw gaping open. When she laughed tartly, she made a shrill twinkling nose, like a tormented crane in its death throes.

I kept myself as occupied as my tortured mind would allow, following Pryce around limply as he showed me what they had already done. I trusted nothing he said, knowing that the course of his analysis had been maligned. As we moved about the lab, Hedra took little notice of me. She did not perceive herself to be discovered. I immediately realized that this was an advantage. And whatever allure she possessed for Dr. Pryce, (and for Quintus, I remembered darkly), had no effect on me. Another advantage. Though she'd done nothing but stare oddly and smile condescendingly at me, I understood with perfect clarity that we were at war.

This bizarre situation eroded my calm and left me entirely vulnerable when they brought out one of the remaining bog bodies. I swallowed the bile that rose in my throat and took mercilessly deep breaths to stop my inclination to hyperventilate.

A large patch of its neck and chest were missing, along with the right leg up to the hip.

"The wounds on his neck are likely animal bites," Pryce pointed out.

"As we can find no other cause, we presume he was mauled to death, the leg most likely carried away after."

I was fairly certain that no animal extant on Britain was large enough to butcher a man thusly, but I continued to observe silently.

"His heart and lungs are not present, but MRI tests indicated that his left kidney and the small and large intestines are still there, badly corroded," he continued.

Just inside my field of vision, I saw a deepened recess, a sunken hole large enough for a hefty oaken stake. Pryce made no note of it as he continued remarking upon the body. In fact, I was positive from his claim that that particular area of the skin was perfect that he *did not see it*. My suspicion of this was goaded by the she-devil, whose lips contorted into a smug pucker as his eyes passed unseeing over it. I had to follow suit and ignore it. For now.

"It's a shame Anglesey Man got away from you," Hedra purred. "Were you able to determine anything?"

"Not really," I answered. "He was gone almost as soon as he was placed in our lab."

"Any ideas where he's gone to?"

"Nope."

"You gleaned enough to earn your doctorate—that must be worth something, surely?"

Damn. It detailed the pieces we had extracted from Quintus's chest, and my supposition about the mingling of practices of bog sacrifice and wicker men.

She interrupted my mental list of all the compromising facts my thesis contained by asking to see it one day. At least, I thought gratefully, Magnusson hadn't passed a copy along to Pryce. If he had, Hedra would have implied its contents with more force. I was beginning to understand her character enough to know that she was overconfident and did not shy away from tipping her hand. Another tick in my corner. She had been allowed to move and operate in this lab unchecked, manipulating the evidence and the data derived from it. Why she did so, I could not yet tell.

She kept me occupied with busy work. I complied, not wanting to disillusion her, if she did in fact believe I was incapable of disobeying. She didn't bother with excuses to be constantly over my shoulder. I tolerated it in silence, my hatred forming a palpable lump in my throat. Aarhaus had not only kept the lion's share of the bodies, but also of the votives and other offerings found on or near them. Even the *cataloguing* had not been completed yet. When I made my way over to the computer to pick up the abandoned work, Dr. Pryce's cheeks reddened.

"We should be a lot further along than we are, I know," he said apologetically. "But with the budget cuts, it's been only me and Hedra here." I really didn't wonder why nothing got done.

I was rewarded for my obedience by a lazy neglect. I wanted to believe what Pryce had told me, but I couldn't take his word for it. Not now. Not under the circumstances. With his back turned to me, I took my phone out of my back pocket, and pulled up Jakob's number.

Are you in Dublin now?

There was no immediate answer. I tried not to jump out of my skin with worry, not to consider the possibility that Jakob never made it to Dublin.

Hedra left the room only long enough to relieve herself. With Pryce's back turned, I peered into the opening in the bog body's chest. With tweezers at the ready, I withdrew a minute splinter embedded in the chest wall. As I angled myself to collect it noiselessly, an amber speck glittered mischievously at me. I snatched the speck, shoving it into the tissue holding the splinter and wadded them into the pocket of my jeans.

I darted behind Pryce and spun him around by the shoulders to face me. I shuddered at how easy it was—the bear of a man I had known was barely there at all.

"Miss Hayes?" he asked, stunned.

"Pryce. Pryce, where did she come from?"

"Who?"

"Hedra!" I hissed. "How did you find her?"

"Find her? Well, she…" He scratched his head, and his eyes stared off into the distance. "You met her before," he insisted, not even sounding sure himself. "She's been here the whole time."

"*No*," I said firmly. "I've never seen her before. Where did she come from? When?"

"I'm sorry, Miss Hayes. I—"

"Think, goddammit! Who is she? What does she want with you?"

He continued to gape at me like a frightened deer. I lowered my voice.

"What did she do to the bodies, Pryce?"

"Do?"

"What did she take?"

Those words seemed to strike a chord deep within his psyche. The light behind his eyes flickered on.

"Asenath..."

"Pryce. Talk to me!"

He opened his mouth to speak again but was silenced by the terse clacking of Hedra's high-heeled shoes on the linoleum floor, coming closer.

"Help me," he whispered.

I nodded and backed away. I was back to cataloguing clay shards when Hedra returned. I turned away from Pryce—I couldn't stand to watch the light fade from his eyes once more as Hedra's hold over him tightened.

My phone buzzed. It was Jakob.

I'm home now. Come over for dinner?

I let out a sigh of relief, my heart only beating half as fast as it was before. Whatever else had happened, Jakob was safe, and I was grateful.

My lips puckered with a tinge of regret as I tapped a reply.

Thanks, but can't. Not a free woman anymore.

He sent back a frowning emoji. I was in the middle of typing a sympathetic reply when he sent me another smiley-face, this one with its tongue sticking out.

Come over anyway.

I smirked, like he probably knew I would. That was the thing with Jakob. He made me laugh and never took anything too seriously. I shot back a face covering its mouth in shock, which earned a laugh from his end. I can't explain why, but the banter lifted my spirits. Joking about something, anything, kept my mind off my day with a demon, and the tension between me and Quintus that just would *not* go away. The pull I had first felt months ago to share my secret with Jakob came back with all its vigor. But it was more impossible now than it had ever been, the dangers even more real.

So, of course, I spoiled the moment.

Jakob—what happened in the lab? Did Pryce let you go?

I was beginning to worry I'd put my foot in my mouth, when the answer finally came.

shrug Ask the red-headed harpy. She's got him wrapped around her finger.

I noticed, I texted back.

Something's off about that one.

His response made my hands shake until the words in front of me devolved into a jittery blur.

What do you mean? I managed.

Idk. Call it a spidey-sense. Just keep your distance. Promise?

I was growing incrementally more terrified about going against Quintus's counsel, and now Jakob's. But, how could I?

I felt a cold breath of wind crawl down my neck, and on instinct secreted my phone away back into my jeans.

Hedra caught the quick movement and arched a thick eyebrow. The result was unsettling.

"Missing you already, is he? And it's only the first day."

My cheeks reddened—it wasn't Quintus that I was texting. I had no idea what I'd say to him when I got back to the house. *If* I got back.

She smiled her hideous smile again. It may have been she was taking a different tack, making an alternative attempt at sympathy based on some unspoken bond between females. I was having none of it. When I didn't respond with a kind look or word, she turned away from me again.

By midday, the multiple layers I had worn to brave the bitter wind outside became a burden, and I stopped to remove a thick pullover sweater. As I did so, my necklace dangled about. Hedra jumped away from me, swallowing a shriek. But she wasn't fast enough to mask her reaction—her whole face contorted in terror before she sprinted out of the room, shouting a flimsy pretext at Dr. Pryce that I didn't even hear. The Eye of Ra had fallen on her, and she ran from it as a vampire does a cross. I grinned widely, thumbing the back of the charm in thanks. I had begun the day with small advantages. Now I had an arsenal.

I walked home in a fuddle. If someone or something was following me, I was too absorbed in my own thoughts to care. I had survived today, but could I bear *another* day, let alone four months?

I was undecided about telling Quintus. What good would it do? Maybe if I could understand what she was doing with Dr. Pryce, what she still hoped to gain from the bodies, I could stop her from harming us, or anybody else. The things I'd collected didn't prove anything other than that Pryce's bodies had at least *some* of the same ritual performed on them. But the chain of artifacts had been compromised. One thing was for certain—she would know Quintus if she saw him, and she knew where we were staying.

Quintus smothered me as soon as I walked in the door.

"Are you all right? How did it go?" he demanded.

"Fine," I said, cursing myself the minute the answer left my mouth. I felt like a coward. My heart hit the floor when Quintus accepted it without question. Utter relief washed over his face, and he hugged me again.

"And the others?" he asked.

"They're dead now," I murmured into his shoulder, gripping him tightly. "That's all I know."

He nodded, his eyes meeting mine. I nearly blurted it out right then. But I didn't. When he released me, I swayed in place, almost collapsing. I had to put my hand on the kitchen counter behind me to find my bearings again.

"Are you hungry?" he asked.

"Sure," I answered, trying to pretend everything was normal "What do you want?"

"It doesn't matter."

"There's an Indian joint up the road. It's not Ravi's, but—"

"Fine. Come." He sighed, beckoning me to his side as he returned to the couch. "I can watch my show in peace now. You know this one, *The Throne's Game?*"

"*Game of Thrones?*" I corrected, resting my head on his shoulder and tucking my legs up behind me. I immediately unfurled again at the sight of Robb eating salt under Walder Frey's roof, and headed for the bathroom.

"Sure you won't watch? It's quite good," he insisted.

"Once was enough for me, thanks," I retorted, locking the door as I sat on the closed toilet seat. I took the wadded-up tissue out of my pocket and uncovered what I'd stolen from the lab. The amber was but a speck, the wooden shard little more than an oversized splinter. I'd felt compelled to take them, to save them from whatever destruction Hedra had intended, though I knew I could do nothing with them myself. I dreaded to think of what else might have been destroyed or tampered with. The entire collection, everything I had left behind for Aarhaus, was tainted. No matter how hard I worked, with Hedra there or not, I'd never be sure my conclusions were without influence. Self-doubt reigned, and there was nothing I could do to shake it.

Dejected, I stood up, stuffing the scraps back in my pocket and turning to face the mirror. I flushed the unused toilet and stared hard at myself. I'd never been prone to lying before. But they'd become a necessity when Quintus had awoken. I'd done with without hesitation, to protect him. Now I was lying *to* him, and I hated myself. The blood-curdled screams of House Stark soaked through the door and mingled with my own dark thoughts. My stomach churned. I splashed my face with water to conceal the redness around my eyes and opened the door.

Quintus sat before the muted screen, his face pale. His head turned absently in my direction. When it came, his voice was a hoarse whisper.

"I've lost my appetite."

"Me too."

$\mathcal{J}$ watched his restful face while he slept, staining my own pillow with tears. I couldn't let it revert back to that state in which he'd first captivated me. I pulled my chain off my neck and slipped it around his without disturbing him. He was still asleep when I readied to leave the next morning.

Locking the door to leave, I was struck by a sudden, almost insane idea, if my circumstances weren't *already* insane. There were traditions in most magical systems for protection, or to guard entryways. Even if I thought there was nothing to them, even if my Eye of Ra had been peddled in a corner stall on a dirt-lined street, a golden trinket bought to placate an excitable daughter, the symbol had resonated with Hedra. So, I made my offering to the only gods I knew. I grabbed a charcoal pencil from my art sack and pulled threads of warnings from memory, scratching them over the lintel: "For all who enter this room to do wickedness, there will be judgment. The wrath of Thoth will seize her neck, and an end be made for her that no priest or doctor can cure." If I believed this woman was truly a witch, then I had to believe that she might behave as certain witches were reported to do, which included appearing in more than one place at the same time. Her being up my ass all day didn't guarantee she wouldn't also be elsewhere. When I was finished, I added a cross in the center. Just in case.

Hedra was warier of me today, unsure if I still had Ra's protection over my heart. She spent the entire day sulking in a corner, complaining of a headache.

"Go home, dear. Azi and I can handle this," Pryce offered multiple times.

"No," Hedra insisted, her eyes flaring. "I'll be fine here, next to you."

Pryce smiled and went about his day, happy as a teenager.

"Look here," he said, splaying out the carbon tests before me for his three bodies. "There's a few hundred years between each of these, even accounting for the range and the margin of error."

"But all were murdered?" I asked.

"Yes, I believe so. This one had his throat slit," he said, pointing to the report on the far left. "This one, head trauma."

"You said this one was likely killed by an animal." I played along, gesturing toward the specimen on the opposite table.

"Yes, but see," he replied, leading me to the far side of the room and pointing with his pinky finger, "this pattern around his wrist and neck. He was bound, then had the animal deliberately set upon him."

That I absolutely believed. Hedra hissed under her breath in her corner, uncrossing and re-crossing her legs. If it bothered her, why didn't she make those clues invisible too? Where did she draw the line between what Dr. Pryce could and could not examine? I wondered about that.

"It's confounding," Pryce said after a pause.

"Not really," I answered, testing the waters. "The place was used by multiple generations. It demonstrates that the place had a deeper meaning, one that was passed down. If there *is* a religious context behind these deaths, then we're looking at more than just one ritual."

"The signs of a tradition," Pryce concluded, catching my train of thought. He put his hand to his forehead, and his eyebrows stretched up into his receding hairline. "How did I miss that?" he gasped, shocked at his own obliviousness.

One guess. But was that the point? Did Hedra *want* us to understand, to appreciate a lost culture and present it to the world? Then why hinder him at all? It was baffling.

"If we look hard enough, we may be able to see how that ritual evolved over this extended period," I said, my eyes shifting back to the reports. "See what changed, what essential elements remained the same."

Pryce's look of stupefaction changed to a wide grin.

"Here only two days and making a fool out of an old hand like me."

"Doctor Pryce, I—"

"Bup! Good for you. Isn't she something, Hedra? We'll *really* get some work done now."

Pryce may not have been in love with me, but he admired me. *That* was why Hedra hated me, and she didn't want me getting *too* close to her secrets. She raked her gaze over me like burning coals and lowered it to my left hand.

"Married already, Dr. Hayes? At such a tender age," she mused, lifting an eyebrow.

"Married?!" Dr. Pryce cried. "You weren't even engaged the last time I saw you!"

"Some things you just know," I answered, warming to the thought of Quintus while fearing for him in the same heartbeat.

"Right indeed. Congratulations!" Pryce shouted in my ear as he pressed me to him. Feeling his ribs through his once-hefty frame sickened me.

"What's the lucky groom's name?" Hedra asked.

My mind went blank. It only took a few seconds for my lips to pick up the slack. "Alex."

"Is he with you, then? We should all have dinner together," she said. I think she saw me squirm in my own skin, for her shark smile widened.

"Yes, I insist!" Pryce turned to me with a mock stern face.

"I would, but he hasn't been very well. It'll take him some time to have an appetite."

"Our fine weather dus naught agree with 'im, then?" The boast, the type made by locals used to the unwelcoming climate, carried a hint more Gaelic than her normal voice let on.

"Shame. Rain check, then," Pryce replied.

The clock was ticking.

I came home not knowing much more than I had the day before and feeling the worse for it. My conversation with Pryce about the bodies had not been stymied, but how long would that last? The ball was in my court, and I had to figure out how to dodge a meeting with Quintus until I could discover more. The warning I'd etched out this morning was undisturbed. I breathed a sigh of relief as I opened the door, sucked right out of me again by Quintus's harsh stare as he sat with his fists on his knees, waiting for me.

"Doing a little dabbling, I see?"

I closed the door behind me slowly, taking the time to choose my words carefully.

"You weren't meant to see that." Those were *not* the right words, from the way he fumed.

"Oh, I see. We've only been married a few weeks, but already the deception begins. What does that say?!" he shouted at me.

"It's nothing bad! It's a warning," I insisted, holding up my hands in front of myself to defend against Quintus's booming voice. There was no use now. "Quintus," I said, stopping more words from forming on his lips. I swallowed my fear and braced myself for his reaction. "Hedra is now assistant to Dr. Pryce. The lab is hers."

His mouth and eyes gaped. I took a step back as he started toward me, but I was caught up in his arms before I could even blink. He shook me hard, his voice lambasting my face until I cried.

"You know what could have happened, what could *still* happen, and you went?!"

I sobbed.

"She's taken everything from me," he said, ceasing his rampage and pulling me close. "I won't let her take you. I *forbid* you to go back there. I mean it this time."

"I can't. It's too suspicious," I said. I wasn't very convincing, even in my own ears.

"Then we'll leave this place. Right now!"

"No." The wave of my emotions passed over me at last. "We might be safe, but who else will she hurt?"

"My only care is for *your* safety. I vowed to protect you until my last drop of blood, and that's what I will do."

"She'll overpower you again," I cried, holding on to him for dear life and preventing him from breaking our embrace.

"I won't be caught by her wiles," Quintus argued. Jealousy burned in my chest, and I had to fight to stomach it. It was a supernatural pull; one he couldn't control.

"It's more than surprise, Quintus. It's power. She has Pryce wrapped around her finger, and she made him fire his staff. They've barely touched their findings. She doesn't want the work to be completed, and she's stealing the amber off the other bodies. I think they bind her victims to her."

"Mine is far away from here."

"That doesn't make you safe!"

He lifted me up and kissed me like he might never again. "I love you, Asenath. I'll love you forever." He spun me around in his arms, tossed me on the couch, and raced for the door.

I scrambled to my feet and gave chase. The doorknob wouldn't turn. He'd jammed it from the other side. I screamed as I tore at the door, trying to rip it off its hinges.

"This goddamn motherfucking stupid machismo *bullshit* is gonna get you killed! Make *me* a widow at twenty-four? Fuck *that* shit!" I screamed. The door was implacable. I was wasting precious minutes like this and turned my attention to the window. The frames were the kind that didn't open, to keep overworked, cracked-out grad students from jumping out. I was in no mood to be delicate about it, so I picked up the chair nearest me and hurled it out of the window.

I stared several stories straight down the flat face of the building—I would be as flat as that if I fell. Quintus was nowhere to be seen, and his head start was growing as I shimmied down the drainpipe. Impatient, I jumped the last few feet. My ankle burned, but I could run on it.

I sprinted through the open courtyards bridging the academic buildings to the student housing. An incoming fog bank on the horizon hastened my steps. I needed to catch up to Quintus before needing to shout his name.

Thin wisps of vapor snuck onto campus like grasping fingers tightening their grip as I bounded toward the lab. The waterlogged air was already draining the color from all things as I raced by, obscuring the face of the figure emerging from the doors until I careened headlong into him.

"Watch where you're going!" he snapped. Then he recognized me, too. "Well, if it isn't the little girl that cost me everything."

"That's Doctor Hayes to you!" I spat, rounding Alex's shoulder to shoot past him into the building. He grabbed me hard by the arm and swung me around to face him.

"Is that all you have to say for yourself? You cost me my position, and Rachael's divorcing me! You ruined my life."

I struggled to break free. I didn't have time for this, but he had stoked a long-burning fire, and I couldn't help myself.

"Serves you right, for trying to steal mine."

He snarled, his tight nails digging into my skin.

"All that was yours should have been *mine*. The house, and everything in it—all *my* hard work."

A cloud bearing my laughter blasted his face in short white puffs. "You're a joke, and everybody knows it—you'll never step out of my father's shadow."

His iron grip on my arm sped to my throat. I tried to rip his fingers away from my neck, but he shoved me hard against the brick exterior, and my vision swam.

"The hell I won't. How does it live, Azi?!" he demanded. Even if I had understood his crazed words, my voice box was being crushed, so I couldn't have answered. "The insect in the amber," he shouted, spit flicking my ear. "I know you know. Tell me!"

I spat in his face. It stunned him enough to make him stagger backwards, wiping the hate from his eyes. I reached for the knife in my pocket. I'd be goddamned if I was going to let *him* kill me. I gave him one warning.

"Stop, Alex!"

He charged at me, and my grip tensed in my pocket.

"A lover's quarrel already?"

Alex's advance on me fell on the empty air between us, and he stumbled at me, the murder in his eyes arrested by the coy shrillness of the interloper's voice. Her eyes locked on Alex as her words fell into place in my head.

Lover's quarrel. She thinks he's my husband.

His hands went lax at his side for a moment, his eyes cloudy, like a robot whose battery had run down. The next instant, he was fumbling over his words, introducing himself. She batted her eyes at him, appearing flattered by his clumsiness.

"No wonder you've been keeping him to yourself," she said, baring her teeth.

"What are you doing here so late?" I managed.

She glared at me but ignored the question, turning back instead to Alex, her eyes boring a hole into the pocket of his tweed coat.

"I believe that's mine," she cooed.

He obediently dug his hand into his pocket and pulled out the amber that had been pinned to Quintus. My eyes grew wide. I started for it, but Hedra was standing closer, and she snatched it from Alex with ease. My heart stopped as she set her eyes on me, not bothering to mask their demonic aspect.

"So, you *were* keeping something useful to yourself. Clever girl."

I stayed silent, not knowing what was going to happen next. Hedra also seemed to consider this a moment, rolling the amber carelessly in her hand like a long-lost toy. Then came her answer.

"Your wife is a little *too* clever, don't you think?" she asked Alex, looking up at him through veiled eyelids.

"She's not my wife," he promptly answered. "She means nothing to me."

It was unclear whether my "husband" Alex was unmasking my lie or simply disowning me. I kept it that way. Hedra pouted.

"She bothers me," she pleaded, her eyes twinkling darkly.

"Do you want me to get rid of her?" Alex offered, seeming eager to ingratiate himself. I tried to remember he was not his own man now and pushed the other possibility away.

"Would you, please?" she said, her tone detached, cold.

He made a grand bow, then turned to me. I set my feet apart and planted them, feeling the sweat creeping down on my spine. He lumbered toward me, his hands outstretched like Boris Karloff, giving me all the room I needed to bury my knife, up and in, right to the hilt.

I shuddered at the sudden rush of warm blood on my wind-chilled hand, and my stomach churned at the soft pressure of flesh as my blade ripped through it. Alex coughed in numb surprise, spraying blood on my face and in my hair. The fog bank in his eyes cleared, showing an even purer malice underneath, before he sank like a stone at my feet. I don't know why, and hadn't noticed when it started, but I was crying.

"I'm sorry, Alex," I whispered, stepping over him. I looked up, expecting a second assailant, but there was none. The campus was deserted in every direction. As I spun around, the lampposts dotting the campus flickered on, but they gave no sign of the witch. She had the amber that tethered Quintus to her, and she would take him from me if I didn't reach him first. I returned the bloodied dagger to my pocket, staining the front of my hoodie as I ran back to the Fellow house and jumped into our rental car just as the fog rolled in from the coast. I could only think of one place she would go.

---

23

*T*he excavation site was empty when I got there. The wheels of our borrowed Jeep jammed themselves into the mud as I leaped out. I surveyed the methodical holes in the sunken earth, as much as I could in the thickening darkness. They were still taped off and tarped to protect from the elements. Puddles of snow remained, floating in darkened pools, obscuring the danger of the pitted terrain and threatening to rip the coverings from their moorings under the weight.

I raced along the treacherous ground, bounding between the trenches, nearly missing my footing and falling headlong into several pits: The ground was so slick from water-packed air and the recent weather that it would be impossible to find the proper footing to oust myself from such a drop. If I fell, Quintus was as good as dead. Though my feet were light and quick, nothing moved but me in these cavernous grounds. Light bounced off my phone, reflecting nothing but dead trees and underbrush, chilling in their stillness. The bog didn't breathe, seeming only to absorb the intensifying fog, making the air thick and unwelcoming. As I traveled like this in a midnight haze, it became difficult to breathe. The moon, too timid to show its pale face, gave no glimmer into these darkened places, no light to belie the depths of these malignant sinkholes that hemmed me in as I traversed the bog, clinging to the untenable surface of the fen.

As I skirted from one unsure-footed step to another, I perked my head up, stretching on my toes and looking wildly in every direction for a sign of movement, utterly defeated by the opaque blackness before me. I started to hyperventilate, feeling the isolation and danger of this place closing tighter around me. I called out for my husband. "Quintus!"

The hair on the back of my neck prickled, and I spun instinctively in the direction of the chill. A bare-footed Hedra, with a single fiery tendril escaping from under a darkened hood, was leading an obedient Quintus, his head hung low, deeper into the bog.

I weaved toward them maniacally, barely staying afloat as I wended a crooked path, but not losing sight of them for a moment. Moving past the tapered chasms, I broke into a run, senseless to the very real possibility of sinking into a depression that went straight to the heart of the bog. Adrenaline pushed me onward, closing the gap between us, when they disappeared before my eyes.

I halted for a moment and flailed my arms about wildly in the freezing mist to stop myself from falling, then ran blindly on, the dim spot where I had last seen them burned into my retinas.

I reached my destination, just as desolate and piled up with debris as elsewhere, hedged in by unruly mounds of sphagnum moss. I couldn't tell how far into the bog I was, but the air was thinner here. I got the distinct impression that I was surrounded on all sides by water, that the slightest misstep would send its fathoms rushing up to meet me. My quivering legs stilled, and I tapped on my phone's flashlight again, pointing it at the ground. Soft, fresh footprints pressed into the muck, and ended abruptly. Shadows danced before my phone, refracting off objects that were not there, bouncing off an invisible forest. I stepped over the depression Hedra and Quintus had made and saw something glinting back at me. I picked my way toward it, and bit back a scream. It was my necklace, the golden Eye of Ra. The chain was unbroken—discarded, rather than lost. I tried to pull it loose from the peat, but it stuck, the chain suspended in the air, pulling away from me as if by a shadow. It was tangled on a twisted root I hadn't seen a moment before.

The thick leg curled upward and then down again, diving back into the bog like an oaken serpent. I unfastened the chain to keep from breaking it, returning it to my neck. The light from my phone had dimmed. When I tried to retrieve it from the ground beside me, it had vanished, swallowed up.

"Shit," I hissed, feeling my knee sink as I groped fruitlessly for my phone. I wobbled, and my hand shot out instinctively to the right. Instead of landing in the mud, I felt an unexpected jolt in my shoulder as my palm made contact with the thick trunk of a tree. I looked up, clawing at the bark as I wrenched my leg away from the bog's sucking mouth. The oak was impossibly wide, and craning my neck straight up, I could not see where its canopy ended and the obsidian sky began. I skimmed around the wide base, hugging the trunk and digging my toes into the roots that weaved in and out of the bog to brace myself. The hem of my pants caught on a dense tuft of bracken at the base. The plant itself was sinking and threatened to take me with it. I flexed my arm to pull it up, and it flew unexpectedly into the bog behind me. It had not been anchored at all, but had obscured a deep, slender well hewn out of the bog, almost into the tree itself. The opening was blocked by haphazard piles of beads, clay-tempered pots now shattered into menacing shards, gold coins, and amber—everywhere amber. But none entrapped Hedra's minions, none caged life. There was no end to the chasm in sight.

It was barely wide enough for me to squeeze through, and there was no clear method of descent, other than falling. I knelt on the ground, shedding my jacket and clenching the knife in my teeth. The iron stain melted on my tongue and ran down my throat. I gagged, clearing the opening while being careful not to cut my hands on the jagged pottery. As soon as it was good enough, I braced my arms into the mud, hoping to slide down, if the walls didn't devolve into sludge and could withstand the pressure of my hands. This worked long enough for me to get my head in the hole—after that, the bog gave way and I plummeted.

Landing in sodden muck, I found myself unharmed. And unarmed. I couldn't fathom how Hedra had gotten here without falling like me, or indeed how far I *had* fallen. The opening into which I had slid was dimly cast in an eerie, phosphorescent blue. The walls and ceiling were so insubstantial that it was incomprehensible that they formed upright structures at all. The muted sound of water lapped in the distance as I trudged in the impossibly cavernous space, pushing up mounds of mud around my ankles as I moved, hauling my straining leg muscles in and out of ditches. Puddles where I stepped filled up with water quickly and my feet were soaked, the cold biting through shoes and socks. My toes were completely numb as I followed a fresh pair of dunes ahead of me. I heard a shore, the muddy surf rushing louder and louder, and then the scraping sound of a small boat pushing off.

I dashed ahead, trying desperately to reach them before they took off into the murky depths without me. I shoved myself out to the shore and waved my hands over my head like a lunatic to get Quintus's attention. Hedra craned her head to glance dismissively at me over her shoulder, her twinkling laugh reverberating wetly off the mud of this underground hell as she dug a long pike into the river, propelling them forward. My eyes dropped to Quintus, sitting opposite her. He stared straight ahead—straight at me—but could not *see* me. His eyes were docile and vacant, but as the darkness of the lake swallowed them up, there was a faint reflection of water trickling down his face.

I stood numb, my mind utterly devoid of a way out of this, when another wooden vessel came into view from the left, drifting aimlessly along the shore. It was occupied by a robed phantom, sitting inert at the stern of the boat, shoulders hunched, knees drawn up tight. It moved not a muscle, made not a sound to pierce the shushing silence of this subterranean river.

It was my only option. I climbed into the back as it brushed against the shore, tripping over an elongated pike that lay at the bottom of the boat, unused. The boatman's eyes sought me out, and he jumped, leaning his hands on the edges of the small wooden vessel with a jerky quickness, lunging menacingly at me. I jumped backed with a scream, and he came right at me. It opened its mouth as if to swallow me up. I held my breath in terror, but he closed his mouth again, and proceeded to turn his head from side to side, a searching sentinel. I let my breath out, and it snapped its head back at me. The hands that had reached out from his sodden, tar-black robes had no flesh on them.

The index finger on the left hand twitched, indicating the pike. The hand was not exposed bone; rather, the flesh shone a dull silver, the moon incarnate. He wore what was once a fine garment, now tattered and worn with age. I took up the staff, pushing its shaft into the river, and it still towered over me. It was incredibly unwieldy, but could move fast if I made it, and I was able to follow the subtle hint of fading ripples as I caught up to Hedra.

I lost all sense of time and space, focusing only on the direction of the ripples as we traveled, left, then right, then left again, now going deeper and lower into the bog, only to rise up again. The boatman sat deathly still. His silence disturbed me more than his sudden outburst had. I shivered when I dug the pike into the river again, and felt the riverbed move under the pressure. The mud level inched up the left side of the boat, threatening to spill over the side and capsize us, then receded again without warning. A few more strokes forward, and I felt a resistant pressure slide across the underbelly of the boat. Something moved beneath us, and it was not the mud. The river was so dense with peat and devoid of all light, I could see nothing lurking beneath its obtuse surface, only knew with a frightening certainty that it was there.

The serpent showed itself, maintaining its cloak of darkness as it coiled around the center of the boat, seeming to separate it in two with an impenetrable shadow. Its head rose up, and I heard the bone-crunching snap of its jaw as it lunged at me, knocking me back with the gale winds of its swift movement. The staff struck me on the chest, robbing me of air. I fumbled for it as the coils around the boat tightened and it reared back, preparing to attack again.

My fingers at last found their purchase on the spear. I stabbed at the serpent with the end of the pike. Inky blackness spilled forth, and the effort to pull the staff out again almost tossed me down the demon's throat as the boat pitched downward.

"Do something!" I shouted at my defunct shipmate. It stirred not, even as I felt the rank breath of the slithering shadow close around me. I scrambled forward, my face landing at my useless companion's feet. I was determined not to be eaten. Even staring it straight in the face, the darkness was so complete that I *could not see it*. The staff lay beside me, and as the wyrm lunged forward, I caught the pike sticking out of its maw and thrust it in as hard as I could, aiming for the brain cavity. A shrill, unholy sound gurgled from its throat and poured like poison into my ears. That sound—I hear it still, in the depths of my sleep. I withdrew my spear, and the menace sank back into the nothingness. The water once again became still.

Too still. I spun all around in the boat, and could see nothing, no glistening trace of movement echoed by the boat ahead of me. I dropped the spear, defeated. I let free a sob.

"Left."

I turned, stunned, angry, almost not believing my ears. "*Now* you're gonna help?!"

"Left," he repeated, his voice quieter than before.

If he was wrong, his guess was as good as mine anyway. I steered the boat to the left.

"Down."

The sound that came forth from the prow was like a dream—not one iota of the phantom before me moved as his voice led us deeper.

"Do you look to it?"

"What?" I said, startled and confused.

"The Eye."

I looked down, and saw my pendant shining impossibly back at me, the sole light in this abyss. "It was a gift," I said.

"From your father," the phantom added.

"How did you—" I stopped myself, for fear of what the answer might be.

"I see all that shines beneath. Right."

My eyelids grew heavy as we traversed the bog's depths, and my mind began to discern the pattern by which we traveled. It was so familiar, I no longer required the boatman's directions, though I had no idea where our prow pointed. The haze over my eyes made shapes and figures visible along the wall, and I could hear my dad's voice thrumming in my ears, pulling me back to a particularly hot spring day.

My dad rushed into the antechamber where I'd been sitting alone for hours in the shade of the cloistered room. I could smell the sweat dripping from his forehead and was thankful to catch the end of the cool breeze he created by swinging his hat in a wide arc before his face. He placed a scroll on the table under my nose and unfurled it very gently.

"*Look, Asenath. Look at this one.*"

"*What is it?*" I asked, my voice small and eager.

"*It's a map. See, the pharaohs were given everything they needed so they would never lose their way.*"

I felt the dry parchment under my fingertips, still smooth on its dyed surface as I traced the path—left, down, right…

The images lulled me. My hands grew too heavy for my wrists, the staff in my hand became a pole of lead, dragging me downward. I woke from my dream and found I had drifted too close to the wall. The mud of the underground smeared on my sleeve. It roused me from my stupor, and I wiped at it vigorously, frantic to remove the stain. I only spread it farther, soaking it into the fibers and assuring its permanence.

I trudged forward quickly now, having caught at last the rippling tides of my husband's captor. We soon arrived at a distant shore. The specter said nothing more as I disembarked. A gloomy pair of unearthly lights marked the way ahead of me. They were flames, inconceivable to sustain in such a place, moored as they were into the sodden wall. Mud oozed down the columns leading forward. The air was thick and oppressive with a permeating cold. A darkened pool became visible in the center of the dimly visible space, the perimeter reinforced with stone. My heart stopped when I saw Hedra—naked but for a feathered headdress, speckled white, and a stag hide hanging open around her shoulders. Her skin was luminescent, and she looked like a vapor, outlined in watery edges, her boundaries indistinct. In one moment, she winked out of existence completely, only to appear again in a sequence of wavy bands spreading ever wider until she was once again visible from the wavering tips of her headdress to her mud-covered toes. She stood before the pool, the amber in her hand. Quintus knelt prostrate at her feet.

"Quintus!" I shouted instinctively.

He flinched, but stayed where he was, his powerful arms hanging uselessly at his sides. Hedra grinned back at me, her eyes flaring maliciously as her hand grazed his cheek.

"You really are a lucky woman, to have tasted this man."

I looked from her naked form to Quintus and shuddered, immobilized as she took the amber that had irreparably changed my life, and shoved it roughly into his mouth, extending his jaw.

She spoke but I didn't understand, and she turned her attention away from me. The ritual had begun. She raised a dagger over the abyss in offering. She meant to pierce Quintus through the mouth, to keep the amber pinned there. She squawked at me, mocking me. "Not so clever now, are you? Come and save him, child, if you think you can, or are you too scared to act?"

I was afraid. What was I doing here, in *her* domain, wearing nothing but a meaningless charm? I had no weapon, no witty plan to counterattack, no knowledge of escape. Quintus would be condemned to the bog forever, and so might I. I was frightened beyond act, word, or thought.

In the cold, still blankness, I heard my father's voice.

"What are you afraid of, Asenath?"

"The mummies!" my small voice answered.

"Mummies are not alive, honey. They can't hurt you. They're just dead things."

"But what if they're not?!" I protested, and started to cry, as I cried now. I felt his arms around me, his fedora pressed to my head.

"Don't ever be afraid, Asenath, of mummies, or sounds under your bed, or shadows in your closet. You have the power to send them away."

I wiped my eyes. *"I do?"*

He pointed at my new necklace, given to me just that morning.

"Call on Ra, and he will send his light into the darkness. Repeat after me: Hail to thee, Amun-Ra, Lord of the thrones of the Earth, the oldest existence, ancient of Heaven, support of all things; Chief of the gods, lord of truth, father of all, maker of beasts and herbs, maker of all things above and below, deliverer of the sufferer and oppressed, Lord of wisdom, the opener of every eye..."

The words issued forth from my lips, stronger and stronger until I was shouting them. They echoed in every open space, cutting through the dense, freezing fog. My voice soaked the bog, bending and multiplying, pouring into Hedra's ear. She put her hands up to her head to block the reverberating sound, swaying in pain as the drums of the underworld sounded without end, beating incessantly on until the ceiling began to rush down the walls and onto the floor, and the stark winter sun stabbed through the darkness.

A cold wind rushed up from behind me, and I saw the boatman, coming to stand stalwartly in front of me, launching the staff across the pool toward Hedra and striking the dagger out of her hands, sending it down into the abyss before her. She shrieked; her face devastated by true terror.

Quintus rose to his feet, blinking furiously as he stood and spat the orb from his mouth. He spun around, catching his would-be enchantress by the feathers and dragging her the short distance to the edge of the pit. She flailed and screeched like a tortured bird, but he wrenched her over the edge, smashing her skull against the stone rim of the well. Her head deflated as he crushed it, reduced to a bloodless husk, an empty pile of skin that he tossed into the pool with trembling hands.

The ground faltered, rising up to meet the collapsing ceiling. The hooded phantom called to me. His shoulders shrugged out of his rags. His skin was not dead or silvery at all—it seemed to shift before my eyes from an impenetrable midnight to a pure, brilliant gold.

"*Doosi Asenat!*"

I raced to Quintus's side, and he caught me in his arms just as the peat beneath my feet swelled to a ridge and swallowed us up.

2 4

QUINTUS

I was brought violently back to consciousness by choking up mud. I rolled over onto my stomach to purge it. I studied my quivering hands and found them whole—not cracking with the decay of untold ages. My chest and face were likewise unharmed, save for an intense soreness gripping my whole body. I stood and let out a shriek of pain. One of my ribs was badly bruised, but not broken, from what my probing fingers could tell. My clothes were soaked through—the stiff wind racing across the sky stole my breath. I peeled my eyes fully open, daring the stark sunlight, and panicked. Azi was not beside me. I stumbled to my feet and called to her, my voice hoarse and garbled with peat.

I called clearer and louder, losing my breath as I caught sight of her form splayed in the surf. I rushed to her, flipping her onto her back. Her face was shaded a sickening blue, and I shook her furiously, devolving into tears as she lay like a broken doll in my hands. We were alone on the bog bank, now collapsed into itself, save for the ibises flying overhead.

"Asenath," I croaked, pressing my forehead to her chest, sobs slicing me down to my very soul. My foolish pride and thirst for revenge had brought me right back into the demon's jaws, and it had cost Azi her life. She had come for me, even after the terrible way I treated her. I wept bitterly, my arms trembling with the dead weight of her.

The flock descended on us, one white, red-beaked bird landing on Asenath's knee. I shooed it away with my arm. I was lost in sorrow, and still the cold-hearted heathens persisted, determined to make a meal of my wife though it were not an hour since she had taken her last breath.

"Away!" I cried, swatting at them and knocking one out of the air. "Leave her alone." I nuzzled her pale face, my soul shattered. A solitary ibis escaped my broad flailing, swooping past my defenses. It flapped its broad wings and settled its small talons into her skin. It screeched, its shrill cry piercing the morning's calm. With a violent jerk, Asenath coughed, grasping for air.

Hands shaking in disbelief, I pulled her torso upright, bracing her over my left arm as she expelled the stain of the lake, and rested her head listlessly on my chest. I wept further, shedding tears of thanks for my soul's joy brought back to me, squeezing her until she groaned in discomfort. I wiped her mud-streaked face as she opened her eyes, her body heavy in my arms as after a long sleep. She stared endlessly at the sky, the sun's beams shining in her pupils as her lips moved silently.

"Asenath. My Asenath," I cried. Her eyes glistened at me, and I brought my forehead to hers.

"Did she...did you...."

"No, my love. No," I answered. She clasped the back of my neck, calling me closer to her. I pulled my wife to her feet, and we stumbled back to the car. Azi favored her right ankle, obscenely swollen. Finally arriving at the edge of the bog, we leaned heavily against the Jeep, catching our breath. Our hands reached instinctively for each other.

"You came for me," I panted, struggling just to stand upright.

"Of *course*, I did. You couldn't have kept me away."

"But how? How did you—?"

Azi smiled then, reaching with trembling fingers to the chain around her neck, thrilled to find it still there. She began to cry and faltered into my arms.

"Forgive me, Asenath. Forgive me."

She squeezed tighter, causing more tears to flow.

"I'm not okay to drive," she said.

"I could make an attempt," I offered.

"No, no," she replied, waving her hand before her closed eyes. "I've had enough excitement today."

"Are you well enough to keep walking?" I asked, unsure. Before she could answer, an anxious voice rang out, carried across the bog by a crisp morning wind.

"Azi?!"

Azi's ears perked up, her eyes peeling slowly open in recognition.

"Jakob! Jakob over here!"

"Keep shouting; I'm coming!" the voice replied.

Azi leaned through the driver's window and laid her arm on the horn. She groaned in relief, relinquishing the pressure as a blue truck came into view.

"Azi! Are you okay?" the young man shouted, rushing toward us. Our eyes met, and he stopped dead in his tracks.

His mouth gaped open, and his finger slowly rose from his side, pointing at me in terror as he backed away, stumbling in the mud. My fatigued heart pounded in my chest. He recognized me.

Azi pushed off from the truck, lunging at him with all the energy she had mustered in her stalwart defense of me. Her eyes snapped into sharp focus.

"Jakob, wait! Stop!" she cried, clasping his arms, both to steady him and prevent him from breaking into a frantic run.

He shouted incoherently as Asenath clapped her hands down on his shoulders. "Jakob! Jakob!" she screamed in his face, trying to conquer his horror. "It's okay! It's okay."

"Azi, Azi, he's...!"

"I *know*, Jakob. I know. Look at me!" She pushed his face to hers, holding his stare. "It's all right, Jakob. Don't be afraid."

He nodded finally, and she took his hand, limping over to me. Jakob's eyes were wild as they came closer.

"Jakob, this is Quintus," Azi said.

He continued to stare at me, standing dumb until I extended my hand.

"Thank you," I said by way of introduction, "for coming to our aid."

"Any time," he answered, shaking my hand longer than was necessary. The shock on his face was soon replaced with amazement. "Wow. I mean...you're really...it's really you."

"Jakob," Azi said softly, "Quintus is my husband."

"Hnn?" he mumbled, not taking his eyes from me as Azi came once more to my side.

"My husband, Jakob. He's my husband."

Jakob's eyes darted between us, then nodded his head slowly, coming down from the frenzy my sudden appearance had produced.

"Well, I'm disappointed, Azi, and more than a little jealous, but—"

"Excuse me?" I interrupted.

Jakob threw his hands up defensively in front of himself. "I didn't sleep with your wife!" he protested.

"What?!"

Azi rubbed at her eyes and groaned.

"I mean, you *weren't*, uh, *she* wasn't your wife, at the time." He scrunched his face. "I'm
gonna stop talking now."

"Good," I answered.

Asenath leaned her weary head on my shoulder and soothed my frazzled nerves.

"Does Pryce know?" Jakob asked.

"*No*," Azi answered emphatically. She opened her mouth to speak again, but Jakob interrupted her.

"You can't tell him. That man can't keep a secret to save his life," Jakob insisted.

"I know," Azi replied. "Just us, okay?"

He looked at me then, and I put my arm around Asenath. Half for support, half as a husband's plea. Jakob smiled wryly.

"You can count on me."

"Thank you," I growled, pushing my agitation down to the bottom of my gut.

"But I have questions," Jakob continued, his voice filling with awe. "So many questions."

Jakob transported us back to the university. Azi took my hand in hers, kissing my knuckles. I knew what she was about—trying to soothe the wound the sudden confession of our erstwhile savior had inflicted. I let her. I wrapped my free arm around her, groaning at the soreness in my ribs as my fingers found a hold on her shoulder, and my lips found their way to her dripping hair.

"I'm yours, you know," she whispered in my native tongue. "Yours alone."

I fell headlong into her dark, pleading eyes, eyes I had thought would never open again. My own stung with tears. I held her tighter, mindless to the wet chill that spilled from her clothes under the pressure.

When we arrived at the laboratory, Dr. Pryce, Jakob's mentor and another unwitting victim of the red bitch, sat wrapped in a cloth on the open edge of an ambulance.

"Dr. Pryce!" Azi shouted, hobbling over to him as he accepted a cup of coffee from a nearby officer. "What happened?"

"Oh, it's nothing. I just collapsed, that's all. Skipped a few too many lunch breaks," he answered glibly.

"You're sure you're all right?" she pressed, cowed by the quantity of flashing blue and red lights.

"Yes, yes. Don't mind all this," he replied, waving his hand at the sirens. "I called them, but they're not here on *my* account."

At that moment, I saw two uniformed men close a black bag the size of a man and lift it onto the back of one of their vehicles.

"Who's that?" Jakob asked.

Pryce looked up at Asenath with baleful eyes. "I'm sorry, Miss Hayes. It's Carew."

"He was here?" I cried.

Azi turned to me, shaking violently in my arms. The look on her face told me all I needed to know.

"Murdered," Pryce explained. "Stabbed right in the gut."

Good girl, I thought.

I pulled my wife closer to me, squeezing her fingers.

"You sure you don't want to come with us, doctor?" an officer asked as he approached Dr. Pryce.

"I'm fine, I'm fine," he insisted, coming to his feet and returning the blanket that had been draped over his shoulders. "This is the post-doc I told you about earlier, Asenath Hayes."

The gentleman turned his attention toward us, handing Azi the blanket and flipping to a new leaf in a small book. She pulled the dark wool tight over her drenched form.

"Dr. Hayes, may I ask you a few questions?"

She nodded.

"Dr. Carew was your mentor, yes?"

"Until very recently."

"When was that?"

"About a month ago. He was fired."

"Fired?" Pryce interjected.

"Do you know why?" the man persisted.

"Inappropriate conduct."

The man narrowed his eyes at Azi, increasing our mutual discomfort. True to her nature, Azi's face betrayed nothing.

"Did you know he was here?" the officer queried, changing course.

"No. I only just got here myself."

"Like I told you before," Pryce said, standing closer to us now, "if he was here, I didn't see him. My assistant may have, but there's no sign of her, either."

"You met this woman also?" the officer asked Asenath.

"Yes."

"Can you give me a description of her? The good doctor here didn't seem quite up to the task."

"It isn't that," Pryce reproached, "it's just…"

My sympathy for him waxed as his voice trailed off, and he struggled, and failed, to recall her. I remembered that feeling very well.

"Let me guess," the officer countered. "Was she a redhead?"

We all jumped at that.

"Yes, of course!" Pryce cried, as if the words had simply escaped him. "You know her then?"

The man's face widened into a strange, furtive smile. "Every so often, a body shows up, under less than usual circumstances, and all anybody can seem to remember is that a redhead had been lurking about. Other than that, no one can say what she looked like."

"It *is* the damnedest thing," Pryce said with a disarming smile.

"Indeed. I suspect the death and her disappearance are related, but," the officer shrugged, "only time will tell." He gave a subtle nod of his head and was gone.

"I never liked that woman," Jakob whispered, drawing our little circle tighter together.

"That makes three of us," Azi replied.

Pryce was about to protest, vehemently, then just as quickly relented, nodding instead in silent affirmation. "I'm sorry, Jakob. For sending you away. I thought it would be good for you. But now, I..." Pryce shook his head. "I don't know anything anymore. All I know is, I'm hungry. Miss Hayes, would you and—?"

"Quintus," I answered for her.

"Quintus," he repeated, shaking my hand. "Would you care to cash in that rain check for dinner now?"

"I think that's just what you need," Jakob chimed in. "Get some meat back on your bones."

"You said it. I feel like an old man. How about it, Miss Hayes?"

"That's *Mrs.* Hayes now." She smiled, squeezing my waist even tighter. "Can I just dry off first?"

Pryce laughed jovially. "Of course! Where'd you two get to anyway, all soaked through like that?"

"To hell and back," Azi answered.

"Right. Well, it isn't much of a celebration, I'm afraid, given the circumstances," Pryce said, glancing over his shoulder, "but tomorrow, we can finally get down to business, I think. Give our bodies the justice they deserve."

"Sounds fine to me," Asenath said, finally allowing herself a full breath.

"I'm in, too, if you'll have me," Jakob said.

Pryce slung his arm around Jakob's shoulder. "As if you need to ask."

Azi and I leaned on each other as we made our way carefully back to Jakob's truck. She ground her teeth as she put weight on her ankle. That is, until I swept her off it, and there it was. The bright, limitless smile I had first seen upon her parents' wall, the smile of a girl without a care in the world. She sighed.

"This is *not* the honeymoon I dreamed of," she murmured.

"Some place warm and dry, then?" I grinned. "I've never seen the pyramids."

***

Thank you for reading! Did you enjoy?

Please Add Your Review! And don't miss more romantic adventures through time like, INFINITE US. Turn the page for a sneak peek!

SNEAK PEEK OF INFINITE US

BY: EDEN BUTLER

The thumping, incessant rhythm wasn't welcome when the headache started.

Brooklyn was loud, midnight dark, full of chaos, adding to my insomniatic misery. But the noise from my upstairs neighbor wasn't the only thing keeping me up. Numbers and algorithms coated my inner vision like some Pollock piece. My body? Stupid with tension—the kind of tight coil that twists your spine and keeps your shoulders from any damn thing but bunching pain.

The numbers, the darkness, all that chaos fought for space inside my head, dimmed by the racket I heard above me. That thumping, hyper noise of a drumbeat from some clueless asshole's speakers in the upstairs apartment, tamped out the jazz pouring from my headphones. Coltrane was wicked, the smooth slip of his sax like the voice of God; the heady mix of condemnation and praise, pain that both harmed and healed in every note. But even the long, sweet whisper of the sax couldn't overcome the thumping of the trespassing drums barging in or keep out the noise of the crazy bitch singing out of tune one floor up. Had to be a woman. No dude's voice could be that high-pitched or whining.

For the fourth damn night.

Insomnia first became my side-piece in college. Every night for four years, the noise of frat brothers stepping in line to DMX and his gravely-voiced barks in "Get It On the Floor" in the quad, the Alpha Phi Alphas and Omega Psi Phis vying for bragging rights of who was the flyest with every step-dance they made, and the general disturbance of new-held adolescent debauchery kept sleep from me. Those Omegas always won.

I'd trained my mind then, let insomnia linger until there was an uneasy relationship between us—me tolerating the elusive hum of sleep and that affliction keeping me from it. I'd wrangle four hours of sleep, plenty for a Computer Science major, enough to ace my classes. Enough that I didn't look like an old man when I left for MIT. By then, insomnia had become the ride-or-die chick that refused to leave me. Got tied down to that bitch. Now I wanted a divorce.

That racket from the apartment above was not helping.

The noisy upstairs woman started a louder chant, something that reminded me of the weird mess my twin Natalie watched every Halloween with her friends when we were kids back in Atlanta. Some movie with three white chicks from Salem, singing about spells and sucking the souls out of children. The one with the redhead woman that my assistant Daisy says likes to burn Kim Kardashian on Twitter. That shit was funny, hell of a lot funnier than the other movies she was in that made my mom laugh so loud when I was six. It was a Broadway phase she kept from my pops. Nothing like the witchy mess from that old movie, that nonsense was crap. And that's what my new neighbor sounded like.

Four nights. Four nights of this rambling, tone-deaf torture. Four nights of the voice of God being drowned out. Four nights too many.

Coltrane fell silent when I pulled the headphones off and moved across my apartment, not giving a damn that my t-shirt was wrinkled when I picked it off the floor and tugged it over my head, not caring whether or not that loud woman would get pissed if I interrupted what had to be some nightly juju ritual.

My skin pebbled in the cool air from the vents at the elevator but I didn't shake or cross my arms to get rid of the sensation. It fed me as I slipped into the car, ignored the quick flash of my reflection on the metallic doors showing the bags under my eyes, the streak of muscle that twitched when I stretched my shoulders. Maybe it wasn't the best idea to confront this chick, but I was tired and annoyed, and before I stopped to think about what I was doing, the elevator dinged and I stood right in front of 6-D's door. There was a constant thump of a drum line bumping beneath the sliver of light at the bottom of the door; the only shadow I could make out slipped around that light, probably dancing to whatever voodoo junk pulsed from those speakers.

Coltrane was music. Spirit music. Deep, heart-aching music that seeped into your soul, filled in all the fragments that life left empty. This garbage? Hell no. This was racket and chaos set to a disjointed rhythm.

Two bangs of my fist and I stood there, arms braced against the doorframe, loops of black tattoos, things I wanted to remember, things I could never forget, visible over my forearms, moving as I twisted my fists on the wooden frame. I didn't care what I looked like, a tall inked black man breathing fire at her door. Not worried that this woman might see something of a threat in me, thin, wrinkled shirt over wide-shoulders, jeans slipping low on hipbones. Instead, I focused on that mean ache of messed-up calm and lack of sleep crowding in my skull. My stupid pissed off attitude amped up the longer it took her to open the door. Waiting, I envisioned that I'd yell, I'd unload on her, then get the hell away before she could react, stalk back to my apartment with my anger leeching out behind me. Then maybe Coltrane would work and I could get at least a few hours' sleep.

The drumbeats stopped. Footsteps. The snick of a lock.

Angry breaths flared my nostrils. My eye twitched. A vein in my forehead pulsed.

With the smallest creak of a hinge, the softest slip of light, the world around me went silent. The silhouetted figure before me sent a whisper straight to my brain. But it was the light cast across her face and the good look I got of her that rattled me, really rattled me. I couldn't shake it. I didn't know this woman, yet she felt freakishly familiar. Like I'd dreamed about her for a year and never caught her name. Like that dream had haunted me and I was only just remembering why. Like there were details about her face that had been branded into my memory and I just uncovered them. One glance, and I stood frozen, unable to squash the rush of memory and confusion that shot at me like a wave.

Sensation overtook me and I got caught up by what felt like a whip of wind moving through the park, of plastic beads and forgotten parking tickets on Bourbon Street the second Fat Tuesday ended, of the spray of waves that had crashed against the quay. It slapped across my subconscious. A whoosh, a break of something that could have been a kiss, likely was a punch in the gut, though no one touched me. Before I finished one blink, there she stood, half a foot from me, staring as though she knew me, like she'd been waiting on me to knock on her door.

"*Oh. Oh no.*" The woman's eyes—bottomless circles I wasn't sure I could look away from even as she seemed to take in every square inch of me—got huge.

It was her.

The girl.

She'd been everywhere—outside my window, soaking up my attention like I had no control over it, and every time she brushed by me on the street, moving like a bubble floating to the deli on Henry Street or the cleaners down past Orange, some fucking specter I wasn't sure was real that kept me standing right where I stood every damn time I spotted her.

Once, coming home, I noticed her walking a block in front of me, and followed her like a stalker, not even realizing what a freak I must have seemed liked. Every time I saw her, it was like her presence had gripped me like a crazy moth to a flame, but I'd been too wrapped up in my work and my own damned mind games to even consider that she was real, and approachable, and living nearby.

And now she stood in the open doorway, only inches from me.

"Honey… just, no."

Her touch brought me from my gawking stupor. At least, it made me move. She touched me and a bolt of electricity coursed through my body. Fingers warm against my skin, pulling me forward like she expected me to follow. Resisting her was not an option.

Her grip tightened as I followed her inside, and a voice started screaming in my head to back up, to get away from this chick before I did something stupid or got blamed for it. But I looked at her again, and the voice quieted to a whimper.

This woman wasn't like anyone I'd ever seen before. She was tall, heightened by the dark tights she wore and the loose, bright top with swirls of green and yellow which might have been flowers that cupped her small waist and drifted nearly to her thighs. She reminded me of a bunch of balloons, the kind that jackass clowns twist into animal shapes to impress stupid six-year-olds. There was so much color and noise in this woman—the whiteness of her skin, the loud shade of her dark lips, the jingle of the stack of bracelets on her wrist, and the thick bundle of long chestnut-colored hair that hung in a riot of waves and curls past her waist.

But it wasn't the chaos of colors she wore that kept me from bolting: It was the stare she gave, the pause before she spoke as though she knew exactly who I was and why I'd pounded on her door.

Hold up. Why *had* I pounded on her door?

I couldn't explain the sensation if I had a billion words to describe it. It was something weird but familiar, something I didn't recognize in her expression, in the slow, sweet smile that moved across her face the longer she watched me. Like she knew me. Like I was supposed to be right there standing in front of her waiting for something to happen.

Hell. I *was* sleep-deprived.

When she stopped watching me, when that little smirk vanished from her features, she squinted, looking over my head as though she was considering something, like she needed to figure out what kind of flaw I had.

"It's bad." She waved her long fingers over my head, swooping one hand up and down my body, breaking the moment and confusing the hell outta me. "It's just the wrong color." Another wave and I finally wrestled my thoughts under control enough to step away from this crazy woman even as she tugged me further into her apartment.

I finally found my voice and my reason. "That shit is too loud," I said, mustering all the good damn sense I could, as I looked around her cluttered apartment.

"What?" she asked, her brown eyes wide, innocent.

My gaze settled on an old ass record player in the corner, spinning, with the needle up. "Your record... that turntable?"

She frowned, but more confused than unfriendly. She had one of those faces that tears and worry and rudeness wouldn't, couldn't, keep from being beautiful. And she was. For a tall, skinny white chick, she was damn beautiful.

"The turntable, the speakers, you got to cut that shit down. I can't sleep as it is, but that fucking ..."

"*Oh,* you shouldn't curse like that."

Again she reached for me, fussing at me, bossy as hell as she led me to what I guessed was supposed to be a sofa but looked like a stack of fluffy mattresses with the loudest looking blankets and pillows thrown around them. The entire place reminded me of a circus caravan—colors that were deep and rich, tapestries and blankets draped over all the furniture, covering the lampshades like some drifter's wet dream. Flowers, both dried and blooming in vases, along the window sill and across the mantel. The thick scent of something that smelled a little like weed clouded in the air, something sticky and sweet, but too flowery to be anything worth smoking.

She stared me down, gaze hard, critical. I brought my attention back her, trying to dismiss the fact that I'd gotten nosy eyeballing her place but not wanting to give in entirely. "Um... mind your business about my mouth..."

"Sit." When I folded my arms, keeping another curse between my teeth for God knows why, the woman moved her brows up, those coffee-colored eyes matching me pound for pound. I meant to tell her to fuck off. I thought about just rolling out without so much as a word to her, but that look on her face, the one that was both severe and tempting all at the same time kept me stuck in place. Damn, it would be a mistake to underestimate this woman, doe eyes or not.

After her glare went on for damn ever, she nodded at the sofa, staring at me like she'd lost her own shit a long time ago and hadn't bothered finding it. A few seconds, several long, furious blinks and I gave up, too damn tired to fight with some woman I didn't know.

I sat, damn the good sense God gave me. No one bossed me but this woman found a way to get me inside her place and on her sofa with half a dozen words, all of them bossy as hell.

"Now, I want you to relax and breathe deeply. I'm going to focus your aura..."

"Look, lady..."

"Just relax. I need to assess where the problem is." Another glare and she relaxed her expression, her nose flaring as she inhaled deeply. "Now, close your eyes." Even as she commanded it, she did it herself. I closed my eyes, but damn if I wasn't still completely aware of her.

The image of her, the long cascading hair, the softly chiming bangles, the blouse shimmering around her body, all lingered behind my eyelids. She smelled like jasmine, a weird scent that I only recognized because Luke, my college roommate, thought he was Erykah Badu's soul mate and was gearing up for the job by shopping at some funky head shop that sold all kinds of crazy essential oils. Jasmine was Luke's scent of choice and of all the nasty oils he brought into our room, the jasmine smelled the least like ass. On her, it smelled... well, better than any damned oil, essential or not.

"There's a misalignment in your auric field, I'm afraid." Her voice went still, deep and as I squinted to peek at her through the half-light , I caught the expression on her face; all studious, the deep line between her eyebrows that hadn't been there a minute before giving her a focused, worried look. She, at least, thought there something serious that needed fixing, and that something serious seemed to be me.

Her face was round, a sort of heart shape that made her look like a kid. But then I got a good look at her eyes and caught something in them that I hadn't before—stories and legends. That's what my gramps used to say of folk whose past was clouded right in their eyes. Stories that became legends; a life so unbelievable or sad, so lived that it showed in the stare someone had, how they held it, kept it as though every story would live in their eyes, but they'd never speak it out loud. You had to look, gramps would say. You had to look hard.

I didn't even know this woman's name, but inside of three minutes, I knew there was something belly deep she kept to herself.

"I just finished cleansing my aura." It came out like an afterthought, something she said to fill up the space between us as she moved her hands around my body, motioning like she meant to rub my skin, but without touching me. Not once. She moved weirdly, hands and fingers stretching all over me; head, shoulders, chest, down to my knees and feet, then back up again, to my shoulders and neck, around my aura, whatever the hell that was, until she finally rested her fingers against my traps, exhaling hard as she worked her nails up and along my neck, her thumbs rubbing in circles just under the back of my head. "It's probably why yours was so easy to notice."

"That right?" I tried for skeptical, but my voice sounded far away. I forgot about the stupid music she'd blared through her apartment over the past four days. I forgot about the sleep that wouldn't come to me. I forgot about all the worries and work that had kept me up, all gone as I gazed at her face. I'd never seen skin that smooth or freckles up close like that, lips that ripe. If I moved a little, brought her close, I could touch her mouth in a fraction of movement.

Damn. Where the hell had that come from? I wasn't into white girls. I wasn't against messing around or hooking up with them, maybe dating for a little bit, but I'd never really been into them. I'd always been into Latina girls or sisters, definitely, but white chicks? Not really. Despite my current tatted image, I'd spent high school locked up in the library or the computer lab, away from everyone but my teachers and tutors. College for me was Howard, a historically black college, before I transferred to MIT. Not a lot of chance for white women to enter my orbit. Not a lot of women, period. There was no reason for me to want to watch her the way I did or think about how she'd taste, what it'd feel like to have that smooth skin against my tongue.

"Oh..." Surprise worked across her features the harder she massaged the muscle of my neck. "*Oh...*"

"Oh?" I saw her expression focus, become determined and deep, and when she licked her bottom lip I almost lost it. Just like that, I forgot about what type of girls I'd always been into.

"It's..." She blinked twice, her gaze moving around my head, as though she saw something I couldn't. "It's changing colors."

"Weird." That was weak but I couldn't think of anything else. I kept the frown on my face, as if that wouldn't give away what was in my head, but I got the feeling this chick didn't buy it. At least she didn't act like it, not the way her cheeks flushed brighter the longer she rubbed my neck.

She paused, and I watched her, wondering what was making her smile like that, wondering why the hell I returned it with one of my own. She noticed.

"You've got a great smile." She moved my face in her hands, revealing the dimples pronounced in her cheek. "I like it."

Then, just like that, she went all focused and bossy as hell again. "Close your eyes." That demand came out soft, the smallest hint of something deep between each syllable, like she wanted to say please, but wouldn't ever. "The tension is here." There was a small graze of nail against skin when she touched my neck and I breathed deep, liking the way she smelled, how that soft, firm touch warmed my tight traps. "There's so much tension... you don't... you don't sleep well, do you?"

When I opened my eyes, ready to answer her, she brushed her fingers against my lids, making them stay closed. "No." I didn't bother sweeping her hand away. She worked some kind of juju on me and for the fucking life of me, I couldn't stop her. Didn't want to. "That's why I came here. Your music..."

"It's the Cistercian Monks of Stift Heiligenkreuz. Well, their chants, anyway. They relax me. You should try listening..."

I opened my eyes despite myself. "That wouldn't relax me. That's why I came banging on your door."

"What would?" She didn't stop me when I looked at her, but her hands relaxed briefly on my shoulders. "What music would relax you?"

"Coltrane." She frowned then, back straightening as she rubbed against my muscle firmer, deeper, as though to avoid looking at me. I couldn't read her expression. "You don't like jazz?" I asked.

"What? No, I do." She corrected that frown, her features returning to the sweet softness again. "My *świenty dziadek*." I frowned and she waved a hand in apology. "Sorry. I meant my great-grandfather. Our people were Polish. Some things stuck. Anyway, he loved Coltrane." She smiled, remembering. "He'd sit in his office, smoking a cigar, sipping on a glass of bourbon, listening to Coltrane's *Spiritual*. Maybe Louis Armstrong if he was feeling 'a little New Orleans', he'd say." She seemed to be lost in the memories, her face both sweet and sad. "He'd do that for hours."

"Why does that make you sad?" That made her glance at me, as if she was surprised that either she had been that open, or that I had been that observant.

"He died. Last month." She moved her chin, her expression evening out as she refocused and stretched and moved her fingers around me, away from my skin. "He was over a hundred years old and I... I loved him a lot." She shrugged, exhaling like she needed it. "Coltrane makes me a little sad now."

"Coltrane is supposed to make you sad." She pushed on my shoulders and I sagged back against the pillows, dismissing how weird it was that I was letting this woman touch me, trusting her to touch me, and not putting up my guard. "That's what good music does."

She moved her hands away, head tilting as though she hadn't heard me quite right. "Good music makes you sad?"

"Nah. Good music makes you *feel*."

It always had for me. Jazz, Blues, especially, really good rap like Rakim, P.E. or Common, old school beats that went deeper than the bragging rights most artists spit out these days, back when lyrics were about fighting the man and celebrating the beauty of who we were and where we were going. Music should be elemental. It should be bone-deep. All those thoughts ran through my head, but I wasn't about to start preaching to some pretty woman I didn't know, the same woman who somehow managed get me on my back with her scent and fingers all over me, working some weird new wave bullshit over me while remembering her granddaddy and his afternoons with Coltrane. Hell, I'd only come up here to get her to cut off that dumbass chant music. I'd done that. I needed to jet.

So why the hell couldn't I move?

"Maybe." The word came out weak, like she didn't buy the line I'd fed her. "Maybe it should sometimes. But I can't listen to Armstrong or Coltrane, or smell those Padrón cigars or catch a sip of Pappy's without it reminding me of him and how he's not here anymore."

I shouldn't care. Not about this woman. She'd kept me up for four nights straight. Looking at her, seeing how she carried herself, how bouji her place was, despite the Technicolor boho mess, how she looked as though she'd never known hardship in her life, I knew we had nothing in common. We were completely different people. But I still wondered what she'd been through, why she felt the way she did. I shouldn't have cared about this woman. God help me, though, I did.

"He a good man?" It was out of my mouth before I could think about how stupid it might sound.

Without skipping a beat, her face lit up with the most beautiful smile. "The best."

There was no doubt in her reaction. She believed no one had a better grandfather and I understood the feeling. I let the moment chill, and when her face started to settle again, I cast around for something to say. "Remind me to tell you about *my* granddaddy one day." My sister Nat and I only got to live with him for four years after our mother died, but those years had made an impact. My mother's father had been a good man. He'd been the best, too.

It was an invitation I didn't mean to make, telling her I'd give her that story, but again, something had spoken for me, some weird, stupid thing that had me itching to let this woman know I'd be back around.

She didn't miss it, and it seemed like my suggestion had pleased her, even as she tried to distract herself with the tassel on one of her bright red blankets. "Does that mean you'll come back?" Before I could answer, she shrugged, fronting like it didn't matter, but there was a wisp of teasing in her voice. "My chanting music or my aura cleansing didn't completely scare you away from ever speaking to me again?"

She went back to fiddling with my aura, all business, or at least pretending that she was. Long, thin fingers moved over my arms, again not touching but coming close enough that I could feel the heat of her body on my skin. She moved closer, and again I saw something a little hungry come into her eyes, a look that housed a thousand legends. Something thick bubbled in my stomach the closer she came and when she glanced at me, reaching forward as though she would touch my face, I realized I hadn't answered her question. "Maybe."

She smelled so good and the heat between us grew, ran into something that felt like a memory, familiarity that made no damn sense to me. Something old and primal seemed to move her and she came closer, leaning on an elbow to bring herself near enough for me to catch a whiff of her breath—spearmint from her toothpaste, gum maybe, enough of a distraction that I didn't think of those lips for half a second. We moved together like magnets, the force unbreakable, undeniable and out of our control. But at the last moment the scent of her breath and proximity of her body jarred me from whatever small spell we'd been under, enough that blinking to clear my head did the job, brought me out of whatever fog I'd stepped in the second I sat on the sofa.

It was as if the air had cleared, and a kind of understanding came to me. After all, pretty women weren't all that uncommon in New York. There were models and actresses, folk coming in from all parts of the world, adding to the melting pot. Pretty women were everywhere and I sat right in front of one of them, but she wasn't what I wanted, not right then, not with everything else bearing down on me. Yes, she was beautiful. She was sweet, weird and bossy as fuck, but she wasn't for me.

Maybe it was me moving back, maybe it was just the spell breaking for her, too, but she went still and stiff, as though realizing where she was and what she was doing. Then suddenly she jerked her hands back, staring at them as if they belonged to someone else.

"I don't..." Her gaze didn't leave her hands, as though she half expected lightning to shoot from her fingertips. There was a hard line between her eyebrows and when she closed her eyes, scooting back to put distance between us, I thought maybe I'd done something wrong, had said something that put her back up.

"You all right?"

"What?" she said, distracted, waving her hand, looking like she wanted to shake something that ached her from her limbs.

She moved her gaze over my face like she'd only just realized there was someone else her apartment. Her confusion was plain, though the low dip of her mouth did nothing to take away the sweetness of her features. Still, she seemed unsettled, continuing to stretch her hand and extend her fingers as though her joints ached. When the seconds lengthened and she went on without speaking, without doing a damn thing but look worried and confused, I figured it was time to make an exit.

"You want me to go?" Before she could answer I left the sofa, moving slow, cautious, only a little worried that she was a dramatic chick that would act a fool if things didn't go her way.

A few more blinks as she watched me move toward the door and she finally got to her feet, holding her arms over her stomach like she needed to keep herself together.

"I'm sorry... it's... your aura is so..." She sighed, head shaking. "There's something about you and I can't figure it out."

"Maybe it's my bitchin' about that." Again I nodded toward the record. The turntable went on spinning and as I pointed it out, the woman moved toward it, flipping down the power button so that spinning stopped.

"It's not that. And I'm sorry." She faced me, curling her arms together again. Her body was stiff and I got the feeling that holding herself like that was something she did to keep her hands off me. Wasn't really sure why that bothered me, but it did. She took a step closer, body still ridged but her eyes held that hungry, eager look again and I wondered what she thought of me and why the look on her face seemed so familiar.

"I'm a little thrown off, to be honest," she said.

"By me?" I tilted my head, not getting what I'd done to throw her off.

She watched as I took a step, that hungry, confused expression not moving from her face. There wasn't any fear or worry in that look, but her stance didn't change. She kept on holding herself together, knuckles white as she balled her hands into fists like she was worried what she'd do if I got too close.

Took all I had to not smirk like an asshole at that thought.

"By your aura... your... presence." She waved a hand, again motioning at something around me, not at me exactly. "There's something I can't put my finger on."

I didn't buy any of this aura mess. I knew I had a body, a good one for how hard I worked it. I knew somewhere inside there might be a spirit or soul, wasn't real sure of the difference, but I suspected there was more than zeroes and ones to this world. I still believed I was part of it. But auras and cleansings and all the hippie crap she seemed to believe in? Nah. That was a pill she offered that I didn't have the stomach for.

But that didn't mean I couldn't shake the feeling of there being more to her. More to the feelings I caught in the half-hour I'd been around this crazy white chick.

My mentor, Roan, had always taught me to listen to my gut, and right then my gut told me not to jet. Not just yet.

"You... you wanna finish?" I grabbed at anything that would keep me in that apartment. The juju shit was weird, but seemed to be strangely... good. "You know, finish with the..." quick wave around my body, at the invisible whatever-it-was that I guessed was supposed to be my aura, "the ju... ah... the aura cleansing?"

The whites of her knuckles returned to their original pink color and I relaxed a little, moving slowly back to the sofa, arms spread wide against the cushions; an invitation to work me over again. Her frown disappeared and she dropped her arms to her side, relaxing as she moved toward me.

She knelt in front of me, still cautious, movements slow as she dragged her fingers to the back of her head to braid her long, chestnut hair. She worked quickly, efficiently, flicking long strands behind, in between, around another as she worked, not watching me as she spoke. "Not sure how good it'll be, now."

"Not sayin' I believe all this," I waved a hand, grinning when she rolled her eyes, "but I'd hate for you to blast that chanting nonsense all night because you couldn't finish the job." She smiled when I shrugged, and I guessed she didn't buy my nonchalant act. "You seem like a chick that likes to finish a job."

She purposefully ignored my crappy attempt at flirting and moved her hands to her lap, sitting straight. "I like solving problems." She was dead serious.

"You think I got a problem?"

"Hello, you can't sleep. Even without my 'chanting nonsense' music playing." Her laugh was quick, a little loud and I liked the way it sounded, even if it was poking fun just a bit. Reminded me of the noises blue jays made when I went to the park on my lunch break. The woman recovered from her humor, head shaking.

"You got a point?"

She moved slowly, but all those colors and sounds came with her as she crawled closer, a few loose strands of hair falling out of the braid as she sat next to me on the sofa. "You offered. And yeah, maybe I do need to finish the job."

"I'm Nash, by the way. Nash Nation." It came out in a whoosh of air, like something I'd kept to myself but wanted out in the open. Had no idea why I'd said that.

"Oh… okay."

She started to say something, and I interrupted her, answering what I knew would be the same smart-ass question I'd heard my whole life. "No, I'm not from Nashville. Never been. Don't much care for country music. Nash was my granddaddy's best friend in the war. I got landed with his name because he'd saved my granddaddy and their entire unit on the beach in Normandy." The small pillow at my feet was blue and red with small sparkling rhinestones edging the seam. I picked it up, to have something to do with my hands as she watched. The silence stretched. "You got a name?"

"A few, actually."

She didn't bother looking sorry for the smartass comment and I didn't bother calling her on it. She knew who she was. "Okay then, wanna give me one?"

She shrugged, a casual gesture I tried to pretend I didn't find hot. That smile, though, even a monk would be affected by that smile. "Willow."

"Like the tree?"

"Like the movie."

For a split second—hell, for longer than a split second—with that teasing look coming from that bold, Technicolor woman, I thought maybe that smile and her flirting might just make me forget about the kind of women I'd dated.

All of them.

○

Grab your copy of INFINITE US available now. Sign up for the City Owl Press newsletter to receive notice of all book releases!

**Want even more time travel stories? Try INFINITE US by City Owl
Author, Eden Butler, and find more from Kathryn Troy at
www.ladybathoryscloset.blogspot.com**

Love is timeless...

Nash Nation loves zeroes and ones, over-sized monitors, and late office
hours. He's too busy taking over the world to make time for
relationships—that is, until his new neighbor Willow O'Bryant barges
into his life, and now Nash can't shake the feeling that this isn't the first
time she's interrupted his world.

Then, the dreams start. And in the dreams—memories.
Memories of a girl named Sookie who couldn't count on love or
friendship, never mind forever. Memories of a library and a boy called
Isaac and secrets made in private that destroyed his world.

The memories seem real, but who do they belong to?
When Nash and Willow discover the truth, life as they know it unravels.

The bridge between this life and the next is shored up by blood and
bone and memory. Sometimes, that bridge leads to the place we've
always wanted to be.

Please sign up for the City Owl Press newsletter for chances to win
special subscriber-only contests and giveaways as well as receiving
information on upcoming releases and special excerpts.

All reviews are **welcome** and **appreciated**. Please consider leaving one
on your favorite social media and book buying sites.

For books in the world of romance and speculative fiction that embody Innovation, Creativity, and Affordability, check out City Owl Press at www.cityowlpress.com.

ACKNOWLEDGMENTS

My heartfelt thanks go out to the team at City Owl Press for their phenomenal support, and especially to my editor Tee Tate, who helped me turn this book into everything I wanted it to be.

I owe a debt to all my beta readers for being generous with their time and giving solid feedback. Special thanks to Melissa Lucas, who has read practically everything I've ever written, and hasn't gotten tired yet of helping me become my best writer self.

To my dear husband Andy: you've earned my unending love and gratitude by reading draft after draft after draft, of this project and countless others. I'm especially grateful for all the heady conversations, and for giving me the brilliant idea that my bog body should be Roman. I love you in advance for all the manuscripts yet to come!

Last but not ever least, this book is dedicated to the loving memory of my grandmother Kitty. She shared her love of reading with me, her nightstand stuffed to the gills with paperback romances and thrillers. I have forever after treated books as treasure.

ABOUT THE AUTHOR

KATHRYN TROY is a historian by day, a novelist and baker by night. She likes to write what she reads —fantasy, romance, gothic fiction, historical fiction, horror, and weird fiction. When she's not writing or reading or teaching, she's either playing a board game, watching a horror movie, travelling, making croissants, or adding some new weird creepy cool thing to her art collection. She lives on Long Island with her husband and two adorable kids.

Facebook: https://www.facebook.com/kathryn.troy

GoodReads: https://www.goodreads.com/author/show/
16571460.Kathryn_Troy

Bathory's Closet Blog: http://ladybathoryscloset.blogspot.com

ABOUT THE PUBLISHER

City Owl Press is a cutting edge indie publishing company, bringing the world of romance and speculative fiction to discerning readers.

Escape Your World. Get Lost in Ours!

www.cityowlpress.com

facebook.com/YourCityOwlPress
twitter.com/cityowlpress
instagram.com/cityowlbooks
pinterest.com/cityowlpress

www.ingramcontent.com/pod-product-compliance
Lightning Source LLC
Chambersburg PA
CBHW031218020726
47499CB00002B/633